Dedication

This book is dedicated to my dearest husband who is whole-heartedly my biggest life cheerleader.

To my loving parents and my sister, who instilled in me kind and honest principles and stretched wide their best capacities in their attempt to carve the best life for me.

To my beloved children whose love has been constant even without knowing much of my history and for my younger son who sparked me with a few ideas for this book.

To those individuals who provided me with their kindness and generosity especially during my most treacherous times in life.

To my managers and mentors who believed in me and have gone out of their way in raising me up.

To my counselors who guided me with their professional wisdom.

To each person I had the privilege to be in a relationship with— those who have enriched my life in different ways whether joyful or difficult, and those who tolerated my mistakes.

To my cousins who demonstrated such kindness toward me.

To my dear friend Joann and beloved aunt Kathy who did not live to see this book.

To all my girlfriends who valued and supported me.

To all my friends who led me to God's light, and most of all, for the mighty God who loved me unconditionally before I was even born.

1

In Waiting

I've heard newborns are as close as we get to God before we leave this world and journey to the next. Some say babies are delivered straight from heaven—they leave the hands of God as they enter this world. Born at morning's first light in Beijing, China, 1962, I wonder what my infant brain was thinking as I approached a new world. The womb is always described as dark, but what if only in the physical? What if we go from light to light—the light of heaven to the light of reality?

If that is the case, then perhaps our journey becomes one of searching for the light that *guides*. Guides us where though? With so much at stake, I picture where I want to be—a place full of safety, full of love. A place I was always aching to be. Right now, I know that what I want most is to be with my parents. I imagine wings sprouting from my back, large, yet delicate, full of bright colors. With wings, I would fly straight out of here and right into their waiting arms.

It's been at least a year since I've seen my mother or father although it's hard to know exactly how much time has passed. The days blend together. Chairman Mao has started the great Cultural Revolution Movement in China, and since Beijing is the capital, the center of this movement happens here. Chairman Mao ordered those deemed intellectuals to be shipped out to rural areas to work hard so they will not forget their loyalty or ever think they are above the common man. A strict prescription of manual labor is meant to remove their sins and renew their hearts to allegiance with the Communist Party.

My parents, who worked tirelessly as teachers, poured their hearts into the success of their students. Father was a psychology professor at Beijing University, and Mother was a math professor at Beijing Teachers' College. They were consistently named the top teacher of the year. Serving as a professor was once considered the most noble career in China, and being named a top teacher was an incredible honor. Now, this only puts us all in danger.

Having no other family in Beijing, when the government sent away my parents, Mother and Father left me here, in this dreary childcare facility built into a large space at Father's former university. I live with about one-hundred other displaced children between the ages of three and six years old. I am five and a half years old.

None of us want to be here, and at night, I can hear the other children quietly weeping for their parents. I was told this is better than joining our mothers and fathers in the rural areas and being forced to work in the fields where the living conditions lack running water and no hospitals exist, but a part of me wishes that had been my fate. Maybe that's ignorant—fueled by boredom, with my imagination guiding my heart, but I want to be with my parents.

I miss nearly everything about my old life. When things were good.

My parents were high school sweethearts and married right after graduating from college. Father was tender and loving, always taking pictures with his camera. Besides teaching, he was passionate about photography and Chinese traditional medicine. He taught himself how to do acupuncture and studied herbal medicine in his spare time. Mother was hard-working, making sure our house ran smoothly with a strict schedule for meals, chores, and play time. She was crafty and sewed our clothes and made our shoes. She was great at explaining why we must do the things we do.

While they taught classes during the day, I stayed home, at our university campus apartment with Nanny. With no other family nearby, Nanny had been hired when I was a baby to care for me. She told me stories as she cooked delicious lunches and would hold me as we gazed out the apartment window, overlooking the University's giant sports field.

We would watch students running around the track or playing games on the field, and we cheered when anyone scored a goal. I saw many other kids out with their grandparents who made tasty food for their grandchildren and knitted sweaters for them to prepare for the winter. The big sisters took good care of their little brothers and sisters, not letting anyone bully them. I had longed for that multi-generational family connection.

Thankfully, Nanny treated me like her granddaughter and made me feel loved.

Now, I wish I could have stayed with her or maybe gone to live with my paternal grandmother in Hong Kong. My older sister Ying-Hong lives with her, but I have never met my sister or my grandmother. Ying-Hong was sent to live with her when she was only ten months old though I'm not sure why. Perhaps it was a better life in Hong Kong, or maybe it was so my Grandma wouldn't be too lonely. Whatever the reason, when I was born five years after Ying-Hong, my parents kept me for themselves. Until now, I was glad they had.

I dream of the day when the Hong-Kong border opens once again, and I can meet this grandmother and sister! Anything would be better than being here. It's freezing here in the winter. The temperatures drop below zero, and even with limited heating inside the facility, we wear heavy jackets padded with thick layers of cotton clothing and heavy boots to stay warm. The summers are even worse. In August it got so hot some days, we'd break out in rashes covering our bodies.

There isn't much to do at the facility. It's so boring. My main event is walking laps around the column in the giant lobby, counting my footsteps on the marble floors. When it was open to students, Beijing

University was one of the best schools in China, the equivalent of Yale in the United States.

I can tell this used to be an important place. The entrance to the lobby is magnificent.

Wide stairs lead to the giant double glass doors framed with thick wood. The handles are made of shiny, golden brass. With its high ceiling, maybe forty feet tall, and giant light fixtures hanging down in the center, I imagine this brightly lit space once felt glamourous and important. I picture the country's best and brightest students carrying heavy books and thinking important thoughts. Now it's just a bunch of us lonely kids, wandering around in circles like lost sheep, trying to keep from going stir-crazy.

On this particularly ice-cold afternoon, I walk around the giant concrete column for what feels like the thousandth time and excavate every warm memory I can of my parents, Nanny, and our time together. My mind wanders to the night before I started Kindergarten.

"Ying-Ying, tomorrow you start school," my mother said with such pride in her voice. I smiled at her. I knew my parents were always at school, so it must mean that I would spend more time with them.

The next day, Father walked me to the long, rectangular school building. Many kids were dressed in matching gray uniforms, and I was excited to play with them. We walked inside, and Father led me to a crowded classroom. He introduced me to the teacher, and that was the moment I realized he wasn't going to stay. He told me to be good and that he would pick me up at the end of the day. My lip began to quiver, and he left. I cried. Everything around me was unfamiliar. I just wanted to be home with Nanny. The teacher told me to stop crying and tried to distract me with toys and art supplies, but I didn't engage. I didn't want to be there.

Frustrated, she asked me to sit in a far corner of the room so as not to distract the others until I was ready to join in on the activities. I stayed there all day, watching them sing, dance, read, and go outside to play sports. None of it made me want to come out of my corner. I was stubborn, and I hoped I would never have to come back there.

Over dinner, my parents' unhappy faces and serious tones told me they were disappointed by my reaction to my first day, and they discussed with me the importance of education.

Mother told me, "Ying-Ying school is your pathway to knowing and to contributing to making our country better. Don't you want that?"

"I miss Nanny."

"Of course you do, and we'll make sure you still get to see her some days after school."

The next day was exactly the same. And so was the third day. I cried the whole time I was at school. My parents expected me to magically adapt and fall in line like the rest of the kids, but I couldn't. Nanny was all I wanted.

On the fourth day, Father recommended the school hire Nanny. She would teach in a different classroom but be allowed to visit me twice during the school day—once in the morning and once in the afternoon. The teacher was hesitant as such a move was unprecedented, but Father insisted that it would only be temporary. He had run out of options. After much persuasion, the teacher agreed as long as Nanny did not do anything to help teach. Multiple authority figures could be confusing for the other kids.

Father told me that if I promised not to cry, Nanny would come to my classroom twice a day. I didn't cry. When Nanny arrived, I ran to hug her, finally feeling safe enough to listen and learn from my teacher.

On the walk home, Nanny would ask me questions about what I thought of school and my day. She would always point out unusual things on our path: clouds that looked like animals, or chipped paint on a run-down building that reminded her of mountains. She would make up stories about the lives of strangers we passed. This became my second education and the pattern of my everyday life.

Once as we passed a store, I noticed a beautiful woman outside. I couldn't help but stare at her. A block later, Nanny said "That was the shopkeeper's daughter."

"Who?"

"The beautiful woman you were staring at outside the store."

"Oh. How do you know that?"

"I just know. Do you want to know a secret about her?"

"Yes!" I squealed.

"Well, the truth is, every day at around this hour, she goes outside the store in order to spot the man she loves. The man she loves is handsome and kind and walks by every day, looks straight into her eyes, and tells her *hello*. On Fridays he stops into the store, and she helps him find whatever he is looking for. While they shop, he places a letter he wrote for her in her coat pocket. When he leaves, she goes to the bathroom so that she can read his letter in secret. They are planning to marry once he can prove himself suitable to her father."

"Really?"

"Yes. But Ying-Ying, you must not tell anyone about this because we don't want to spoil it before they are ready to tell her father."

"I won't say anything."

I wondered then and still do now, what it is like to love a boy.

I didn't finish the kindergarten year before my parents were sent away from me. For weeks before, I could feel my parents' anxiety and overheard them whispering at night, often mentioning my name.

Nanny came the night before I was to be taken to the facility. She helped pack up the few clothes and belongings I was allowed to take with me. She held me as I cried. "Ying-Ying you are braver than you know. Remember who you are while you're there. Make friends, keep learning, and keep noticing what's around you. That's how this time will pass."

My parents put on strong faces for me as they said goodbye, promising to visit as soon as they could.

I didn't cry that day, too shocked to produce tears. I was quiet, taking in every corner of the building. I found I felt less trapped in the lobby, and so I spent hours every day walking the wide-open hall. And this is where I have remained, walking, waiting, wondering when it will end.

My parents have visited me four times. But this feels like the longest stretch so far since I've seen them. I stare up at the concrete column again. I have memorized every mark on it but still always look to see if anything new has appeared. Amazing how something can stand day in and day out and not appear to have changed in the slightest. I feel a kinship to this column. Even after everything changed, it feels as though nothing in the past twelve months has happened at all.

These are my thoughts as I count my steps, walking around the column over and over again. *One step . . . two . . . three . . .* I notice a mark on my hand. How did that get there? My investigation into this is my most personal feat of the day, and yet I can't help but know it is unimportant. I wrack my brain until my only conclusion is that perhaps I scratched unknowingly in my sleep. I'm not satisfied with this answer, but even a hypothetical answer is an answer.

At eight o'clock we are all meant to be in bed. I try to sleep, but the rhythmic orchestra of my peers' snoring does nothing to soothe me. I toss and turn, hoping sleep will overtake my loneliness, but it does not.

Instead, my mind wanders, remembering the arms of my mother

wrapped around me, my father taking pictures as I danced around our apartment, and Nanny winking at me as she cooked the most delicious food. I want to play again; I want to use my mind to create a world different than this. I sit up, trying to see if anyone else is having trouble like me.

No one stirs, everyone in a consistent rhythm of the comfort only deep sleep brings. Next to me is the toy cabinet. We are under strict orders not to play with the toys at night, but I don't care. Play is my only option.

I open the cabinet. *Creeeaaaaak.* I crouch on the cool floor.

Please let this sound wake somebody.

Someone snores louder.

I grab a couple of dolls—one male, one female. I have them dance with each other as I hum a song. I hum louder. No one makes any effort to tell me to be quiet, and I'm disappointed.

I toss one of the dolls at the girl sleeping next to me. It lands on her small face, and she jolts up.

Her short black hair is sticking up in several directions and she squints at me with her tiny eyes. "*Ugh.* What's wrong Ying-Ying?"

"Do you want to play with me?"

"No, I'm sleeping." I throw the other doll at her, and she shrieks before saying, "Fine, I'll play."

She begins getting out of bed, and I feel such electricity pulsing through me. *Finally!* I grab another toy from the cabinet and another and another until all the different sports balls and wooden building blocks are sprawled in front of us. Having a friend to play with is nice, but it is hard to keep whispering.

"Watch this," I tell her.

I throw a ball at the bed next to us. The two girls in that bed wake up and see the toys. They join us. I go around throwing toys at everyone until all twenty of us are awake and playing. We are laughing and running around the room, and I believe this moment is my crowning achievement. My cheeks feel sore, and I realize I haven't smiled this much in months.

BANG.

The door flies open and our teacher, dressed in her winter sweater and thick black cotton pants, is there looking at us in shock.

"What are you doing? Get to bed everyone!" We all flee back to our beds, and she continues, "Who is responsible for this?"

The other kids don't say anything, but they all look toward me. The teacher doesn't miss a thing. "Ying-Ying, is this your doing?"

I nod my head. My smile has vanished. "Come with me, Ying-Ying."

Forehead pinched and spindly arms military-straight, she marches me down the hallway in silence until we arrive in front of Principal Yang's door. The teacher knocks and waits. She stares directly at me but doesn't say a word. After a minute, which feels like ten, the door opens slowly.

Principal Yang, a fat man who never smiles, takes in the scene. He stares down at me as my teacher recites the evening's events to him. I feel like the ultimate rebel and am terrified at what might happen to me. Will I be sent away to work in the fields like my parents? The principal dismisses the teacher and ushers me into his office.

He has me sit down and takes me in, plotting punishment.

"Ying-Ying it is important you never do that again." I nod my head in understanding. He opens his desk drawer, and I'm terrified that he has something in there that will hurt me. Instead, he hands me a piece of sour apple candy. My eyes go wide.

"Here you go. Now return to bed quietly."

I'm surprised, but relieved he has nothing else to say to me. When I get back to my bed, I break the candy into a bunch of tiny pieces, and save it, allowing myself one sliver of sweetness each day. I never wake the other kids again, but as I walk around the column each day, I often relive that night, and my smile comes back. It was worth it.

2

The Return

Goodbye, boring column!

After eighteen months, my parents' time in the rural area is up, and they return to the city. I can see that the year has been hard on them. Father is not as communicative as he once was. When I ask mother about it, she tells me that for about a month his lungs got very sick while working, and he had to be hospitalized. To help him, they were giving him antibiotic drops through infusion.

One day, she had gone to visit him in the hospital and heard the sound of a faucet running. In his bathroom, she noticed the sink had been left on. When she asked my father about it, he said he hadn't heard it running. It was far too loud to not be heard so she immediately got a nurse, who stopped the infusion drops, citing it may be an overdose that could be impacting his hearing. He was having a hard time hearing high-pitch sounds in one of his ears, and it would take a while before he was back to normal as he learned to adapt. *Just show him a lot of kindness Ying-Ying,* she'd said. *And don't ask him about it.*

So I don't ask him, but I can tell that it wasn't better, and often it makes me sad that he doesn't talk with me as much as he once had. But I am far too happy that life is getting back to how it used to be to focus on that. Nanny is with us, we are back in our old apartment, and now I am ready to catch up on lost time.

That is, until my parents drop another new chapter on me. When they come to pick me up, they bring an older girl with them. I learn this is my sister. My biggest dream come true!

No one explains to me why she is back, or why exactly she left in the first place, but I'm so overjoyed to see my family, I do not ask questions. We move into a gigantic apartment building where one-hundred other families live and settle in. Ying-Hong brought with her many beautiful clothes that no longer fit to give to me as well as my first Barbie doll. I look at Barbie's blue eyes and golden hair and love how unique it is. I have hope that having a big sister will be the best thing to happen to me.

I realize quickly, though, that this transition isn't going to be easy for Ying-Hong. She is nine years old now, and hasn't seen my parents since she was a baby. She doesn't know our dialect, and thus, is often teased by other kids. She has a soft, pretty face but is very quiet and shy. I do my best to make her smile, but it is getting harder as I see how my parent's main focus is on whatever she needs and wants. My own desires aren't heard in the same ways hers are, and I bend and bend my voice in order to be "accommodating."

My loneliness, though, is obliterated as not only do I have my family back, but the giant apartment building we live in has many other kids to play with and plenty to do. There are playgrounds, basketball courts, trees, space to run around, and, my personal favorite, ping pong tables. I am getting good at ping pong, playing whenever I can. One afternoon, as I play with a friend, a group of older boys, all of them dirty and dressed in dull army-green cotton clothing, come up and watch. They laugh at us. The tallest of them says, "You little girls almost done? It's time for the real players to play."

My friend remarks, "We are almost done, but you need to wait your turn."

He comes up right next to the table. "We are done waiting. You girls need to leave."

Furious, I place my hands on my hips, "You want to play that bad, huh? Well, I challenge any of you to a game." I don't care that they are all bigger than me.

Laughter courses through their group.

A boy with a mean smile steps forward, takes up a paddle, and boasts, "Okay, but I'm warning you now, this isn't going to be pretty for you, girl."

I don't even flinch but calmly ask, "Do you want to serve first or should I?"

We begin to play, and I notice he's a worthy opponent, one of the better players I've battled so far. His return is quick, and the ball lands nearly out of reach. I focus harder because he's a jerk and he didn't deserve to win with his arrogant attitude. I beat him eleven to nine.

"You're a cheater." He tosses the paddle on the table with a hard thwack and storms off. Two of the other boys decide they're up to the challenge, and I beat them both.

Humiliated, the entire group leaves, cursing at me. I go home smiling. Justice was served (literally).

None of the universities are open because students are serving as part of the Red Guards. The Red Guards are a youth paramilitary group focused on reporting and persecuting those who are unfaithful to the Mao regime—people who favor the old ways of China or anything that could point toward capitalism. With the older students gone, I have the ultimate gift of my parents being out of work and at home with me. They are dedicated to making the most of it. Mother and Father play with Ying-Hong and me, helping us with our schoolwork and taking us to parks and the zoo.

On one of our trips to the park, I see a plethora of vibrant butterflies flitting around a bush. I've always loved butterflies. They live uninhibited, dancing as they fly. Overjoyed at the sight, I burst into laughter as I chase them. My chasing turns to dancing, following the painted butterflies, full of hope and ease. My parents smile at me, and Father takes photos with his camera. I'm twirling and jumping, trying to reach the height of the butterflies, when I notice a handsome man wearing a blue cap that matches the color of his blue "Mao" outfit talking to my parents. He is a journalist, I soon find out, and he is asking my parents if he can take a picture of me to publish in China's national children's magazine.

I shrug and turn back to the butterflies, but there is only one left as the others have flown away. This blue one with yellow spots is unapologetically beautiful, and I want to be her. I can feel my face light up in a giant smile as I imagine being the butterfly. I picture never having to live in fear of drawing attention to myself or my family and getting taken away by the Red Guards. As I dream of this freedom, a giggle escapes my lips.

I am told my picture was in the magazine later that year.

One warm summer day nearly two years after I leave the facility, we go canoeing in a pond. My parents are paddling while my sister and I try to spot fish. Suddenly, giant thick gray clouds roll in and sprinkles of rain land on my face one by one. The sprinkles turn to fat droplets of water, and my parents hustle to row us back to shore. We are almost there when a large silver fish catapults straight out of the water and into my lap. I scream and my sister screams too, and my parents yell at us to be quiet and hang onto the fish. I do my best, but he is thrashing and slippery. Ying-Hong grabs him and holds his wet, heaving body tight to her chest.

I'm disappointed I'm not holding him, wishing I could have another chance to prove I could do it. As I think this, I'm hit in the arm by another silver fish. "ANOTHER FISH JUMPED INTO OUR BOAT!" I squeal, but this time, I'm determined to hold him. He's in shock and doing his best to navigate this airy space he finds himself in but failing.

"*Shh*. It's okay little fish. It's okay. I have you."

We are almost to shore, completely soaked, and mother tells us to hide the fish under our coats so no one sees that we have them. In these times, each family is rationed only two pounds of meat per month, which means we rarely have any. Mother tells us this is a miraculous blessing and that tonight we will have a special dinner!

We walk quickly, and I try not to look suspicious, but the fish is slipping and beating against the inside of my coat. I hide behind Father as we walk, and luckily, since it is pouring rain, there are few people around. When we make it home, we burst into laughter and hand the fish over to my parents. Ying-Hong and I change out of our wet, fishy clothes. I take extra-long because I don't want to see my parents killing the fish.

I'm sad we don't get to keep our fish friends alive, but it's worth it when I taste our salty, delicious dinner. That night we feast, and we tell the story over and over again of the two fish who braved the open air to join us in our canoe.

In February we celebrate the Chinese New Year, and our parents each set before Ying-Hong and I a gift that came in a flat, fabric-covered box. Ying-Hong opens hers quickly, but I take my time, enjoying the anticipation of a surprise gift.

Inside are kites made together by bamboo and silk! Ying-Hong's is in the shape of a colorful dragonfly. It's beautiful and intricate.

Mine is a butterfly and looks just like the bright blue butterfly with yellow spots that I loved so much that day in the park. I feel the silk between my fingers, letting it glide over my skin, and am in awe of such a gift. I can't wait to try it out.

After we eat lunch (I barely eat, too anxious to try out the kite), our parents take us outside to see if there is enough wind to put the kites to use. We walk to the nearby college campus sport fields, and Mother determines the wind to be just right. *Yes!* They help us place bamboo sticks in the frame of each kite and then slowly begin unraveling the string connected to the handle.

Father holds the butterfly part of the kite above his head. "Looks like we're about ready for takeoff. Ying-Ying, make sure you hold on tight to the string. If this catches wind, it'll want to take off fast. You ready?"

"Yes." It takes everything in me not to scream that word. I'm so excited.

"Okay, start backing up, Ying-Ying." I do so, step by step, and when he determines there's enough distance between the kite and me, Father releases his hold, pushing it toward the sky.

I feel my butterfly kite jerk rapidly to the sky and I think I might just get caught up in the sky with it. But after a few seconds, I manage to get a solid grip on it and look up. *Wow.* There it is, swaying majestically from right to left, right to left, its colors lighting up the gray-blue sky. As I stare up at it, fiercely determined to not let go of the string, I can't help but feel a piece of myself is in this butterfly kite. She is abiding by her role. She stays connected to the string, connected to me, but I know if given the opportunity she'd take off, her beautiful silk wings jetting to faraway lands I could only imagine seeing someday. I almost let go of the handle, wanting that for her. But my own selfish desire to keep her brings me back to reality. I don't want to let her go.

3

Hidden

The older I get, the more I realize life isn't all play with my parents. Mother and Father are originally from Hong Kong, and most of our relatives from Father's side reside overseas. Those facts alone would make one a target for the Red Guards. Many of my parents' friends with similar backgrounds were accused and persecuted as capitalist spies. I find out years later they were forced to kneel on broken glass until they bled, eat feces from the toilet, and worse.

To keep us safe, my parents tell Ying-Hong and I that when people ask us about our grandparents, we must say either that they are dead or that they live in Shenzhen, a city about two-thousand miles away in the southern part of China. I'm afraid if I slip up, the Red Guard will take us away too. It's a heavy burden to carry.

My parents take all sorts of precautions. I watch Mother cover her entire, beautiful gray wool coat in a cheap, blue cotton fabric to make it look muted. That was what most everyone wore. Anything that could make you stand out must be hidden.

"Ying-Ying, you must blend in and not let anyone know you have nice things, or they might think you are an enemy instead of a friend," she says to me as she makes me wear old, tattered dresses instead of the ones Ying-Hong had given me. My shoes have developed holes on the bottoms of them. Though I know I could have a better pair of shoes, Mother patches the holes with fabric. This does very little to prevent rocks and dirt from getting in, but I know never to complain.

Father covers the Nikon logo on his beloved camera and etches out the company name on his bike—signs that point to products received from capitalist countries. I learn from there on out, that my protection depends on hiding where I come from. That is survival. That is my priority. My other priority is to excel in school. My parents urge Ying-Hong and I to focus on our education as the pathway to success and security. We set out to be perfectionists, allowing not a single mistake. It could be deadly!

One morning I wake to Mother making breakfast for us. As I take my first bite of congee, a delicious rice soup, I notice a basket filled with goodies. I try not to squeal because I know this means we get to go visit Nanny! Though she no longer works for us, during holidays, Mother often packs up a basket of gifts for her. Today she asks Ying-Hong and I to deliver them for her.

Nanny lives about a mile away, and it is freezing out, but as Ying-Hong and I walk the sidewalks, shivering, watching our hot breath rise up in billowing clouds, I know it will be worth it as soon as I see Nanny. I can't wait to tell her about our neighborhood friends and the games we've been playing together!

As we get close, my heart quickens. I notice a crowd of people are standing around her house, looking and pointing. I see red tape on her door and a sign. We take cautious steps closer, pushing against an elderly man so we can read the sign . . .

Capitalist Spy: The sinners deserve to be dead a million times.

I don't understand the words on the sign posted on Nanny's door, so we ask a woman in a tattered bathrobe, "What happened to the woman who lived there?"

Her eyes stare blankly ahead, unblinking. "She's dead."

My vision bleeds out and I feel that I might collapse. It hurts to breathe.

Ying-Hong stays calm and asks how she died, and the crowd

ignores the question except for a scrawny man in the center. He stands with his arms crossed over his sunken in chest. "She worked for a capitalist family earning dirty money," he says with hate, "and became a spy herself. The Red Guards tortured her publicly for weeks, and she couldn't take the shame any longer and hung herself."

My heart sinks further and my body shakes. *We* were the family. Nanny couldn't be a spy. She wouldn't have killed herself, would she? What was happening? Would they torture us next? My sister and I look at each other, tilt our heads to say *let's get out of here quick*. We can't risk being recognized. Dropping the basket, we run as though our lives depend on it because they do.

We know we can't lead them straight to our home, so we make detour after detour. I believe at any moment they'll catch up and grab us like Nanny. I have no idea how long or how far we've been running. All of a sudden, my sister stops and pulls me behind a small store. We crouch low next to some trash bins looking to see if anyone is following us. I realize this is the store Nanny had pointed out when she told me the story of the shopkeeper's daughter. My heart beats fast and I try to keep my breath from being too loud, but the pounding in my head thumps like a gong being rung over and over and over.

We don't spot anyone who seems to be searching for us. The few people we do see in the street have no intention of caring about two frightened girls. They are far too preoccupied with their daily routines.

"Okay, I think we're safe." Ying-Hong creeps out from behind the trash and reaches for my trembling hand.

When we enter our apartment, the tears come. My breath is too tired to sob, but silent waterfall tears fall on repeat. I realize nothing will be the same. The safety I felt from Nanny's love is gone forever. This can happen to anyone now, and now all my parents' precautions I understand. Worry overtakes me, and I vow to say my Mao chants at school louder and focus my energy into being the best student in my grade.

My body gives me no option but to go straight to bed. My last thought before tears usher me into sleep is to wonder if the shopkeeper's daughter ever married her love.

Is such happiness possible in a time like this?

From then on, we avoid Nanny's neighborhood, afraid to ever walk in that direction again.

4

School

So much of my world feels uncertain after Nanny's death, and I'm constantly afraid the Red Guards will come for me or my parents next. I have nightmares, and have come to depend on school as the ultimate distraction. The little brown brick schoolhouse three blocks from home feels like the only place where I control my destiny. I know if I work hard, listen to my teachers with enthusiasm, and obey the rules without question, I will succeed. I am often chosen to be the spokesperson for our classroom during school-wide events and am awarded the highest achievements in my grade.

All of our curriculum is centered around the statements of Chairman Mao. At school we recite throughout the day the chants of Mao. "Obey the Communist Party! Obey Chairman Mao's instructions selflessly to serve the country!" We must memorize and recite each word of *The Red Book*, which is a printed record of Chairman Mao's statements. Every single song we learn to sing, and every single dance we are allowed to dance, are centered on praising Mao. We never read fairytale books, and though I want to learn about flowers and animals and love, the students are never asked for our opinion on learning.

My second passion is dance. I lose myself while I dance, alone in my room to our box radio, feeling such a connection to my body when I hear music. The natural ability I have to dictate each move of my body makes me feel strong and powerful. When I dance, I'm not worried about hiding who I am or protecting my family. I have no choice but to be present in the moment, all thoughts on aligning my arms, legs, head, chest, and hips to the established rhythm. I think it is this escape that ushers me into the world of dance.

I am excited when they announce auditions to dance in a giant celebration for The National Day of the People's Republic of China. The two best dancers from each school in Beijing will be selected to train as dancers for the Independence Day celebration, which will take place in Tiananmen Square. To be selected means you will dance in front of Chairman Mao himself, which is an incredible honor.

For the audition, a dance teacher comes in the morning to teach us a routine, and then we perform it as a group after lunch. I don't eat lunch that day and instead use the extra time to hide out in our empty classroom to practice the routine over and over. My mind is sharp, and I move through the steps like clockwork.

As I walk back to our dance room, I see one man and a woman dressed in blue and gray conservative Mao-style suits, sitting at the front of the room. They've obviously been sent by the government. A shiver of fear takes flight up my spine, but I know they are only here to select the dancers. That's their job. I'm nervous before the audition, but I focus my mind on being present and dancing with everything I have. *If I am chosen, my family will be safe,* I tell myself.

They bark, demanding us to repeat the dance five times. I am in the middle of the room, so I fight to be seen, putting emotion behind my dance. The two discuss in whispers the results after each round. After the fifth round they bring over the dance teacher and whisper to her as well.

She walks over and grabs a girl who is a couple years older than me and sets her before the man and the woman. They nod in agreement and ask the girl to sit next to them. The dance teacher goes to grab the next dancer, and I feel like I can't breathe, I'm so nervous.

The next thing I know, my teacher's small feet are right in front of me. I look up, and she's summoning me to the front of the room. I walk straight toward them. They nod at me as well, have me sit, and then dismiss the rest of the room.

They tell the other girl and I that we have been chosen as the two dancers to represent our school, and my insides might burst with joy! The officials tell us that for the next few months, we will need to train in a dance studio in the city center instead of attending school.

My parents are furious when they find out. Dancing instead of continuing my education is not the future they have in mind for me. There's nothing they can do, though, as refusing this honor would look suspicious and could result in imprisonment or worse.

Before training begins, my parents are told to return to their schools although they will no longer be teaching. Instead, the government is teaching the teachers about how to love Mao. While they go for their re-education, I wake myself extra early every morning to take a bus into the city center, and I don't return home until evening. The days are long and intense. The instructors critique every precise movement and make us repeat them until we get them perfect. There are short breaks throughout the day, and I'm beginning to forget why I loved dance to begin with. I'm always tired, but I'm committed to getting through this so I can perform for Mao and bring honor to my family.

One autumn morning, the leaves reflect brilliant shades of red, orange, and gold outside the windows of our dance studio. I am working on leaps and pirouettes in what will be the first of five workouts that day. I've been training here for a month now, and I'm exhausted, but that's normal. I go to do a leap, and as I land, my back twists incorrectly. Intense pain shoots through my lower back. I fall to the ground in agony. A young teacher with kind eyes comes over to help me up. She tells me to walk it off, but I'm cringing as I walk. She instructs me to sit this class out and just watch. I do so, but at the end of the class as we are walking out of the studio, she notices me still limping and comes up to me.

"Ying-Ying, your injury is going to keep you out of training for weeks. I'm sorry, but we are sending you home for good."

I walk into our apartment, my back still in terrible pain, and my ego bruised with disappointment. My parents, who come home hours later, are ecstatic when I tell them I will no longer be dancing.

"That works out great, Ying-Ying! I was getting worried you'd be behind forever. You have to catch up in your studies. You're going to have to work harder than ever," Mother tells me.

"My back really hurts."

"Just rest it, and it will get better."

I start crying, fearful for what will happen next. "I don't know if I'll ever be able to dance again."

"Ying-Ying there is no future as a dancer. Once you get older, they will replace you with someone younger and better, and you will have no other skills to help you. Plus, you are too tall to be a good dancer anyway. In fact, please don't grow anymore. Otherwise, no man will marry you!" At eleven years old, I already tower over my 5' 3" mother, who is considered a tall woman by Asian standards. Most of my father's male friends stand about 5' 5". I will eventually reach nearly 5' 8", a giant among women in China. Being different is difficult enough without my mother's criticism.

I cry harder and run to my room. Crawling into my bed, I cry from the pain, from the embarrassment, and from the lack of sympathy from my parents who are beyond happy I am no longer dancing. As I fall asleep. though, an overwhelming feeling of relief comes over me. I really am glad I don't have to train tomorrow.

I never go to a doctor, but over time my back no longer hurts. I don't dance much after that. My focus goes back to school, and my parents seem to breathe easier. I can now finally work toward their perfect image of me.

I do have to work tirelessly in order to catch up on the schoolwork I've missed, but it feels good to be back in the classroom. My teacher seems happy to have me there, and I pour all my energy and brain power into excelling again, seeking the thrill of great grades.

It is a mile walk to school, and because I'm in elementary school, I get out a couple hours earlier than my sister and walk home by myself every day. I like this time to myself, my mind able to wander, my breathing calm and steady as I take in my surroundings without having to answer to anyone.

One afternoon as I arrive home, I notice the door is unlocked. This is strange because usually my parents are still at work when I return. As I open the door, my eyes are met with an unsettling sight that pulls a scream from my chest. Our apartment is turned upside down, ransacked from every corner, and with just a glance, I can tell that many of our prized possessions are missing. Mother's rosewood armoire, the one with a full-length mirror, has been knocked over and smashed. Our best clothes, silk tops and cashmere sweaters bought in Hong Kong, are nowhere to be seen. My father's camera, a radio receiver—the only communication conduit available to the people— and even our electric iron, are gone.

We've been robbed. Being the only one home, I wrack my brain for options. It is too far to get to my parents' school by foot, and I don't think taking my sister out of school would be helpful. Maybe I can take the bus, but I have no money to board. That's when I remember that, just the other day while on the bus, Father pointed out the closest police station. I'm not sure how long it'll take me to get there by foot, but I know it's close by.

I sprint out of the apartment and onto the busy street. Bicycles whiz by as people sit on their front stoops, taking in the summer sun and slurping down bowls of soup. Tantalizing scents of garlic, onions, and sweet ginger distract me for the briefest moment, but I quickly regain focus. Amazingly, my brain remembers exactly the street I need to find, and I run straight in that direction. Block after block I run, ignoring the weird gasps and stares of people watching me. An elderly woman blocks my path.

Normally, the respectful thing would be to walk cautiously behind her, but I don't have time for that. She's sauntering at the pace of an inch worm. I approach her, slowing down, hoping she'll feel my presence and move to the side, but she doesn't seem to know I'm there. I decide to sprint around her, but this startles her, and she yells, "You foolish child. Come back here and learn some respect!" I block out her words and keep running. If she knew why I was running, she'd understand. Who wouldn't rush to help their family?

I run for nearly an hour until I arrive at the police station, drenched in sweat. It was farther than I thought, but I made it. I burst through the doors and am met by a policeman in the foyer. My breath is so rapid from exhaustion that I have to repeat myself several times before he understands what I'm saying. "Our apartment was robbed. My parents aren't home. Please come quick!"

He asks me a thousand questions, but when I tell him who my parents are and where they work, he contacts their schools, notifying them of what's taken place. When this happens, I know I've done the right thing. "Okay Ying-Ying, we are going to your apartment. I'll take you there on my motorcycle."

I'm thirsty now, but I don't dare waste time to ask for water. We need to get back to my apartment.

The policeman puts me on the back of his motorcycle sans helmet and tells me to hold onto him. He goes at a temperate speed as we travel to the apartment, but my hair blows erratically behind my head. I've never been on a motorcycle before, and at once I feel both exhilarated and important. We pass the elderly woman I had pushed past, and I smile at her and wave as we drive by. She looks at me quizzically as she waves back.

We arrive at the scene, and two other policemen are already there. We all go up to the apartment, and I tell them exactly what I found when I came home, walking them through the apartment carefully, describing how backwards everything is. "Normally, the table is over there, and my clothes are in the drawers. I made my bed this morning too." I feel this is important to add since even my bed has been tampered with. They ask me more questions and keep writing down notes vigorously.

My parents come home, bursting into the scene. They both come straight to me and hold me tight. "We are so proud of you Ying-Ying. I can't believe you knew just what to do," Father says. Ying-Hong comes home a few minutes after that, and mother fills her in on what happened. She looks straight at me and glares.

After the police leave, we spend a few hours straightening up our apartment as best we can. We sit down to dinner, and Father says, "Ying-Ying, thank you again for your quick thinking. You were the hero of the day." I smile. It feels like it's been forever since special attention has been shown to me, and it's nice.

Ying-Hong doesn't think so, though. She scrapes her chair backwards and stalks away from the table. I don't see her the rest of the night.

My sister's reaction troubles me, but what's worse is the reality of the day's events.

We've been so careful to hide our lives from the outside world and the Red Guards so as not to put our family at risk, but even in our home, we've been violated. Nowhere feels safe anymore.

We have no idea who robbed us until two years later when the police finally find enough evidence to prove it was the younger brother of our next-door neighbor.

5

Shenzhen

The years fly by on the calendar: 1973, 1974, 1975. Always, I dive into my studies, excelling in every grade. My parents continue to emphasize that my hope for the future rests in how well I perform. Not only am I selected as spokesperson for my grade, but also sometimes I am selected to make a speech at school-wide assemblies. This is my part in the battle to protect my family.

As I enter middle school, the cultural revolution is still strong in Beijing. Thankfully, because of my parents' careful efforts, we are safe, with no one suspecting our ties to Hong Kong or the United States. But there is always a risk, and my parents' plan for us begins to change. For the first time, they tell my sister and me they are thinking of moving us to Shenzhen, a much smaller, safer town, far from Beijing.

Two years pass, and the freedom in our city continues to dissipate. The government now dictates every avenue of a person's future, from if and where they will go to college to their career path and even who they will marry. Most marriages are arranged by representatives of the Communist Party. These representatives are sent to watch over a group of people in a school, factory, or any of numerous other entities, and then recommend who will marry who in that group. My parents believe in the right to choose your future, and know that will be the best for each of us.

My father's grandparents live in Shenzhen. My great-grandfather had lived in the United States for over sixty years, sending money back to his family in China. Now that he's retired, he has finally returned

29

home. He and my great-grandmother are suffering from ill health, and my parents feel it is their duty to get to Shenzhen as quickly as possible to help them.

The timing couldn't be better. Shenzhen is located in Southern China, close to Hong Kong. Not only is the weather much nicer, but also, there are more families with similar backgrounds to ours, and Shenzhen is much less politically monitored compared to Beijing.

It's 1975, and the universities are finally opening back up to students. Father applies to transfer for a teaching position at a local university in Shenzhen. This process takes over a year, and unfortunately our great-grandfather dies while we are waiting to move. When this happens, Father doesn't want his grandmother to be by herself. He decides to send Ying-Hong and I before his transfer is approved. This way we can be of service to his grandmother, and we can begin assimilating to the schools in Shenzhen. It worries me because I know my sister stayed with my grandmother in Hong Kong for eight years, and I don't want to go that long without seeing my parents. But Father and Mother promise that this is different and they will join us in a few months. Ying-Hong seems certain they will, and that also makes me feel better.

I am thirteen years old when Ying-Hong and I arrive in Shenzhen. I am shocked when I see my great-grandparents' house. It's a mansion! Great-grandfather worked his entire life, always sending money back to his family so they could purchase such a grand home. It is three stories high, located in a beautiful neighborhood with both a front and backyard and a rooftop patio. There is less pollution here, so you can see the entire city from that rooftop.

One of the first things I notice is a giant fig tree in the front yard that covers most of the space. Shenzhen is extremely hot and humid in the summer, and this tree is large enough to create glorious shade for us. I am entranced by it. I play and read under its foliage on a mat made of bamboo. When I spot the figs among the leaves, I can't help but to climb the branches and pick the juicy, sweet fruits. This is the first time I learn about figs. The Cantonese believe figs are extremely nutritious for one's body, and I eat plenty of them the first few weeks living there.

At this point in my life, I've only seen families living in tiny apartments, many of which have three generations living together in just a studio space. As I unpack the one bag of possessions I brought with me, I feel that I need more just to fill out the room I am staying in. I unpack my clothes—a few boring outfits—and place them in a chest of drawers that could fit quadruple what I have with me. The last thing I grab from my bag is my butterfly kite. The colors have faded since I was first given it on that Chinese New Year years ago, but it still brings with it memories of happiness. As soon as I feel the silk in my hands, I'm hit with how much I already miss my parents and how nervous I am for this new chapter. I close my eyes and let myself get lost in the memory of flying the kite for the first time. As I watch the silk wings flap in my mind, I begin to calm down. This is simply an adventure. I can do adventure. I'm sure this kite will love new skies to explore.

I still can't believe this entire house is just for our family. Of course, our parents tell us to never inform a soul we live in that house. "You are not allowed to have any of your friends or classmates over. Ever," Mother emphasized constantly before we left. She only sent us with our most humble clothing, nothing that can stand out, and many things which have tears and holes in them. I long to wear beautiful things, but Mother didn't want anyone to suspect us of having capitalistic connections. Even in Shenzhen, our family connections could endanger us.

We begin school immediately. The dialect in Shenzhen is Cantonese, which is different from the Mandarin dialect I used in Beijing. I am able to speak the language but have a heavy accent that my classmates make fun of. I stay particularly quiet in class for the next few weeks, which makes it easy to keep knowledge of where I live and who our family is at bay.

Great-Grandmother is fascinating. Unlike us, she wears beautiful clothing and seems to always exude elegance. She has outfits custom-made for her from local tailors, and she carefully selects the perfect jewelry and hair pieces to accompany her outfit each day. I'm amazed by the look and feel of the clothes she wears. She has the tiniest feet I've ever seen on a woman, which my sister tells me is because of foot-binding practices she must've done as a child. I can't imagine doing that to my feet although I am worried that a man might think mine too large, like Mother tells me I'm too tall.

Great-Grandmother is also kind and extroverted. She is always having visitors over, many of whom come from faraway villages, bringing with them all sorts of unique, fresh produce that Great-Grandmother adores. She in turn gives these visitors red envelopes filled with money or some of her jewels.

She sits in a chair by the door until I come home each day. We chat about the day, and sometimes I read to her. Then she retires to her bedroom with the help of the housekeeper. I wonder if she misses Great- Grandfather terribly, or if she is used to being alone. For most of their marriage, they lived on separate continents, and yet, she never talks about it.

My seventeen-year-old sister goes into her room and studies as soon as she comes home from school. I am lonely, missing my parents and my friends from Beijing.

One humid day, as I'm reading in the front yard under the fig tree, soaking in the summer sunshine and the warm breeze, a woman from across the street waves at me. I wave back cautiously. She walks over to me. She looks like she is around my mother's age, perhaps in her forties. A few strands of gray streak her jet-black hair, and her eyes are kind. "Hello! I'm May. I'm your neighbor from across the street. I noticed you just moved in recently. What's your name?"

"I'm Ying-Ying," I say, thinking she has a big house too, so it's probably safe that she knows I live here.

She gives me a friendly smile. "It's nice to meet you Ying-Ying. And you have a sister who came with you?"

"Yes."

"Well, I'd love to meet you both. Anytime you want to stop by for tea, you are both welcome. I just live by myself now and am always eager for visitors. I can also answer any questions you may have about the neighborhood."

"Thank you very much," I say.

"Well, goodbye for now! Hope to see you soon!" She jaunts off with a slight skip in her step.

I watch May walk across the way to her house. It is smaller than ours but still bigger than anything I had seen in Beijing. I like that she made no comment about my accent. She's the first person I've met so far in Shenzhen who hasn't mentioned it.

The next afternoon, I walk across the street and knock on May's door. I'm not sure what my parents would say about this, but boredom gets the best of me and my gut tells me I can trust May. I didn't tell Ying-Hong because it was a rash decision, and I don't want to be talked out of it.

May answers with hesitation, opening the door with a stern expression. When she sees me, her entire face transforms. She's beaming. "Oh Ying-Ying! It's a pleasure to see you! Come in."

Her house is cozy. All of the furniture looks old but well-loved as if a careful life has been built within these walls. There are many plants inside. I've never seen someone have so many plants indoors.

We pass by a small room with a chair and about five large baskets of yarn. "What is all the yarn for?" I ask.

"It's for knitting. Knitting is one of my favorite hobbies. I make all sorts of blankets and clothes by knitting and send them to my friends."

"I've never knitted before."

"I would love to teach you! Why don't you come over sometimes, and I'll give you lessons. It's a very handy skill to know."

With no other friends yet, I go to May's house at least once a week after school. We have long conversations while she teaches me to knit. She also makes tea and brings out cookies for me. I never tell Ying-Hong or Great-Grandmother about the visits, and they don't pay enough attention to ask. I can't fathom them telling me not to come here, though, so I don't worry about it.

I'm at May's house for another knitting lesson when I go to use the bathroom. I notice there is blood in my underpants and my pee is red as well. I scream and scream.

May rushes in. "What's wrong Ying-Ying?"

Tears flood my eyes as I give her the news that I am dying. As she sees the blood, she smiles. How can she be so calm in a moment like this? "Ying-Ying, you are not dying. You've begun your period."

I'm confused. My parents had never given me a puberty lesson. How in the world can blood coming out of you be a good thing? Thankfully, May breaks it down for me, teaching me the how and why of a woman's period. This is a lot to take in before lunch. I figure I must look shell-shocked because May asks, "Ying-Ying, are you okay? Does that make sense?"

I nod yes but only because I feel that's the answer she is looking for.

"Good. Well, let me know if you have any more questions or need anything. I'm here for you."

She turns to exit the bathroom when I blurt out, "But what am I supposed to do when this happens? Do I have to stay still? Can I walk? Can I eat? Can I go outside?" I ask her.

She laughs such a deep laugh that my whole body jumps. "Dear girl, just live like normal because this is *normal* for a girl your age. Maybe don't run around quite as much as normal since you might need to get used to this, but all healthy women experience a period and still go about their life as if nothing is different."

May exits the bathroom, and I take my time slowing my breath, doing my best to process all this new information about my feminine body as well as try to get over the embarrassment of not knowing something that is supposed to be "normal."

I finally summon the courage to go into the living room where May gives me a bag of treats to take home. "Go on home, dear Ying-Ying, and celebrate this new part of your life. You are blossoming into a woman!"

She quickly sews a cotton holder and fills it with paper towels as women normally use for this purpose. With a bag of replacement paper towels in one hand and a bag of freshly steamed roast pork bao in the other, I return home calmer but still uncomfortable. I try to get used to the feel of the pad, but I'm worried something is wrong. I wonder why my sister has never talked about a period. Perhaps this is supposed to be kept a secret. Though May assured me it's normal, I can't help but feel like this is some sort of weakness, and I know that one must never openly state their weaknesses.

That night before bed I'm in the bathroom for a while, trying to figure out how to change the pad correctly. Ying-Hong knocks on the door. "Hurry up Ying-Ying! I need to use the bathroom."

"Hold on! I still need a minute." After a couple of minutes, Ying-Hong bangs again.

"I'm almost done!" I yell at her, and at that she flings open the door. She sees me hovered over the toilet figuring out the pad.

"Get out of here!" I shriek, but she stays staring at me, taking it all in. Her face goes from annoyed to disappointed to furious. She looks disgusted with me and slowly backs out of the bathroom, slamming the door as she leaves.

Her reaction affirms that something must be wrong with me.

If Ying-Hong had treated me bad before, now a whole other level has been unlocked. I find out later that though she is five years older than me, she has yet to start her period. Her jealousy grows. My parents still haven't moved to Shenzhen yet, though I pray they will be here soon. In the meantime, Ying-Hong believes she has authority over me, and I do my best to submit to that authority so as to not upset her further.

She now monitors my every move, making it hard to sneak away to see May, but her primary focus is on inhibiting me from my studies. She blocks me from doing my homework, often taking my worksheets and shredding them.

One day I have an idea. I hide my homework in my skirt so that she will not find it. As soon as I get home, I hide it under my bed. I wake up in the middle of the night, so no one will catch me. I take out my math homework and begin solving the problems. I'm halfway through the exercises when Ying-Hong barges in.

"Why is the light on, Ying-Ying?" I try to hide my homework, but I'm not quick enough.

She sees the pencil in my hand. She barges over, grabs the pencil and stabs my hand with it. Blood bursts from my hand, and I scream from the pain.

"Shush. Be quiet, Ying-Ying. Don't wake up Great-Grand-mother." At that she dashes out of my room. I grab a gray cloth and hold it against my hand as it turns to crimson. I cry and I do not sleep at all that night.

My grades are slipping since I have missing assignments. My only hope is to get a near perfect score on the final exam to make up my math grade. One Saturday, I prepare to study all day so I can nail the upcoming exam on Monday. I wake up early to begin but can't find my math textbook anywhere. After nearly two hours of searching through the entire house, I feel doomed. I know I carefully placed it into my backpack right before I left school, so it has to be here. I begin to panic, and as the tears begin welling, I frantically run over to May's house. After she listens to my dilemma, she suggests, "Why don't you borrow from your classmate?" The thought hadn't occurred to me as asking for help wasn't something usually encouraged. She walks me a few blocks away to one of my classmate's houses and convinces the parents to lend me the math book for a couple of hours. Filled with relief, I'm able to focus all my energy on a cram session of studying.

The relief continues as I receive a saving grade on the exam! When I arrive home after school that day, I find the textbook right under my bed. I had searched thoroughly a hundred times there, which convinces me that someone deliberately placed it back there when I no longer needed it for the exam.

Thankfully, my parents are approved to make the move shortly after the pencil and math textbook incidents. With my parents back, Ying-Hong backs down, although she still makes threats, and I must be careful about hiding my homework. I'm afraid things will get worse if I tell my parents, so they never find out about the way Ying-Hong has treated me. They never notice, or at least they never ask me about, the scar on my right hand.

Within a few months after my parents return, my great-grandmother dies from a stroke at eighty-six years old. I am saddened but will remember her elegance, kindness, and love for beautiful things.

We mold into a familiar rhythm, and our collective mission is in full force to get my sister and me into reputable universities. At this time, less than three percent of Chinese high school students are being accepted into universities due to the shortage of schools and faculty members after the Revolution. Yet, the only way to have a successful career is to get into college. No one rises up to high levels of success in any other route. That would not fit into the government's plan. If you don't have a pathway through your education, you are subjected to government assignment for work. This means working in factories, strict government entities, or on farmland in a region you do not get to choose. The only semblance of choice comes from the college degree you select if you are accepted.

Remarkably, my father's career skyrockets in Shenzhen. He is promoted to vice president of a local college and is well-respected among his colleagues. I go to visit Father at work often after school, and every time I do, he is surrounded by students who admire him. I've always loved him, but seeing him so intentional with the students makes me swell with pride. He speaks to them with such wisdom, and I, along with them, hang on to his every word. He believes education is the pathway to a future I've never seen, one where possibilities are limitless. I want the freedom to carve my path and thus, adopt my parents' dream as my own. I have no other choice but to get into a great college.

Also influencing my passion for academics is the community that surrounds us. I become friends with the children of Father's colleagues. All of us are the offspring of university faculty, and thus, I'm surrounded by the brightest, most intelligent kids on track to be the most successful. We push each other to be more, and I have no doubt that my life will have meaning. I want to make an impact on the world. I want to be somebody who counts in society. I will stand out and find my way.

As part of this path, not only am I excelling and winning over my teachers, but also, I've finally overcome my embarrassment over my accent and am even befriending my classmates. Father's role is to hire multiple tutors for me. First, he hires a music professor, one from France who has impressive credentials from his university, to teach me violin. Father has noticed my love for music (whenever music comes on, I dance and hum along in tune). He believes I may have a knack for it if developed properly.

The music professor is awful.

Every lesson he yells at me until I cry. I barely play my first note on a song before he criticizes my form, my stance, my brain, and my dedication. I don't know if I'm his therapy session, using me to work through his worldly frustrations, or if he believes degradation creates a musical prodigy, but it doesn't work. After a year, I quit violin and am forever too traumatized to touch a musical instrument.

Father then hires me an English tutor. Strangely, this man finds the English language dull and repulsive. He says, "Honestly, if you learn any language, it should be French. French is the poetry of all languages and feels delightful on the tongue."

We meet once a week for months, but he dominates the lessons by singing French songs and reading to me in French. I wonder why French follows me. His son, a couple years older with a full head of curly, dark-brown hair, always sits next to me and makes funny jokes. I find it ridiculously cute and enjoy his attention. He becomes my incentive to continue with the lesson. After months, I don't know a sentence in English, but there are a few French songs I have memorized. I never rat out the tutor to Father, and as time goes on, I realize it would look foolish to tell him now after he's spent months paying this man. Luckily, he doesn't often ask me how my English is coming along. I don't think he's keen on me learning it after all.

My favorite chore is feeding and tending to our backyard flock of chickens. Each day I must feed them and check to see if any of the hens have laid eggs. I always get excited to see the hens lay eggs, but I feel terribly guilty taking them away from them.

What's worse is that on holidays, our housekeeper kills a chicken for a special meal. This overwhelms me with sadness, and thus, I refuse to eat it and usually go into my room to eat something else so that I don't have to witness my family eating the chicken either. Poor innocent chickens.

Another part of my education revolves around dating. And by dating, I mean a clear lack of that. Dating is not par for the course once in college. There is one consistent speech from Father on this subject. "No dating. Men are not to be trusted, and as you are going to college, a college which may not be here in Shenzhen, you must not lead on any boys. That is not respectful by any means."

Mother's lecture is slightly different. "When it comes time, make sure to marry a man whose mother you like. Getting along with the mother-in-law is even more important than liking your husband." I realized then just how toxic her relationship must be with the grandmother I'd never met, the grandmother who raised Ying-Hong for the first few years of her life.

I take my parents' advice and ignore the possibility of dating, even the attractive English tutor's son! It's easy as I know now is not the time to be distracted by the opposite sex. Thus, I continue to excel in my classes, but my education in the male gender remains elementary at best.

6

The Decision

The outside world is changing. While I'm in high school, President Richard Nixon comes from the United States to visit Mao and focuses on revising the relationship between the two nations. This begins to transform everything. For the first time in my life, the gate to the western world is beginning to open up. The American concepts of freedom and the pursuit of a happier life penetrate our society.

Chinese people everywhere are now looking for ways to get into the U.S., but immigration to the U.S. is a battle. It is only made slightly easier if you have relatives already living there, or if you are a pretty woman that an American might consider marrying. I realize quickly, though, that I might be in line for such an opportunity.

One night after dinner, my parents tell Ying-Hong and me that they have something important to discuss with us. We are both anxious to leave the table and get back to our mountains of homework, but they assure us this cannot wait.

Father begins by telling us that with this new relationship between the U.S. and China, his sister who lives in New York City has been writing to him, advising him that we should all apply to emigrate to the United States. He has applied, but the visa happens in a type of lottery that could take five to ten years, and that type of visa only allows him to take with him his wife and children under twenty. Even if it only took five years, Ying-Hong would be older than twenty, and would not be able to join until my parents became official U.S. citizens.

They believe emigrating to the U.S. will provide us with the best opportunities for a prosperous life, but they tell us this plan must never be spoken of to anyone else. It might not happen, and even if it does happen, it could still put our family at risk. Not everyone in China is on board with these new ways of thinking, and though people are more open, there is always the reality that another revolution could happen at any time. If that does take place, anyone who is looking to move to the U.S. would be in danger.

This conversation with my family gives me a fierce hope like none I have experienced before. From then on, my heart is in the United States. I regret not telling Father about the French-loving English Tutor.

I spend countless hours daydreaming about a future in America.

The idea of meeting my extended family keeps me in a constant state of excitement.

Grandmother moved to the United States right after my sister came home from living with her and I've longed to meet her, my cousins, and aunt. We have a few colored print photos of them at home, and I stare at them, taking each detail in so I can recognize them in person. Their clothes and hairdos are so different and stylish, and I imagine myself being the same. I am most intrigued by my grandmother, who looks as young as my mother in the pictures. I can't wait to walk down the streets of New York alongside this grandmother, my arm wrapped around hers, signifying to everyone that we belong to each other.

My curiosity grows ravenous for answers to a thousand questions. Does this family like Chinese food? Will they like me? Will they think I have a weird accent? How often will we explore the city together? Will they want to teach me how to mimic their hairstyles? What was it like for Ying-Hong living with Grandmother?

The thing I daydream about the most, though, is no longer having to hide my identity. I could be free and safe without worry and dress and do as I please. This becomes my American Dream.

After a couple weeks of this, though, I realize the daydreaming is interfering with my ability to focus on school. My parents tell me there is no guarantee we will move to the U.S., so we must still keep the plan of going to college here in China. I struggle to stay motivated because all I want is to go to school in New York, but my parents keep pushing me to avoid distraction.

Three years later, we are still waiting on the visas. I am eighteen and have been accepted to multiple universities. My parents are thrilled but cautious. Father urges me to accept a spot at the university in Shenzhen because he feels it is safer and thinks it would be good for me to stay close to home. My score on the college entrance exam was not high enough to meet the requirements of the physics department. I'd had my heart set on this path, but as I always do, I listen to my father and enroll anyway. Ying-Hong has been attending a law school in Shenzhen as well.

In mid-August I move into the dorms on campus and begin my studies in chemistry. I am excited about the newness of college and the ability to explore more of my independence even though my parents don't live far. Eager to make friends and get involved, I decide to join a student leadership group on campus.

At the first group meeting, I find myself noticing a tall, handsome student across the room from me. I feel so connected to him, even though we have never met, that I end up staring at him. He turns his face toward me, and I quickly turn my head the opposite direction, my cheeks burning. In the meetings, he speaks up with passion and authority. I find out his name is Wei Chang. He is an upperclassman, highly intelligent, and a model student. I like all these things about him, and I have a feeling we would be a good match.

I get more and more excited to go to the meetings each week, but

I always make sure to sit as far away as possible from Wei Chang. Thankfully, he is one of the group's leaders, so he always arrives at the meetings early, grabbing a spot before I get there. It's strange to be so aware of another person. I've never felt this way about a man before, and I can't tell if this is a good thing or not. I decide to not speak to him directly if I can help it until the jury in my head decides it is a wise thing to do. I must keep the perfect plan of mine.

My studies keep me plenty busy, so my brain doesn't go to mush thinking about Wei Chang. In late August, with the heat and humidity as oppressive as it has been all summer, I'm about to head to the library to study when I open my dorm room door to see Father standing outside it about to knock. This is a surprise, but I invite him in. He looks nervous. I instantly think of my mother.

"Is everyone okay?" I ask, the bright sun shining in my eyes.

"Yes."

"Mother?" I ask, just to make sure.

"Yes, she's fine."

"Then what is it?" I ask as he walks inside and takes a seat at my small dining room table.

Father takes a deep breath and sighs it out before answering. My stomach is in knots. "I just found out your aunt applied for a student visa for you to study in the U.S. It's gone through except for needing the approval from the American Embassy here. If they sign off on it, then you can go to New York City and continue your undergraduate studies there. My grandfather told me he saved money to fund Ying-Hong and your higher education. Grandmother in New York is holding the money. If you go, your aunt also says you can live with her in exchange for helping with some chores as she is confined to a wheelchair now."

I am shocked and thrilled and barely breathing as I take in what he's said. He continues to speak rapidly.

"I don't know if this is the best idea. On one hand, by the time our family visa is approved you will most likely be past the age limit just like your sister and will have to wait even longer to come meet us. This student visa would be a way to get you there first, but I don't know for sure if that will help or hinder our own visa case. I think this will be good for your future, but navigating a new country by yourself isn't smart. You don't even know the language, and I worry that—"

"I want to try."

"What? How come your reaction is so different than Ying-Hong's? I asked her first to take the opportunity, but she didn't want to go by herself, choosing to stay here to finish law school instead."

"I want to try to get to New York," I say, bursting with confidence.

His eyes flicker, and I can't tell if it's fear or pride he is feeling. He starts verbally processing once again.

"At this point, I hear the embassy is rarely approving any student visas. They are suspicious of the motives. Many have tried to fool the system and abuse the privileges of a student or marriage visa just to get to America. They know this, and it'll take an epic stroke of luck to be approved. And historically, they have never signed a student visa with a pending immigration visa already." He pauses and takes in my unmoved expression. "But alright," he concedes. "I will take you there on Monday."

In the following twenty-four hours, I encounter numerous stories of people being denied a visa by the embassy. I read multiple stories about this in the newspapers, and overhear a professor talking with a colleague about his brother's application denial. Getting this visa approved seems nearly impossible, but I have to try. I must do my best to make my dream of freedom a reality.

I spend the next few days researching everything I can about American history. As it feels like the only piece I can control, I am determined to not be denied a visa based on a lack of preparation. I go to my parents' on Sunday and plan to spend the night so Father and I can head over to the embassy early the next morning. When I get there, no one is home.

My parents must be out grocery shopping or out to lunch with friends. I grab one of my American history books (a rare find) from our home library and continue studying when the doorbell rings.

I open the door to discover it's *him*! It's Wei Chang at my parents' house. My breath catches for a moment before I drag him quickly into the house before anyone can see that a boy is here to see me. Or at least I think he's here to see me. *What is he doing here? How does he know where I live?*

"What are you doing here? You must leave immediately. My parents will kill me if they find you here!"

He chuckles at me but says nothing else. He just stands there very calm, looking straight at me. My eyes have been avoiding him but I finally get the courage to look straight back at him. As I do, our eyes connect, and I feel something so extraordinary, it makes it hard to breathe. It's like laser beams are shining from his eyes straight into mine. I'm filled with warmth, which quickly turns to fire, and a passion develops in me, rising through my stomach. My heart pounds with lust for this man, and my body shakes. This overwhelming sensation takes flight, making me want to bury my body into his chest and feel his strong arms around me.

But I don't. This feeling is interrupted by the words of my Father in my head, telling me never to forget my mission and where I am going and to not allow a man into my life until I am settled and happy with where I am.

"You have to go," I tell him again.

"Oh, please don't make me go. I've been wanting to talk to you for weeks, but you always leave the room so quickly after our meetings."

"I'm sorry. I can't explain, but you have to go."

I shove him back out, his expression puzzled but slightly amused, and I slam the door. I don't breathe again until I see him walking on the street, away from me.

Get a grip Ying-Ying! You are probably moving to America, I lecture myself. I try to go back to reading the list of American presidents, but my mind keeps wondering why Wei Chang came to see me and replaying the way my body reacted to being close to him. I wish I could've let it be, let him say what he had come to say, do the things he wanted to do, and I could've held on to what was happening in me. But I know I must not play mind tricks on a boy right now when my heart is yearning to move to a separate continent. That was the responsible choice, and I'm sure if he knew my plans, he would've thanked me for saving him from wasting his time.

Between the impending visa interview and the burning desire I have to see Wei Chang again, I don't sleep that night.

The next day is September 8th, 1980. I enter the American Embassy shaking. Father and I check in at the front office, and they ask us to wait until my name is called for my interview.

Sitting next to us is a father and son duo, handsome and tall. "Hi, my name is Yang Hu," the son says and then asks me what school I'm planning to attend in the U.S. We find out that we are going to the same school, starting at the same time. Out of thousands of schools in the U.S.—what a miracle! The father is so excited, he makes us exchange contact information and repeatedly requests that we promise to take care of each other in New York. My heart wonders what the outcome of this coincidence with this handsome and intelligent boy might be.

A few moments later, a young lady calls out my name. I stand, give Father a weak smile, and follow the lady to a room labeled #4.

Inside the room is the consular officer. The consular is older and bald with a large, muscular build that suggests he was once a star athlete. He asks me to take a seat as he looks over my student visa application. In my head, I'm going over the names of former presidents and the biggest cities and the rules of democracy as I await the long list of questions I'm sure is coming for me.

Instead, he takes a deep breath, pulls out his pen, signs the visa, hands it back to me, and then motions for me to leave. "Good luck," he says in a deep timbre as I stare back at him, stunned before I turn to exit the office.

I can't believe how easy that was, and my first inclination is to deny it. There's no way he signed. My legs are still shaking when I return to the waiting area. Father sees me, surprised how quickly I've returned. A look of relief flashes over his face.

"Did they deny it?" He asks. The truth hits me.

"No."

"What?" His mouth falls open as he holds out his palms in shock and disbelief.

"He signed it."

"He signed it, as in he approved it?"

"Yes. He did. I can go to New York."

Father grabs the paper from my hand to see for himself. "It's a miracle," he says, and his face is dumbfounded. I see in his eyes that he was sure I would be denied.

Seeing the reality set in on my father's face proves to me that hope is coming. I restrain myself, though, from displaying the excitement building inside me because I know my father would think it inappropriate. My parents always tell me it is selfish to outwardly show feelings of happiness, and I've gotten used to hiding my truest self in order to survive.

We leave quickly, forgetting to check on Yang Hu's visa signing status. I guess I'll find out when I arrive at school in New York. We arrive home and write to my aunt to tell her the news. She's enrolled me in a university that begins on September 22nd, two weeks from today, and the deadline to confirm my attendance is tomorrow. I have less than twenty-four hours to decide if I am going to uproot everything I've ever known. What makes the decision even harder is that if I leave my university, I will never be able to go back to college in China because of age restrictions made by the government. Oh, and Wei Chang. I will never be able to find out what that feeling meant when I saw him yesterday.

The truth is, this opportunity is what I've dreamt about for years. Unfortunately, nothing prepares you for the moment your dream comes true. No one tells you that arriving at the destination of the thing you've wanted forever feels like it just might kill you. I wasn't a novice dreamer, but I'd never had a course in how terrifying and sacrificial the road to my dream life could be. I toss and turn all night but awaken at six in the morning startled by the light shining through the gaps in my curtains. I marvel at the fact that, somehow, I'd managed to fall asleep.

I stay in bed as my eyes adjust to the hazy sunshine. Something about the way the light dances across my room makes me smile. My body feels weightless, and I want to laugh out loud. I think this must be what hope feels like.

In that moment, I make my decision.

The next two weeks are a blur of moving out of my dorm, packing, and buying anything I might need to take with me to a foreign land. My luggage is mostly filled with gifts for the family I will soon be meeting. There isn't much room for my own things, or for any sentimental packing, but I manage to sneak in my butterfly kite, folded into the original fabric box.

I've not said goodbye to anyone, not even Wei Chang.

My parents drop me off at the train station, where I will board the train to Hong Kong. I'm too excited and full of adrenaline to understand or appreciate this moment fully.

"Work hard, Ying-Ying," Mother whispers as she hugs me. "Our family's future depends on you now." It's a lot of pressure but I'm truly honored she believes in me, and I feel like I'm going to make it. What choice do I have? Father looks teary eyed.

I assure them I'll make something of myself. "I will be okay. Not just okay, but I will be amazing. And I will see you there soon." These are the last words I say before I must walk toward the terminal, the last words I say before I must turn to mask the tears that begin to well. It hits me then how crazy this is. My life is about to change forever.

7

America

The train ride is one hour long. My Hong Kong relative picks me up and escorts me to the Hong Kong International Airport. The pit in my stomach stays as I walk through the airport to my boarding gate, but part of me knows that this feeling is excitement. I'm eighteen years old, and for the first time, I am in an airport, and by the end of the day, I will be in the United States of America!

I approach my gate and stand by the giant window as I wait for boarding to begin. I marvel at the giant United Airlines plane before me. Entrancing me are the other airplanes that I watch land and take off in a seamless rhythm. I can't believe that shortly I will be on my first-ever flight!

That thought invites my nerves to make themselves at home, and they are growing in intensity. I start to worry about the airplane and what it will feel like to be thirty-thousand feet in the air. I worry about landing in New York and not being able to find my way to the baggage claim where my aunt's husband is supposed to meet me because I barely know any English. I wonder if school will be harder in America and if I'll be able to pass my classes. I wonder if I'll be able to make my family proud like I told them I would. One thought leads to another until they're all intersected in a web of anxiety.

I shake my head, hoping to push these thoughts away, and take a deep breath to ease my mind. I can do this. My internal monologue takes over:

Ying-Ying you've experienced such luck and success all of your life.

Your teachers, friends, and even parents would not be surprised that out of all your peers, you would be the one to study in the U.S. They would believe in you, and you know that anything you've set your mind to you've been able to accomplish. In America, this will be no different. This is just a next level challenge. A challenge you're ready for. You are intelligent and have a determined spirit, and that's all you need.

This rationale eases my nerves slightly, just in time to board my flight. As I board, a beautiful American flight attendant, who reminds me of the Barbie doll my sister gave me when we first met, kindly helps my lost-self find my seat. I have a spot next to the window, which feels like another drop of good luck!

A middle-aged American couple sits down in the two seats next to me. They smile and say hello, and I smile back at them and then turn to stare out the window, taking everything in.

I hold tightly onto my armrests and hold my breath as the plane begins taking off, moving down the runway at high speed before beginning to ascend. I close my eyes until the plane steadies in the air. As the plane gets into a smooth pattern, I finally remember to breathe and look out my window. I see the land beneath me grow smaller and smaller as I become one amongst the clouds! I let out a giggle as I take in the miracle unfurling before me.

A little while later, the same blonde flight attendant comes by each row asking passengers a question in English. When she arrives at my row, I am embarrassed that I have no idea what she is saying. The American couple by me try to explain, and the wife begins drawing on her notepad to help me understand. She draws what looks like rice and noodles and then gestures to me which one I prefer. Ahh! They are asking me what kind of meal I want. They are patient with me, and when the food comes, I meekly utter a "thank you" to the flight attendant. This is one of the few phrases I know in English and have heard others on the plane say as they receive their food.

I am so grateful and surprised by the kindness of these Americans.

Father, who was always overprotective, especially around men, told me not to talk to or accept help from strangers. But what a blessing this couple is. I remember when I first moved to Shenzhen and how terribly people treated me because of my accent. Here I can't even speak the language, but both this couple and the flight attendant showed me no animosity. The couple also gives me their contact information if ever I need anything in New York. I can't believe they would do such a thing without knowing me. Are all Americans so nice? I put away their contact information in my little wallet and thank them politely even though I am not planning to contact them. My parents' voices telling me not to depend on anyone ring through my mind.

Twelve hours later, staring out my window, I see it for the first time—*New York City*.

I do everything not to squeal aloud as the sensation of being on top of the world overwhelms me! I look down on the infinite city lights, and I feel a powerful sense of peace. Here I am looking down on this city I have dreamed of for so long, able to take it in from a heightened perspective, looking at it in real time, knowing that, in just a few minutes my feet will be planted on American soil. It is so extraordinary that my breath catches. It takes me a long moment before I finally release my breath, and as I do, I can't help but wonder what divine being has delivered such a miracle for me. At this moment, I believe there must be a force more powerful than I who is looking down on me just as I am looking down on this city, whispering that more is ahead of me than I've ever let myself imagine.

The plane lands with a jerk, making me jump. They open the cabin doors, and the other passengers begin moving to exit the plane. I follow, and though my brain is in a daze, my feet know what to do. They step off the plane. Slow and deliberate, they continue through the boarding tunnel, and make it onto the tiled floor of John F.

Kennedy International Airport. For a moment, the world pauses as I take it all in.

I, Ying-Ying, am officially in America. I made it.

The pause only lasts a few seconds, though, as the jostle of people hustling around me jolts me back to reality. Having no idea what to do next, I follow the other passengers who navigate with purpose toward the Customs exit.

After a lengthy wait in Customs, where thankfully they found me an agent who spoke Mandarin, I find myself in the baggage claim area, scanning the crowded space for the face of my uncle. Since my aunt is confined to a wheelchair now, Father told me my Uncle Richard will be picking me up. I had spent the last couple of weeks staring intently at the few pictures we had of this family so that I could memorize their features. As I search the crowd, I notice a taller than average Chinese man with a very handsome face. I know immediately it is him.

I rush over to him, introducing myself in Mandarin, but he responds in English, which I barely understand. He leads me over to the baggage claim carousel to look for my luggage. I've never seen one of these before, and I'm amazed at the system of a machine circling our luggage around as people dart around each other to grab a bag and then lug it out of the crowd. I spot my two suitcases, and Uncle Richard grabs each one for me. I'm grateful because I'm intimidated by how fast one has to push past people to grab their bag.

After getting my luggage, it's nearing ten at night. We stand outside in a long line to get a taxi. I marvel at the newness of everything as I witness it. It is loud, and people are rushing to and from. Though it's early September, it's already cold outside, and I can see my breath cloud the air as I notice the different ways in which people are greeting each other. Some are filled with warmth and strong embraces. Others yell at each other and quickly hop into cars that speed off. Everything feels purposeful, as if each person has a very important place to be where they should've been fifteen minutes ago. My senses are overloaded as I take in the novelty of it all: honking horns, loud voices, the scent of someone's broken bottle of red wine on the sidewalk, and women wearing exotic perfumes. I can't help but smile. My soul has needed this kind of adventure for too long.

It is finally our turn to hop into a cab, which will take us to my aunt and uncle's home. In the taxi, Uncle Richard is quiet and reserved. I can't tell what he is thinking and if he is at all happy I am here. Perhaps he just isn't speaking to me due to the language barrier, or maybe he's tired. I have no idea how long he waited for me to arrive. My parents told me that Richard was born in the United States but that his parents were from a remote area of China where they speak Taishanese, a dialect used only by a small number of people. He is a successful architect and designed a famous music hall in New York.

Forty-five minutes later, we arrive at their Midtown East Side Manhattan condo. I stare up at the height of the upscale apartment building as we enter through a revolving glass door. We are met by a large lobby with beautiful marble flooring. There is a counter where a bellman, clad in a business suit, sits and watches a few television consoles that monitor different parts of the building. He nods at us and says something I don't understand. Uncle Richard smiles and replies as he leads me to the two sets of elevators on the right side of the lobby. There is a beep, and an elevator opens. He motions for me to enter, which I do with caution. We ride up five floors until the elevator stops and the doors open. I follow him as he walks down the windowless hallway, pulls out his keys, and opens up the door to their three-bedroom condo, my new place of residence.

As we enter, there is my Aunt Danielle sitting in her wheelchair, waiting for us. I am shocked she no longer resembles the pretty woman in the photograph I had memorized. She is missing most of her hair, her eyes lack any spark, and she has gained quite a lot of weight. She was such a stunningly beautiful woman, and I'm saddened by all that she must've suffered to make her appear like this. Immediately, compassion overtakes me and, in my head, I commit to doing everything I can to make her life easier and to repay her for the opportunity she's given me to be here.

"Welcome Ying-Ying. I am glad you made it safely." She doesn't crack even a small smile, but she speaks my dialect, and I want to burst with gratitude for the ability to communicate with her.

"Thank you so much, Aunt Danielle, for this opportunity. I am so very grateful. I've brought with me many gifts for you all from home."

"That is great Ying-Ying, but I'm sure you are exhausted from traveling. Richard will show you to your room so you can rest, and in the morning, we will talk and do gifts and go over the plan for you being here."

"Of course. Thank you, Aunt Danielle."

She nods at Uncle Richard, who grabs my suitcases and shows me to a bedroom. He gives me a half-smile as he leaves, closing the door behind him. The room has a bunk bed, desk, bookshelf, and a rocking chair facing a small television. The entire space smells of cigars, and I'm sure this was my uncle's study before I arrived. I sit on the bottom bunk bed and feel relaxed for the first time in twenty-four hours. I'm in a home with family, and I feel like everything is going to be okay. This beautiful apartment is a safe harbor in a foreign land, and with that thought my adrenaline surrenders to exhaustion. I lay my head down and fall asleep instantly.

I wake up the next morning to voices outside my bedroom door. I'm coming to consciousness in a dreary fog, and it takes me a moment to remember where I am. The smell of must and cigars is so unfamiliar, and the voices make me think I'm back in my dorm room. As I open my eyes and see the bottom of the bunk above me, it hits me—I'm in New York.

That's all it takes for me to jump up. The last thing I want is for my family to think me lazy, sleeping in for hours upon end. I have no idea what time it is, but if my family is up, I should be too. I swing open my bedroom door to see my aunt and little cousin Luca, a short, round child, standing there.

"Oh, you are awake," Aunt Danielle coolly states.

"Good morning," I say timidly in English.

"It's afternoon actually!" Ten-year-old Luca, Aunt Danielle's youngest child and the only one who still lives at home, tells me in English, which I spend a moment trying to understand.

"Come to the living room, and we will talk," Aunt Danielle directs me.

I follow her to the living room and sit, waiting for her to begin. She sighs and begins speaking slowly without much inflection. The monotone of her voice sends shivers up my spine.

"Now I want you to know my expectations. You are allowed to stay here, but for my kindness in getting you to the United States, I expect you to help with all household chores. This may include running errands and occasionally helping out with Luca. I have put off your enrollment into the English as a Second Language Program at Hudson College until winter term. That way you will have time to get adjusted and make yourself useful."

"I'm not starting school yet?"

"No. You are not ready. You must learn your role here, and then you can begin the program."

I am extremely worried and disappointed that I won't be starting the ESL program right away because I have to pass the Test of English as a Foreign Language (TOEFL) exam by March in order to complete college applications to start in the fall. Starting the program later will mean far less time to study and improve my English.

Without any other option, I agree to her terms and am determined to do everything I can to be helpful and productive. The next few days I spend getting familiar with the house and learning how to use the stove (so different from what we had in China) so I can help cook. I do the laundry and look all around the house for what I can help clean, washing countertops, floors, tables, and bookshelves. There is a giant picture window from floor to ceiling that covers the entire width of their apartment. One afternoon, I notice the blinds of this window are rather dusty and spend hours cleaning them, one leaf at a time, until they are pristine. After a day full of chores, I go to my room and do my best to study English on my own.

Though I am grateful to be here, it doesn't take long for me to feel incredibly lonely. I miss home, my family, my friends, and familiarity with the culture. Everything feels off here. My uncle and young cousin only speak English, and Aunt Danielle doesn't like talking with me.

She mostly stays in her room, watching television. The three of them usually act as if I'm not around, and I'm hurt by the lack of warmth and companionship here. I am also bored and craving anything fun or entertaining.

My biggest excitement the first week comes when Uncle Richard takes me to the grocery store so I can pick up groceries for them in the future. Afterward, we collect Luca from school. His friends all crowd around us, asking if I am Luca's mom. I guess they've never met Aunt Danielle before.

The next week gets a bit better. Aunt Danielle wants me to have a pair of nicer shoes and asks Uncle Richard to take me to the Macy's on Fifth Avenue to buy a new pair. I'm in awe of the giant department store and extremely excited to see clothes that will actually fit me. Since I am so much taller and have much larger feet than most Chinese women, it has always been hard finding clothes that fit.

Mother would have to make my clothes, but they were never very stylish or form-fitting. I often felt like I looked like an elephant wearing them being taller than most of the people in China.

But here, in Macy's, there are limitless, beautiful options! Uncle Richard notices how in awe I am and encourages me to try on some clothes. I try on a few items and am in heaven when I find a pair of jeans with length that fits me perfectly! I imagine they were tailor-made for me, and I feel like royalty.

When I go to look at shoes, I am floored at the amount on the price tags. I can't imagine spending so much on a pair of shoes! I can't accept this, and try to tell Richard this is far too generous, but he insists I pick out a pair. I go to the clearance section and look for the least expensive shoes in my size, which are a pair of plain navy-blue flats. They're pretty ugly, but I choose them so that at least I know they are far cheaper than anything else.

When we exit the store, it feels magical as I pretend to be a native New Yorker walking down the city streets, holding a Macy's bag that consists of the shoes and the pair of perfect jeans Uncle Richard let me buy. Since we are close to the music hall that Uncle Richard designed, he suggests we go take a look, and he can give me a tour.

My mouth drops open as we approach the glamorous, modern-style music hall. The design screams of movement as various geometric shapes all flow together in a perfect sync of art and inspiration.

Uncle Richard is pointing out various aspects of the building and describing the process as we enter the inside, but I can't understand most of what he says. As I take in the brightness of the space, I unconsciously tune out his words and feel an immense sense of pride in him and all that he has accomplished.

I've been told that Chinese Americans can't expect to be successful and achieve careers beyond service industries. But here I am, standing in an extraordinary building that shows the big name my uncle has made for himself. It allows me to hold onto my dreams of making something of my life here in America. I owe it to my family, my culture, and myself. It is possible.

What a day! We are on our way home when Uncle Richard makes one last surprise detour, taking me to see the Empire State Building. He pays for us to ride the elevators all the way to the top, and as I step outside and look out over the city, I am immediately captivated by the vibrancy of this extraordinary place. It is beautiful, and I'm reminded of all the miracles that happened so that I could be standing here, literally on top of the world. I tell myself that though it might take some getting used to, this place is going to be my home.

A few weeks later, I've developed a rhythm to my days. One afternoon, I head back to the apartment after going to the grocery store but am not allowed in. As I go to enter the lobby of the apartment building, the bellman blocks my entrance, refusing to let me pass. I try to get around him, but he doesn't budge. He yells at me in words I don't understand. I shout back, "Richard and Danielle, Richard and Danielle!" I still don't know much English, but I hope that saying their names resolves any confusion he has about my being there.

He keeps sternly saying something I can't make out and blocking my path. Dread begins hitting me hard in my core. What is going on? Earlier, this man had waved at me as I exited the building. What changed in the past two hours?

He chooses a different phrase next, one I do understand. "No more," he yells as he forcefully pushes me out the door, making me drop all the bags of groceries. That's when it hits me. I am being kicked out.

Tears well up in my eyes. I have no idea why this is happening. What did I do to upset my aunt and uncle to the point that they are throwing me out on the street? I have no idea where I will go. All I have with me is a purse with a few dollars and, thankfully, my passport.

I breathe hard and fast, trying to calm the million anxious thoughts that are hitting me like a hailstorm. The endless acreage of New York City feels claustrophobic right now. I don't know in which direction to step next. I have nothing with me, and I realize I may never see any of my possessions again. The one that hurts most is my butterfly kite. Picturing that bright blue color makes me think of my parents and opens up a floodgate of tears.

People walk past me rapidly, trying not to stare at the girl who has her head in her hands, trying to calm her breathing and tears. No one is stopping to ask if I'm okay. No one knows that my world has just been turned upside down, my options nil. Humiliation and loneliness stab my heart.

As I start to realize it is going to be dark soon, my brain urges my legs to move. I begin walking and thinking. Making my way in some direction is all I can do to spark a pinch of hope. A few blocks down, I see a phone booth. I try to think of any phone numbers I know that could be helpful. I remember the kind Americans that gave me their number on the plane. I go into the phone booth and search my purse to see if I still have the paper with their number on it. I do! It is crumpled in my wallet. I place a few coins into the payment slot and slowly punch in the numbers matching them from the paper to the phone buttons.

I realize how different circumstances are now than when I was first landing in New York.

Never did I think I would call those Americans, and yet here I am holding my breath as the phone begins to ring. It rings and rings and rings, but no one answers. An operator says something I don't understand, and I hang up. I will try one more time. It rings and rings and rings, and then—oh, no, it's just the operator again. I hang up.

I don't want to waste any more of what little money I have, and I know the chances of being able to connect with that couple without knowing English will be almost impossible anyway, so I continue walking.

I start to think about my grandmother and Yang Hu, whom I met at the American Embassy. I've never met my grandmother, but I know she lives in Chinatown. I can't believe I listened and accepted Aunt Danielle's strict orders that I was not allowed to contact and tell my grandmother I was here. My Father had given me her phone number and address, but it was in a folder that was still in Aunt Danielle's apartment together with Yang Hu's number. I begin to fume as I think of how much my aunt has hurt me. Not only has she kicked me out, but she made sure I didn't connect with any other relatives here. She made sure she would be the one handling my fate.

With no other options, I go to see if I can track down Grandmother. I don't have her contact information, but I will go to Chinatown and inquire around to see if I can find someone who knows her. I've been told that her husband, my step-grandfather, is the head of a village association in that part of the city, so I am hopeful that they are well known.

I take a bus into Chinatown and am disappointed in what I find. The place is filthy with trash all over the street and is wreaking with the smell of fresh seafood on top of crushed ice lining the storefronts. The sidewalks are taken over by vendors displaying fresh fruits and vegetables as well as dry goods. People are cramming into each other as they hurriedly pass one another on the overcrowded and smelly street.

The lack of sanitation overrides any comfort that an edge of familiarity brings. I must admit that though it is called Chinatown, this place doesn't look much like Shenzhen. It is nice, though, to see Chinese writing, food that looks like what mother makes, and people who look like me. As I take it all in, I hear a couple speaking Mandarin and immediately turn behind me to talk with them.

"Hello! I am looking for my grandmother. Her name is Mrs. Cheng, and her husband is Edward Tang. He is the Tang's Village Association chair. Do you know them?"

They shake their heads no and quickly walk away from me.

I realize there is no real graceful way to do this, but desperation doesn't tend to move with grace . . . it just ushers in the need for it.

I decide to pop into every store and ask the owner if they know my grandmother. This is the most strategic plan I can come up with, and so that's what I do. Most shoo me away quickly with a resounding "No." Others don't speak my language. Some try to sell me souvenirs from their store in exchange for information, but I don't have enough money for that.

Then I walk into a salon and see an older Chinese woman behind the counter, cleaning up. It's late, and it looks like she is about to close shop for the night. She looks at me and gives me a quizzical smile. I'm exhausted and lacking any encouragement that my plan will work, but I ask her too if she knows my grandmother.

"Why yes dear, I do know her," she answers in perfect Mandarin. "She's been coming here to set her hair twice a week with me for the last fifteen years. I never knew she has such a beautiful granddaughter who lives in Red China!"

"Do you happen to know where she lives? I wasn't able to communicate with her about my arrival, and I must find her."

"Why, yes, I do! She lives in the high-rise building at the end of Canal Street. I'm not sure which apartment number is hers, but the doorman can ring her for you."

I thank her, and though my legs are burning with fatigue, I jog to find the building.

Luckily, it's the only one of its kind in Chinatown, so I spot it within minutes. I'm out of breath when I approach, and I pray the information I received is correct. It's ten at night now, and I can't imagine what I'm going to do if this doesn't work.

I enter the building and find a Chinese doorman behind a counter who also speaks Mandarin. I give him my grandmother's name and ask if he can ring her for me. He smiles at me and takes the phone, dialing a number. The phone rings for a minute, but it feels like ten, when finally, a groggy "Hello" comes through the phone. The doorman tells her someone is here to see her and then hands me the phone.

"Hello? Who is this?"

"Hello, Grandmother. This is Ying-Ying. I'm in New York. I was staying with Aunt Danielle, but she just kicked me out, and I have nothing with me and nowhere to go."

There is a long pause on the other end, and I feel that I might collapse. Finally, she gives a short, "Come up. Apartment 2308." With a surge of relief, I hand the phone back to the doorman who signals me to the elevator.

As I ride the elevator up, I try to calm my breathing. This is about to be the moment I've dreamed of my whole life. I am about to be in the arms of my grandmother. I knock on the door, and as she opens it, all my positive fantasies vanish.

Her pretty face is twisted in an angry scowl. "How dare you arrive here unannounced! This is the most disrespectful and selfish thing you could do. No wonder Danielle threw you out. You need to learn better just like your mother. Never do something like that again. You understand?"

I stand there shocked and desperate. She is yelling at me in the hallway of her apartment building, and I'm completely humiliated and ashamed. I'm terrified she is going to slam the door in my face, but instead she opens it wide and walks back into the apartment. I follow timidly, closing the door behind me.

She points toward a bedroom, and sternly says, "You can sleep in there." Then she walks into her bedroom and slams the door. I lie down on the bed in the room and cry myself to sleep in a tearful mixture of shame and relief.

8

Grandmother

The next morning, I wake determined to apologize and make things right with Grandmother. As soon as I hear my step-grandfather leave for the association meeting, I find Grandmother making tea in her kitchen.

"Grandmother, I am sorry about last night. Thank you for taking me in. I never imagined meeting you like this, and realize how wrong it was. But I was desperate. Thank you for your kindness."

"Ying-Ying, you look just like your mother with the big round face. What a pity. I've long hoped to meet you, but surprising me like that was in poor taste. Tell me why you're here, though, and I will see what I can do for you."

I sit across from her and tell her my journey to this moment. She sits and nods but shows no emotion. After the story, I sit quietly as she stares, taking me all in.

"Alright, Ying-Ying, you can stay here for the time being. I will write to your father."

I soon realize that Grandmother is unlike any woman I've ever met. She is in her late seventies but looks twenty years younger. She is remarkably stylish and elegant, owning a plethora of custom-made clothes, which I admire. Her nails are always impeccably manicured, and she gets her dyed hair set in the salon twice a week. She's also an incredible cook, and goes to the market every day to buy fresh ingredients. Everything she makes tastes delicious. She keeps her apartment pristine, and the entire space is decorated with tasteful furniture. I'm amazed at the life she lives.

Living with her personality, though, is far less glamorous. For the next few weeks, I hear an earful about the history of my family, embedded with all my grandmother's opinions on each family member. My ears get the slightest relief when she plays a round of mahjong, a tile-based game originated from China, with a group of four ladies for a few hours daily. One especially friendly woman from the group adores me, and every time she sees me, she says I must meet her son who is a surgeon and unmarried in his early thirties.

Other family members stop by to see Grandmother, and I get to meet them too, and then hear all the gossip about them from Grandmother afterward. The most consistent character in her monologues, though, is my mother. She's never warmed up to her, thinking it is Mother's fault that Father didn't marry a Chinese American woman and move to the U.S. to become a successful doctor or lawyer. I realize now why Mother always emphasized I should marry a man whose mother I liked, and why anytime we received a letter from Grandmother, she was always upset. I remember hearing her and Father argue about his mother often, Mother hurt by the harsh comments Grandmother had written about her. I wonder what it was like for my sister to live with her. Perhaps Grandmother was nicer to her because my sister looks more like my father. As Grandmother was quick to notice, I look more like my mother.

I also wonder why Mother never divorced Father, to relieve them both of the pain caused by Grandmother. I think that's what I would've done as a sign of love for my husband, freeing him from such a tangle between wife and mother. But Father treats Mother well, and is a good husband, and I believe they care deeply about one another.

I learn that Grandfather died when my father was just seven years old, and there were few options for Grandmother after that. At the time, cultural traditions prohibited Grandmother from remarrying, and, as a widow with four children, most Chinese men would not want to marry her anyway. Thus, she put her hope in the marriage of her daughters.

When each daughter was sixteen years old, she arranged a marriage for them with American men. This would lay the path for herself to make it to America. Love was never the driving force for their marriages; rather, marriage was the vehicle to fulfill the American Dream. My Aunt Danielle was the eldest daughter, and was stunningly beautiful, but at sixteen was in love with a boy that lived nearby. When a man twice her age from America came to take her to New York, she tried to run away. The village they lived in was so small, though, that she was quickly found and forced to marry the man.

Aunt Danielle did become an American citizen, and many years later sponsored my grandmother so that she was able to move to the U.S. as well. It was at this point Grandmother dropped my sister off with my parents and flew to the United States. When she arrived in New York, Grandmother met and married a younger man to whom she is still married—my step-grandfather. He lives with us and always greets me with a gentle smile but never speaks to me.

By the time her mother arrived in NYC, Aunt Danielle had four children, had divorced her first husband, and had fallen in love with and married Richard (her first husband's cousin).

Grandmother constantly criticized Danielle for getting divorced and marrying Richard. Eventually, I believe Danielle could no longer handle Grandmother's controlling and abusive nature, and they got into a huge fight, which is why they no longer talk. Grandmother says it is because Danielle is mentally unwell, but I don't blame Danielle for wanting separation from the constant criticism from Grandmother. I have another aunt also in the U.S. who is married to the man Grandmother had arranged for her, and has two children, but I haven't met them, and from what I remember hearing from Father, she isn't very happy herself. Piecing together all of these accounts is my initiation into the numerous complexities that make up my family.

A few weeks into my stay at Grandmother's, I am in my room studying English when Grandmother barges in.

"Ying-Ying, listen here! Tomorrow I have a wealthy businessman coming to meet you. You must wake by six a.m. to clean yourself up. I will style your hair, and you must wear the Qi Pao I brought for you."

My first week living with her, she had taken me to her favorite tailor to get me a custom-made Chinese dress, known as a Qi Pao. When it arrived a few days later, I was stunned. The bright red silk fabric was so beautiful. I had never owned something so elegant.

The idea of having an occasion to wear it sounds wonderful, but I'm confused by her urgency of my meeting with a businessman.

"What?"

"We will meet him for a dim sum brunch! I have shown him your picture, and he is very interested in marrying you. The Qi Pao will make you look presentable. I need you to—"

"No!"

"What did you say to me?"

"I said no. I will not meet this man. I am going to college, I'm going to find out who I am here, and someday I will allow myself to fall in love. I'm not ready for marriage!"

"Ying-Ying, you need to face reality. You will never be able to get a college degree here with your English, and no one has any money to pay for your tuition! A marriage like this is the only way you're going to be able to make it here in this country. You may have been something special in China, but here you are nothing except a young, pretty face."

"That's not true, and I will not allow you to destroy my dreams like you did your daughters'!"

Her mouth falls open, as if what I have said stuns her. She replies with disdain. "Then you can leave here immediately. You are not welcome in my home if you do not meet this man."

My heart sinks to the bottom of my stomach. I didn't see this coming, but my fury kicks in fast. I picture an older man who wants to use me for his baby machine. There's no way I'm going to let her marry me off like she did her daughters. I'm only eighteen years old. I can't let her take my entire future away from me.

Ten minutes later, before I even have time to get scared, I am, once again, out on the streets with nowhere to go. I regret that in my rush, I didn't grab the beautiful Qi Pao. This time I just have twenty-five dollars in my wallet—a little better than last time I got kicked out, thanks to the cash Grandmother's mahjong friends gave me as welcome gifts. But it's still nowhere near enough to get by for long in New York.

I can't believe this is my family, so broken and manipulative. I will prove them wrong though. I will make it here. But Father is right. I can't rely on anyone else to help me. My future relies solely on my own capability and determination. I'm on my own and will find a way myself. Without many options, I go to sit in the beautifully maintained garden just down the way from Grandmother's high-rise building to regroup myself and come up with a plan. I sit and people watch, noticing ladies sunbathing on lawn chairs, a couple of older men playing a game of chess, and a group doing qigong. I'm zoned out watching them, and I don't notice the friendly lady from Grandmother's mahjong group approach.

"Ying-Ying?"

"Oh, hi! I didn't see you."

"That's all right. Are you okay?"

"I will be. Grandmother and I had an argument, and she kicked me out. I don't know where to go."

She looks at me with concern and purses her thin red lips in thought. "I have a friend who is a recent widow and very lonely. She could use some company, and I believe she has an extra room. Let's go see if she can house you."

I follow her to the widow's home. On the way she informs me that though she tried to convince him otherwise, her son, the surgeon, is not interested in meeting me. Somehow that news feels like another blow. Will anyone want me in this country?

We approach a small house, and an older woman opens the door. My situation is explained by Grandmother's friend, and the widow asks me a few questions. It doesn't take long before she determines she likes me and that she will allow me to stay in a small room for a very low monthly rent. I'm grateful for a place to sleep and for a lengthy evening discussion over tea with the widow. We both seem relieved to have such amiable companionship.

This agreement is short lived, however, as two days later, the widow's daughter comes to visit and is horrified to find me living there.

I overhear her yelling at her mother.

"Mom, how can you be so careless! You are allowing a stranger from Red China to live in your house? She is probably plotting ways to steal from you. You need to make her leave here immediately."

The widow tries to defend my case, but it is no use. Nothing she could say would convince her daughter that a stranger from China with no other place to go is a suitable housemate. After the yelling match, the daughter comes to find me and says I must leave at once and never come back.

I leave, but that night, once it gets dark, I'm scared to be on the streets. I walk back to the widow's house and sneak into her backyard from the side door. I curl up on a bench there to rest but am too scared to sleep, and I have no plan of action for the next day. The more exhausted I become, the more dire I feel my situation is. How could this happen to me? How can this be my American story? I rest my head on top of my small gym bag filled with school books and a couple pairs of clothes, and I close my eyes for a bit. As the sun comes up, I pray for a miracle.

The next morning, I walk into a bakery in Chinatown to grab something small to eat. The familiar scents of roasted pork and morning tea make my tummy rumble. Before I can order anything, though, I recognize a woman who strolls into the shop. She is a distant middle-aged cousin who I met recently at Grandmother's. I say hello to her because, thankfully, she speaks my language.

"Ying-Ying! I heard your grandmother kicked you out. Are you okay?"

"Yes, I'm okay." I lie. The truth is, I'm terrified. I'm worried about how I will get my next meal, take a shower, sleep at night. I've only been in this country a month and still don't speak the language or have a single friend to call for help.

"What happened between you and your grandmother?"

I try not to let my guard down. I cannot cry. "I just couldn't marry a stranger and give up my whole reason for coming here."

"I understand. We aren't our grandparents' generation. So, what are you going to do?"

I shook my head. "Honestly, I have no idea."

"Well, I have no extra space in my place, but you know, you do have some other relatives who live here. Let me see if I can find any that can take you in. Stay around here, and I'll come back and find you with an answer in an hour."

"Really?" I smile, feeling hopeful. "Why would you do that for me?"

"Well, I've had help in my life many times that allowed me to be here. It's time I return the kindness."

"Thank you much."

She smiles in return and leaves. I walk outside the store and snack on a roast pork bao and a cup of hot milk tea as I wait for her to return. Hours go by, and with each hour my hope is diminishing. I don't think she's coming back. All these potential relatives must've heard how much trouble I bring with me and refused. My cousin probably feels too sorry to face me with the bad news. I tell myself I will wait thirty more minutes before I try to figure out a different plan. I have to find somewhere to sleep before dark.

The thirty minutes pass, and I begin walking away, when I hear my name.

"Ying-Ying! I found a place for you!" My cousin approaches, out of breath. "Come with me. Your great-granduncle Sui Hong and great-grandaunt Ling have agreed to house you."

I am in disbelief that she's found a solution. "How much will they charge me for the rent? I don't have any money right now."

"It will be free. They don't want you to pay for anything, not even food. Sui Hong is your great-grandfather's blood brother, and he's heard a little bit about you and Ying-Hong from your great-grandfather before. He knows you and your sister's names are listed on the family tree! Plus, he is very grateful for your great-grandfather's help when they were struggling to take off in their business years ago. You can accept this kindness."

I'm in shock. It is hard to fathom all the good luck given to me from a great-grandfather I never had the chance to meet.

I grasp the handle of my gym bag tighter. "What will happen when they find out Aunt Danielle and my grandmother have kicked me out? Won't they think I'm bad news and untrustworthy?"

"Ying-Ying, most of our relatives here talk all the time about how crazy your grandmother is. She has a terrible reputation about the way she treated her children and grandchildren. We know what they did to your sister. Our family knows it isn't your fault."

I'm skeptical but extremely curious to know what she means about my sister. I follow her as she leads me to the apartment of these generous relatives. I pray this works.

Sui Hong and Ling are in their eighties and live in an apartment above an Italian deli. They moved to the United States around the same time my great-grandfather did and never left. They didn't have kids of their own but have one adopted son who lives in New Orleans with his family. He is only able to come visit once a year, so I will probably never meet him.

Most importantly, they seem thrilled at my presence on their doorstep. I quickly find them to be two of the warmest souls I've ever met. They treat me with such generosity and care, always asking about my favorite foods and my preferences for every meal. I feel like royalty.

"What is your favorite kind of cheese?" Sui Hong asks me not long after I arrive.

"I'm not sure," I respond. "I've never had cheese before."

He is shocked, and after that, Sui Hong makes it a point to go down to the deli to pick up a different type of cheese and salami for me to try each day. He thinks it a pity I haven't explored these foods before.

"One of the greatest things about New York is the delectable variety of meats and cheeses!" he often exclaims.

I honestly had no idea there were so many kinds of cheese. After weeks of taste-testing, I determine blue cheese to be my favorite.

During dinner one evening, Great-grandaunt Ling tells me Grandmother called her earlier to inquire about me. "I told her to never call us again and hung up the phone. She's such a bitch," Ling says with a look of disgust.

I do my best not to laugh. It is such a relief that someone accepts me and sees the right and wrong in my situation. I feel such justice! I also finally find out what happened to my sister.

My great-grandaunt tells me she heard, through trusted sources, that all those years ago, when Ying-Hong was an eight-month-old baby,

Grandmother took a secret ferry ride over from Hong Kong (it was only about an hour trip) to Shenzhen. Grandmother came in the afternoon when she knew my parents would be at work and Ying-Hong would be alone with her babysitter. At the time, citizens from Hong Kong were permitted to travel to Mainland China back and forth, but mainlanders weren't permitted to leave without special papers. Grandmother took Ying-Hong and ferried back to Hong Kong before the border closed completely.

I would later learn from Father that this story was true. There were several theories as to why Grandmother did this. Some thought it was to punish my mother, whom she didn't like. Others in the family said it was because Grandmother was very vain and wanted to appear younger than she was by having a little daughter who called her "Mother." Another theory was that she could use my sister as an excuse to make our relatives in the United States feel sorry for her burden and send her money. Some even said she may have thought it was the best for Ying-Hong's future to stay away from Red China.

Whatever her reasons, my parents couldn't do anything to get Ying-Hong back, and Grandmother never allowed my sister to communicate with them. My sister thought my grandmother was her mother until one day, when Ying-Hong was nine years old, Grandmother took the train with her to Mainland China, handed her to my parents without explanation, and left for the United States.

After learning everything about Grandmother, I know that Grandmother is a cruel woman, and she probably damaged my aunts and Ying-Hong to cause their current outrageous behaviors. I finally feel permission to stop questioning what I did wrong to make my family hate me.

9

Settling In

It is a supreme blessing to finally have a safe place to call home, but I still need to come up with money for my tuition. Father told me that I should have education money saved for me from my great-grandfather, but Aunt Danielle and Grandmother both denied such a thing when I asked them.

What makes this even more difficult is that in order to keep my visa, I have to be registered as a full-time student, but according to the law, that means I'm not allowed to work outside of school. If I don't work, though, I will never have enough money for tuition. My only option then is to find some sort of underground job, but it isn't going to be easy.

Not only is my English minimal, but I've come to find high levels of discrimination from those from Mainland China. Most of the Chinese in New York came from Taiwan or Hong Kong, or were American born, and they treat those from Mainland China horribly. If a business owner finds out you are from Mainland China, they won't hire you. Thus, I am told to do everything I can to not act like Mainland Chinese but to act like I grew up in Hong Kong.

I spend extra time studying how to appear like I am from Hong Kong. I style my hair like the girls in Hong Kong, borrow a new outfit that wasn't purchased in China, and even try to give myself a slight accent. I had taken acting courses in school before I left, and because of this, I am good at pretending. I'm determined to do whatever I can to make this work because I have no other option. If I go back to China, they won't allow me to return to college. I lost that chance when I left the country. If I want a college degree, it has to be from here in the U.S.

Knowing my predicament, another relative begs one of her friends to hire me for a sewing position at a garment factory. Normally, owners can only afford to hire skillful workers to occupy their highly sought-after sewing stations, but as a favor to my relative, an owner hires me to sew zippers on pants and skirts. I will be paid ten cents per item, the standard price, and the owner has agreed to pay me under the table in cash since she knows it's illegal for me to work while having a student visa.

I have zero sewing experience to begin with, and being paired with an industrial grade sewing machine is almost too much to bear. The obnoxiously loud noise that occurs every time I hit the foot pedal terrifies me and makes my hands shake, and the results are dismal. I make only twelve dollars my first week of work, because I am slow and constantly keep sewing outside the lines. I have to take the zipper apart and start over time and time again in order for my work to pass inspection. The hardest part is that not only must I make sure to sew the line straight and on target, but also, at the same time, I must coordinate the timing of pressing my foot on the pedal and releasing my finger at just the right moment when the machine needle rapidly drags the zipper to completion.

One day, as I'm sewing, my rhythm is off, and I don't move my finger in time. The needle presses deeply into my finger, cutting off a good amount of flesh with the skin. Blood spurts out everywhere. I'm trying to stay calm and contain the spurt when my co-worker notices.

She yells at me, "Go to the bathroom and pee on it or it will get infected!"

For some reason the idea of peeing on my hand pushes me over the edge, and I begin to cry uncontrollably.

My finger ends up being okay but makes it even harder to sew until it heals completely.

For all of these reasons, which show just how unsuitable I am for this job, I am sure the owner is going to fire me any day. But by some act of God, she has pity on me and allows me to stay. Not only that, but one day she brings me a few bags of clothes, shampoo, lotions, and school supplies. For the first time ever, I have beautiful, warm clothes that will be perfect for the upcoming New York winter! Her patience and kindness touch me immensely and motivate me to improve my sewing skills so as to not disappoint her. I get better with each day, and within a couple of weeks, I am making about three hundred dollars a week like the other experienced workers. I save every single penny I make and am thrilled that I save enough to pay my tuition for the upcoming semester!

January is here, and that means I begin my ESL program at Hudson College, a small school just a quick bus ride from my new home! I am so excited to start learning again, but it also requires an ambitious workload. My schedule will consist of going to classes during the day and then working in the factory from three to nine p.m. After work, I will go home to study until about midnight. I will have to do my best to get some sleep each night, and then repeat, day in and day out.

I look hard, hoping to find Yang Hu from the embassy, but he is not at the school. One teacher says she taught him in the last semester. Luckily, school is my playground, and I put all my energy into excelling. It is so fun to be in a classroom setting again, asking questions and learning, feeling a sense of purpose and drive. My English teacher is a beautiful woman with gold, short, curly hair and a pair of big blue eyes. She is gentle and patient and reminds me of the couple I met on the airplane when I first arrived. Her care is exactly what I need to succeed in this new style of learning.

I meet a few other students from Mainland China and develop new friendships. There is one handsome Chinese boy, Frank Chao, in my class who is always very chatty and friendly toward me. I find him attractive but am too overwhelmed with my situation to consider dating. I sometimes have thoughts about accepting his numerous invitations for a date, but the idea is quickly extinguished by the reality of my life. I'm so imperfect now, I'm afraid that if he finds out about my crazy family, he won't like me anymore. More than that, after work, school, and studying, I have no energy to spare for thoughts about dating. On top of everything, I need to study for the TOEFL as I have to pass in order to get into a good college. College applications are due by the end of March, and I have no time to waste. Now is not the time to be distracted.

One day, though, as I'm on my way home, I spot Frank Chao holding hands and dining with a beautiful woman in a restaurant near my apartment. I'm immediately hit with a dollop of sorrow that runs through my body. Sad, shameful, and hopeless feelings bubble up inside me. At that moment, all I want is to pity myself. If my life was different, that could've been me taking the time to enjoy a date and the affections of a handsome man. I let one hopeless tear slide out of my eye before I take a deep breath and shake the thought out of my head. I must move on!

I have the generosity of Sui Hong and Ling to keep me encouraged and well fed. Every night, they leave out an amazing three-course dinner for me on the dining table. They cover it with newspapers so that no flies can get into it as it sits out once they go to bed. This beautiful daily gesture fills me with love and motivation to continue.

The months pass by in a blur, and by the time the first hint of summer arrives, I have completed the ESL program, passed the TOEFL, and been given admission to SUNY University. SUNY has multiple campuses, but they are all located outside of the city, at least a two-hour car ride away, and I don't even have a car. Thus, in the fall, I will have to move out of Sui Hong and Ling's place and find money to afford tuition and room and board.

The owner of the garment factory has given me a promotion to a non-sewing position in the factory, but unfortunately, it still isn't enough to pay for all my expenses at SUNY. When I tell my friends from the ESL program about my predicament, Frank Chao mentions his sister is moving to another state next week and her hostess position in an upscale Chinese restaurant will be available. The pay is more than double what I make at the garment factory, so I take him up on the opportunity. I'm determined to work as many hours as I can, saving everything I make in order to pay for the coming semester. This is the American Dream.

I work at the restaurant all summer to save up money for the school year. My mother's cousin Katie hears about my situation, and that I've been accepted into the SUNY University system, and insists that I go to SUNY Binghamton, near where she and her family live. Not having any better plan, in September I move to the town of Binghamton, New York, and begin college.

In September, I say a tearful goodbye to Sui Hong and Ling, and Aunt Katie drives to Chinatown to pick me up and take me to my next big destination, helping me move into my dorm. On the two-hour drive to Binghamton, I come to know Aunt Katie's story. She is such a warm, caring, and intelligent woman. She is tiny and beautiful, and though I can see the fatigue in her eyes, her happiness overcomes it. She has four daughters, and the youngest is just eight years old with some disabilities. She has a master's in education from Cornell, but chose to stay home to take care of her family, especially since her youngest needs extra attention. She learned sign language to communicate with her and managed all of her schooling.

Aunt Katie met her husband George in college. She told me she had quite a few suitors in college, but George had caught her eye in a math class they shared. They were the two brightest students in the class and competed with one another to get the best grade. By the end of the semester, she beat him by one percent, and he asked her out to dinner. They'd been inseparable ever since.

She tells me she's a Christian and goes to church every Sunday with her family. She offers to take me with them whenever I want. I've never been to church and am curious what it's like. In a flash, the drive goes by and, as we enter Binghamton, Aunt Katie exuberantly says, "Welcome to your new home!"

As I take in the town, I feel I'm in a completely different state. Everything is orderly, clean, and quiet. Each yard is lush and green, and the homes look peaceful in their suburban bliss. I'm relieved to breathe clean, good smelling air, and I quickly realize I will not miss the constant chaos of the city.

Katie helps me move my belongings into my dorm room, and as I fall asleep that night, I feel safe and at ease. For the first time in my American experience, there are no sirens, horns honking, gun shots fired, or people yelling as I drift to sleep. This is the dream.

10

College

School starts with many challenges since my English skills are minimal, but I still manage to get mostly B's and a couple of lucky A's. My hardest class is Calculus because the professor is from Japan, and he speaks with a heavy accent. Since English is still hard for me, it becomes almost impossible to understand someone speaking English with such a thick accent. I end up skipping many of his lectures and just learning on my own through what he assigns on the syllabus, finding this to be more effective. And I still get good grades in his class!

I am on a very tight budget with the money I saved over the summer. Thankfully, I have access to a kitchen in the dorm building. My weekly food budget covers a dozen eggs, a bag of hot dogs, and some ramen noodles. I get fruits and vegetables, depending on what is on sale each week.

I befriend a few fellow students and get along really well with my roommate Mary. Her family originates from Greece. She's incredibly kind and loves fencing. She invites me to watch her practices and matches, and I am hooked. I fenced some in China, but it is very different from the American style. Both are enjoyable, though, and since all the equipment and outfits are free, I decide to join her on the school team later. We have a blast!

The first couple months fly by as I adapt to college life, and that's when I learn about Halloween. Mary invites me to go with her to a party, and I'm in awe of the students clad in costumes. Every single person is dressed up as a character, the decorations are all creepy, and even the food is made to look like spiders, fingers, and blood. I've never seen anything like it! I don't have a costume, and didn't realize everyone would be dressed up, but I have so much fun seeing everyone else in their costumes. What a night!

By the end of the semester, I am asked to declare an academic major, and I'm at a loss. For the first time I have a choice in what I study, and honestly, it's stressful! Where do I even begin? In China, it was all decided for me. But now I'm having to stop and ask myself, "Who am I and what do I want?"

In this process of choosing, I remember being five years old and thinking to myself that I could write better books than the ones my parents were reading to me. I loved books, and one day I asked Father, "How long does it take to write a book?"

Father, being a writer himself, responded, "Two years."

I was flabbergasted. "What?! How can it take so long?"

As I grew older, my writing in school was consistently applauded. Many of my essays were published in school newsletters. These articles were focused on praising Chairman Mao, largely the only topic of article allowed to be published. I often won composition competitions throughout my schooling in China.

Father knew this strength of mine but rarely celebrated it. Instead, he said things along the lines of, "Ying-Ying, there is no future in being a writer. Successful careers come from math and science, and that is where you should focus your studying." I still wonder why a liberal arts professor was opposed to my being a writer, but thankfully, I had always liked math and science, especially physics. In high school, I was one of the only students who got the extra credit questions on physics tests, and it made all the high school boys jealous. But now I have a dilemma. I'm taking the required liberal arts courses such as

American History and English. As I explore my options of study, I begin to feel stressed. There are the things I love, the things that come easy to me, and the things that follow the voices of my parents. Not all these things coincide with one another.

I'm riding on the wave of the beginning of the electrical engineering era. And though I am conflicted in my path, I can see the enormous career opportunities awaiting graduates of electrical engineering and computer programming. I can envision the pride and financial rewards post-college in such fields and want to be part of something that has an impact. I'm taking one electrical engineering class called "The Computer Operating System." It reminds me a lot of physics, which I love, and which comes easily to me. I'm excited to learn more, and when it's time to register for the following semester, I add more such classes and declare my major as electrical engineering.

Aunt Katie picks me up on the weekends and holidays and brings me to her house. We often go to church on Sunday, and though I don't fully understand Christianity, I respect it, and I feel peace when I'm there. Katie's daughters are so friendly to me, and I love listening to Katie and George's love stories from when they were dating. I hope I can find a love like theirs someday.

Christmas comes, and I stay with Aunt Katie and the family over winter break. We sing Christmas songs and eat tons of traditional holiday foods. For the first time in my life, I try turkey. Honestly, I don't like it much because it's very tough, but at least I've had an authentic American meal. Aunt Katie bought and wrapped gifts for everyone, including me. I receive my first big, brown, stuffed teddy bear and a red cashmere sweater. I love the gifts so much and can't believe this is my life. It's so fun celebrating the holidays this way in America! Most of all, though, I'm insanely happy to have a family who cares for me, and I feel I can finally settle in and acknowledge this place as my home. I'm safe and thriving.

By January, I am running low on the money I had saved to live on, and I need to find a job. I don't have a car and therefore can't work off campus. Plus, it's not Chinatown, so no one will risk hiring me under the table.

As I'm walking to class one afternoon, I spot an ad for a teaching assistant position for a professor who teaches Chinese classes at the university. This is perfect for me! I want the job so badly that I immediately go to the classroom where he teaches. I wait until his class lets out and students begin to pour out of the room. I enter and see him talking with a student. He is a well-built, clean-cut, middle-aged Chinese man. I wait patiently as they finish their conversation, and as the student leaves, I make my voice heard.

"Professor Wong?"

"Yes, can I help you?"

"My name is Ying-Ying, and I saw your ad for a teaching assistant position. I'm very interested."

At this, he smiles a giant smile. Somehow though, this makes him look off, like his smile does not fit on his face appropriately.

"Yes, the position is still open. Can you come to my office on Thursday at five p.m. for an interview?"

"Yes, that works great!"

"Great, I'll see you then." He smiles again, and I give him a small smile before quickly leaving the room. As I leave, I shake off the weird vibe I got from him and instead focus on preparing for the interview. This is such a perfect opportunity!

On Thursday, I arrive at his office at 4:55 p.m. I take a deep breath, and right as I'm about to knock on his office door, it opens.

"Oh, good evening, Ying-Ying! Do come in and take a seat."

I sit on a sofa he has next to a bookshelf stacked with countless books, half of which are in Chinese.

"I've made some tea for us. Would you care for some, Ying-Ying?"

I don't really want tea, and Father always told me not to take anything from strangers, especially men, but I also don't want to be rude or appear unkind.

"Yes, please. That would be great." He places the teacup on a saucer and hands it to me. "Thank you."

He sits in a chair across from me, and does a "cheers" motion as he takes a sip of his tea.

I blow on mine to cool it down and take a tiny sip.

"Now, Ying-Ying, why are you interested in the position, and what skills do you bring with you?"

"I'm looking for work on campus while in school. Being Chinese, I'm a perfect fit for . . ."

Something isn't right, and as I try to continue to speak, my eyesight starts to darken. I feel like I'm on a rollercoaster all of a sudden, spiraling downward at a warp speed. I think I'm going to pass out.

"Ying-Ying? Are you all right? Maybe take another sip of tea?" I hear Professor Wong say this, and that's when I know for sure this isn't right.

I know something is happening that is out of my control, but I am determined to save myself. I see black spots everywhere. The room keeps spinning, and yet I keep shouting my name in my head so I don't lose consciousness. "Ying-Ying! Ying-Ying! Stay awake! Stay awake! Ying-Ying! Ying-Ying!"

I don't know how long this goes on for, but I start to recover, I'm gradually getting sober, and my first reaction is anger. I've never felt anger like this. I remember reading in novels about violent outbursts of rage, but such a reaction was foreign to me until now. I begin to scream at him.

"What did you do to me?!"

"Nothing. Uh, I did nothing. Let me take you out for dinner. Make this up to you. You need food." His voice is frantic, nervous, shaking—nothing like the confident professor he appears to be. Thankfully, his horrific smile is no longer plastered on his face. I'm disgusted.

"No! No! No! I just need to get back to my dorm. Now!"

I'm still out of it. It's hard to tell exactly where I am. The world feels like a bubble, and I'm inside it, but I'm hyper aware of his presence as he guides me back to the dorm building. From there, I leave him, and though it takes me longer than normal, I find my room where I collapse on my bed, hoping tomorrow I'll wake up and realize this was just a nightmare.

But it wasn't. As the sun rudely makes a scene in my room the next morning, stirring me from the last few hours, I have to pretend this didn't happen. My brain flashes back to the night before. And in that moment, I begin gasping for air.

My heart knows it is miraculous that he did not succeed in what he had planned to do. I don't know what he drugged me with, but I showed incredible strength in overcoming it. These are not the thoughts, however, that dominate my mind. Instead, I am depressed, confused, and even ashamed. I hate this professor, I hate this place, and I hate my life. Time after time when I finally think that something will work in my favor, I am doused with abuse. It must be my fault. I'm too careless, a troublemaker, and I am being punished. I am unlucky and always will be.

Did I mislead him when I smiled back at him? Did I wear something that gave him the wrong impression? What happened in our first conversation that made him think he could do this to me?

I think about telling someone, possibly Aunt Katie, but I'm too scared she'll blame me for this, too, and think I am unlucky and not want me around her family anymore. I can't fathom losing this family I've grown to love. Plus, she has been so good to me that I don't want to add any extra burdens to her life by telling her this. It's the last thing she needs. I decide to stay quiet.

For two weeks, I'm severely depressed and anxious, and I rarely leave my dorm room. After that, I force myself to begin to function more normally, but it's difficult. Everywhere I walk on campus reminds me of the incident.

One evening, a friend I know from Hudson College, Collin, calls me, and I find out that he studies at SUNY Albany, which is about two hours away from where I am. Collin raves about the school and tells me I should consider transferring as Albany is a far superior campus to Binghamton.

It takes very little to convince me. I have to leave Binghamton, and this is the first gleam of hope I've felt in weeks. This is a chance at another fresh start.

The hardest part is telling Aunt Katie. I've avoided seeing her the past few weeks, blaming it on school exams, but really, I couldn't face her with the shame I'd been feeling. But every student needs an adult to sign off on their application to Albany, and since I don't have any parents or relatives to do so, I need her signature for my paperwork. When I go over there she comes up and hugs me, and it takes everything in me not to burst into tears and tell her everything.

I stay calm and reserved and tell her that I've decided to transfer to Albany because of their top-ranked electrical engineering program. I see it in her eyes: worry, confusion, disappointment. She is searching my face for an underlying reason, for some give away of what is really going on.

"I want to make sure you're okay. We care a great deal about you, and Albany is harder for us to come quickly if you need anything."

"Please don't worry! And don't think for a second this transfer has anything to do with you. I will miss you all terribly, but this is what's best for my future. And I'll be fine. I have friends from Hudson College that will help me settle in."

She notices my determination and reluctantly signs all the papers she needs to.

"Okay. But if things don't work out up there, please promise to come back here. We are always here for you, Ying-Ying."

My application to Albany is accepted just as the school year ends in early June. I decide to go back to New York City, to work at the restaurant I did last summer and stay with Great-granduncle Sui Hong and Great- grandaunt Ling again to save up money for my move to Albany in September.

It is so good to be back with Sui Hong and Ling, but sad, too. Their health is deteriorating, and they need more help than they'll admit. On my one day off a week, I take them to doctors' appointments or to a dim sum lunch, or on a slow stroll in the nearby park. I cherish these moments with them, and I am happy to return the kindness they've given me. They tell me often that they're glad I'm here.

One evening I come home from work around midnight and sit at the dining table, enjoying the dinner Ling left out for me. I glance at the nearby trashcan and see something that looks like a check. I take it out to see and realize it is a check for $40,000 made out to Sui Hong! I place it on the table and wonder if it's a real check or not, and why it was in the trash.

The next morning at breakfast, I ask Sui Hong about it. He waves his hand casually as he says, "Yes, yes. I sold some stocks recently."

"Well, you should deposit this in the bank."

I know it is hard for Sui Hong to walk these days, and the idea of trekking to the bank must sound exhausting.

"No. You can go deposit it. Maybe I can sign something so that you can deposit it in your account."

I pause for a second to imagine the possibilities. That much money would make my life so much easier, but I shake my head to say no. Accepting this kindness is out of the question. "Today is my day off. I'll go with you, and we can deposit it together into your account."

"All right, all right." He waves his hand. "After breakfast, we can go."

The walk is excruciatingly slow but good for him, and I'm happy to know I helped him deposit such a large check. It's hard to imagine he would have just thrown it away. I feel like I have helped give something back to the people who have been so good to me.

The greatest gift of the summer, however, is Emily. A co-worker introduces me to her when she comes into the restaurant one day, and we get into such a fun conversation about travel. Emily is an immigration lawyer and co-owns a firm in Chinatown, and she has been to more places than I can ever dream of! She is an American-born Chinese woman who speaks fluent Chinese as well as multiple other languages, including French. She graduated from Columbia University, has been divorced twice with no children, and is currently single.

We bond immediately, and I love her strong spirit and independence as a woman. I'm grateful that the fact I am from Mainland China doesn't seem to matter to her at all. I feel appreciated for who I am, and I love that she treats me as an equal friend despite our differences in age, background, and economic status.

She calls me her God Sister, and she shows me the New York I've been missing! We go out to movies and long dinners and even see a Broadway show together. She introduces me to her friends, and for the first time, NYC isn't all work and struggle for me. Finally, I'm seeing the city come to life!

With my newfound view of NYC, I almost forget how dark the city can be. One night I get off work at 10:30, head to the subway, and get off like normal at my stop in Chinatown, only a block away from my great-grand aunt and uncle's apartment. As I step out of the subway, I notice a tall, well-built man in my peripheral vision. It is only he and I at the stop. He unnerves me, so I begin to walk fast in order to get out of there, but he matches my speed.

Then I start to run, and he begins to run, too. I realize I'm his target.

I get outside the station and run as fast as I can toward the apartment. I get my keys out of my purse as I run. I can see the apartment. I'm so close, but I can hear his feet pounding on the pavement behind me. I run faster, my lungs burning as I sprint. This chase feels like life or death.

Half a block later, I realize I can no longer outrun him because I can hear his breath huffing directly behind me. I quickly turn around to evaluate my situation and am shocked to find he is over six feet tall with a body like a heavyweight boxer. At the realization that I stand no chance against my attacker, my entire body shakes uncontrollably, almost like I'm possessed.

With no other option but to try and mask my fear, I dramatically channel Bruce Lee and make a karate forward stance with my right fist high above my head and my left fist in front of my chest. I try to be still, but even my face is shaking with panic.

I am pondering what else I can do when this giant of a man immediately stops, a look of utter confusion and horror flutters across his face, and he immediately turns and runs away from me.

I'm confused but relieved and waste no time sprinting straight to the apartment, where I slam the door shut and lock it as quickly as possible. My breath is coming up in heaps. Thankfully, Sui Hong and Ling are already in bed, which is good, because I don't want them to worry about me. It takes me a solid hour, sitting on the floor right inside the doorway before I realize I am safe.

I replay the incident over and over again, wondering why he ran away from me, until it finally clicks. He must've actually mistaken my shaking body pose to be some mysterious and terrifying karate move from the likes of a master like Bruce Lee! I laugh out loud, relieved that I am safe, and amazed that such a man could find me so terrifying.

The next day I tell my co-workers what happened, and my manager, who is about five years older than me, begins to pace back and forth in anger. He's only a few inches taller than me and a little overweight, but his concern makes his soft face a little more attractive. John insists that I need someone to accompany me home at night, and volunteers himself the next couple of nights. I hate that at twenty years old I feel frightened to be alone on the streets after dark. But that's the way it is, so I accept his offer.

On the third night, when John gets ready to say goodbye to me at my apartment door, he asks if he can take me out on a date the following night. I have mixed feelings, but I'm mainly gratitude for his help and caring. That makes it hard to reject him, so I say yes.

John is gentle and respectful. The one date turns into a few more over the summer as he takes me to places in the city I've never been before. We love going for walks in parks and discussing films we've recently seen. I like his companionship and am grateful to spend time enjoying the city I live in.

For many reasons, I try to keep my distance and let him know I am not interested in being anything more than friends. Though I am enjoying our time together, I can see that our lives will be moving in completely different directions after the summer. John is happy in New York as a restaurant manager, and I will be leaving in a month to go back to school and pour myself into preparing for a career that could take me anywhere. I made promises to my family to leave a legacy that will make this world better, and no man is going to stop that.

Even still, when he leans in and kisses me one night, I let him because I feel it's the least I can do for his kindness toward me. It's my first kiss, and I'm happy for the experience. It's exciting in a physical way. I finally get to see what it is like to do something intimate with a man.

Each time he does it, though, when we break apart, I look at his face and know that I am not in love with him. The kind of a burning desire that combines spiritual and physical doesn't exist with him. Thus, as the summer progresses, I make a point to prevent him from kissing me again. I don't want to lead him on.

On our last walk, before I head back to school, I can tell he is nervous. "What is it? Why are you fidgeting?" I ask him.

"Well, I'm realizing I'm going to miss you when you're gone. Can I call you while you're at school?"

"Sure, but John, I want to clarify something. I've really enjoyed our time together. It has been such a highlight of my summer. But we are heading in separate directions, and when classes start, that will be my focus."

"I get that, of course, but I'd still like to talk to you." I can't really deter him from here. I do like talking with him.

11

Men

I feel hopeful as I arrive for my first semester at SUNY Albany. The historic buildings, the peaceful atmosphere, that allows me to pour myself into my studies—everything is exciting and new. I move into a dorm building with two long hallways of twenty rooms on each side. One hallway for the women, another for men. My room, which I share with my roommate Jennifer, is in the middle of the girl's hallway. There is a common area with sofas, dining tables, and a kitchen. Since I'm on a very tight budget, I cook almost every meal in the kitchen.

Between classes, adjusting to life in Albany, and developing a social life with Jennifer, the semester flies by. John often calls me from the restaurant to say hi, but I keep missing his calls. I mean to call him back, but my schedule fills itself, and the days turn to weeks, and before I know it, it has been a month.

One Saturday night, I'm studying in my dorm room when I hear a loud banging on my door.

"Ying-Ying. It's John!" He sounds vile and not like himself. I don't know how he found my dorm room, but I don't answer, hoping he'll go away and think I'm not home. He keeps banging relentlessly.

"Open the door, Ying-Ying! I know you're in there!" The tone of his voice scares me, and I'm not sure what to do. "Okay, you give me no choice. I'm going to break down the door."

Finally, I answer. "John, don't! Please leave. I'm not interested in anything more than friends. You're scaring me."

"You don't mean that! Come out and talk to me, now! I am a U.S.

citizen and am opening my own restaurant. I want you to work with me. Our life together will be promising, and I can take care of you!"

"No! Leave, or I'll call security."

At this he starts kicking the door with shaking force. I'm pretty sure the door is going to fall off the hinges at any moment. I have no choice but to call campus security. They tell me they're on their way, but as I wait, my body starts trembling. All I can hope is that the door resists his advances. Thankfully, security arrives and escorts him off campus.

An hour later, there is a soft knock on my door. It is Collin, my friend who convinced me to attend Albany. I've only seen him a handful of times, but I'm relieved it's just him.

"I heard a man was banging on your door, threatening you," he says, voice laced with concern.

"Yes. He was this guy I went on a few dates with in New York. I don't know what got into him. It was awful."

Collin wraps his arms around me. We've never hugged before, and it is weird. "I'm so sorry," he says, "but I'm glad you're okay."

"Thank you."

He takes out an envelope that holds a ten-page letter he wrote, addressed to my parents, and a photo of himself. He presents them to me and says, "Ying-Ying, I've loved you ever since the first time I saw you a year ago in our ESL class, and I want to marry you. I am an U.S. citizen, and if you marry me, you can become a legal U.S. resident. Then you don't need to work in the restaurants, and I can protect and provide for you. In this letter I wrote to your parents, I introduce myself and my family. I also listed the top ten reasons why I'm your best choice as a husband. I know they will make you marry me once they receive this letter. Here I have prepared $2,000 for you to buy some warm clothes and food for the upcoming winter."

He keeps his arms around me for a few minutes. Then he loosens his grip and looks at me, and there is something in his eyes I don't like. He presses me firmly onto my bed, until I'm lying on my back.

"Collin, what are you—"

At this, he starts kissing me. I'm trying to push him off me when Jennifer and her boyfriend open the door, and he breaks away from me.

"Ying-Ying, I just heard what happened! Are you okay?"

"Yes, I am." I say as I run my hands through my hair and try to stop trembling. What is wrong with these men? They are awful.

"I'm so glad you're back though," I tell her.

"Well, I'll let you all hang out," Collin says. "Glad you're safe, Ying-Ying. Let me know if you need anything." He quickly scuttles out of the room.

I decide I'm never going to talk to Collin again after that. I'm so disgusted by men and now understand all of my father's warnings about them. I wonder if any men are decent human beings in America. The next weekend, John comes back and does the same thing, threatening to break down the door. Then he does it the following weekend too. I'm terrified and begin to worry he could show up at any time, anywhere, and hurt me. My roommate urges me to talk to a counselor who helps me file a restraining order against him. Security knows to look out for him, and they tell him if he breaks the conditions of the restraining order, they'll have him arrested. I never saw him again after that. I'm thankful, but I also wonder what happened to bring out this aggression in John. He was so gentle with me over the summer, and I never saw this side of him before.

A couple of weeks later, I received a letter from my parents. In the letter, Mother tells me that they got Collin's long letter along with his photo. "Although he seems highly qualified to be a husband," she writes in her elegant penmanship, "it should be your decision, Ying-Ying, as to whether or not to marry him. I trust your judgment." I set the letter down in shock. I didn't imagine that would be her reaction, and I am touched that even across the oceans between us she is showing me understanding and support. I finally feel that I'm being treated like an adult!

A few weeks after the restraining order incident, I go into the kitchen to cook dinner, and see an Asian man washing dishes. He sees me approach and gives me a head nod and a smile. I need to use the pan he is washing, and as I awkwardly stand there waiting, I study him.

He's only a couple inches taller than me, but he has an athletic build. There is a gentleness in the way he speaks that makes me want to talk to him more.

Plus, he's pretty cute.

I don't have many friends at SUNY yet, and especially not many that are also Chinese.

As I wait and watch him scrub the pan, I can't help but blurt out, "Are you Chinese?"

"Yeah, I am. My name's Francis."

"I'm Ying-Ying."

He reaches out to shake my hand and as I shake it, I note the softness of his soapy hand. "Well, Ying-Ying you are making dinner?"

"Yes."

"Well, when you're done, feel free to join my roommates and I at the table over there." He points to a group of guys horsing around, tossing popcorn into each other's mouths from across the table.

"Okay, I think I will."

When I finish cooking my stir fry chicken and mixed vegetables, I take up his invitation. I sit next to him, and as I watch and chat with him and his friends, I laugh more than I have since I left China.

Over the next few weeks, I visit Francis's dorm room to play computer games with him and his friends. Francis patiently teaches me how to play, as it's new to me. He always cheers me on as I battle against his roommates. I become addicted to the game Pac-Man, and one day before a final exam, I play for countless hours, almost missing my class! Thankfully, I look at a clock just in the nick of time. I can't believe I've been playing all day!

School is definitely keeping me busy. My classes are getting more advanced. But now, my life feels lighter. Definitely, the highlight of my day is the chance to see Francis. He introduces me to a life of routine fun I haven't experienced since moving to America. He teaches me bowling, and our group goes to the student union to play often.

When we play, we usually bring our own snacks. One cold winter day, while we keep warm in the packed student union, a friend of Francis's brings a box of bagels and cream cheese.

"Ying-Ying, what kind of bagel do you want?" Francis asks me.

"I don't know," I respond. "I've never had one before."

The entire group looks at me, flabbergasted. To have lived in New York and never eaten a bagel is basically blasphemy. They determine that they will cut each bagel into pieces so that I can try every flavor. After three rounds of bowling, the jury looks at me expectantly.

"So, which one was your favorite, Ying-Ying?"

"It's tough, but I have to go with the poppyseed one!" They cheer as if I just discovered the cure for an infectious disease, and I laugh heartily. Bagels will always hold a special place in my heart after this night.

Francis's family lives in NYC, and he usually goes there on weekends. I don't ask, but I wonder if he has a girlfriend he visits when he drives home every week.

Soon, final exams are over, and we are on winter break. Francis is heading back to New York City to be with his family, and I am too so that I can see Sui Hong and Ling and work at the restaurant over the break (luckily John no longer works in this restaurant).

I can't get Francis out of my head. Every moment as I walk the crowded, snowy city sidewalks on my way to work or run an errand or see a friend, I am on extra alert, hoping I'll run into him. I miss him, and I can't tell if he likes me or not. I wonder about his family, what they are like, and what traditions they have during the holidays.

Before I go back to school in January, I buy myself some new clothes, and I even perm my hair for the first time. I'm hoping he notices. Aside from that, I'm not sure what else I'm hoping for from him.

Spring semester starts up, and January flies by in a blur. February is upon us, and Jennifer and the rest of the girls in my dorm hall keep talking about Valentine's Day. I never knew this was such a big deal, but apparently Valentine's Day is supposed to be the most romantic day of the year. They gush to me about their plans with their "sweethearts" and ask me about mine. I tell them I have none, but deep down I wish Francis would ask me on a date. I sometimes daydream about kissing him. It would be my first kiss that I wanted, and it deserved to be somewhere magical, outside, under the moonlight, a giddy feeling overwhelming me. But alas, it is February 13th, and I still have not been asked out on a date. At this point, it feels hopeless.

I'm walking back to my dorm after class when I see Francis jaunting over to me. I like that he often skips as he walks. He tones down his skip as he gets next to me, though, matching his steps to my own.

"Ying-Ying, I have a question for you!"

"And what would that be?" I ask, full of hope.

"What are you doing tomorrow night?"

"Hmm..." A tiny grin escapes my lips. "I don't have any big plans."

"Would you want to go out to dinner with me for Valentine's Day?"

My insides want to burst with giggles, but I keep my cool. "Sure! That sounds nice."

"Sweet! I'll meet you at your dorm at seven tomorrow!" With that, he skip-walks to the science building, and I can finally let a giant smile overtake my face.

The next day, though, I'm crazy nervous. This is my first real and official date with a man I like. My roommate and the girls in the hall are all very encouraging. They can't believe I'm still a virgin, and they all want me to have a magical time. Since I don't have many clothes, let alone dress-up clothes for a hot date, they each search their own closets and pull things out for me to try. It's cold out, so I settle on a purple sweater dress and a pair of high boots. They help me do my make-up and hair. It's fun being able to get ready with all of them!

Francis arrives promptly at seven and whisks me away to a fancy steak dinner complete with red roses and a few gifts of perfume, chocolate, and a silver bracelet. I feel like a queen! We savor each bite and laugh throughout dinner, and I nervously anticipate kissing him later.

I imagine it will be similar to the way I felt about Wei Chang when he showed up to my door right before I left China. I'll never forget the feeling that overtook me, that made me want a man so badly, that trickled down from my head to my feet. I hope I will feel that again tonight.

As we step outside the restaurant, a full glimmering moon and twinkling stars light the night sky. It's exactly how I envisioned the evening would go. I'm hoping he will take my hand, lead me somewhere beautiful outside, where we are alone, and kiss me.

Instead, he hails a taxi. We get inside, and he grabs my hand. It feels nice. He leans close to me and right then, kisses me deeply. Sadly, I am so embarrassed. Here we are kissing while the taxi driver sits right in front of us and can easily see us in the mirror. I can't get into it, and I so badly want it to stop. I am severely disappointed. This isn't what I wished for at all.

We arrive back on campus, and Francis walks me to my dorm room. He kisses me again outside my dorm. He looks confused as he tries to take in my reaction. I kiss him back, hoping that will ease his mind. This is better than the taxi, but I am still nervous that someone will see us. I figure he can sense my hesitance, and I know it will be a turn off, but right before I am about to go back to my dorm, Francis asks, "Ying-Ying, will you be my girlfriend?"

I've dreamed about such a thing, but am surprised he is asking. Apparently, I didn't turn him off. I smile and feel chosen. "Yes, Francis. I will."

He kisses me again and says good night with a sheepish grin on his face. Damn, he is cute. I go to bed happy, but also confused. Tonight isn't exactly what I'd hoped, but now I have a boyfriend. Maybe my romantic expectations were unrealistic. Francis is a great man, and he wants me. That's what matters.

As boyfriend and girlfriend, our time together grows. I feel the freedom to be myself around him, and it is special being adored and appreciated for my authentic self. We go to see movies and for walks at the lakeside. I enjoy learning about my desire to be physically connected with him. We end our date nights cuddling and kissing passionately. Although, I expressed to him my desire to save my virginity until marriage, and he respects it. I can explore and be close with him but also feel safe and respected.

Two months later, it is Francis's birthday. After a celebration with his friends, we stroll back to his room. Alone, we keep kissing, pushing the limits further and further. Since it's his birthday, I don't want to stop him from what he wants. Plus, I can feel my body desiring all of him. I want to know what it's like to connect deeper and experience what's so special about sex.

That night I let my guard down completely. He's so happy, I pretend to climax so he'll think I enjoyed it as much as he did. This is also my way of saving something special for my wedding night, something that will set that future day apart from all others.

I do love the fact that I experienced the connection of lovers though. It's like nothing else I've known, and I can feel how it brings me closer to Francis. I wonder if I will marry this man someday. Either way, I am excited for the day I'll be married and will get to experience sex fully without any boundaries. The next morning, I tell him how special last night was, but that I want to go back to holding off on sex until marriage. Thankfully, Francis is understanding.

A few days later, we are heading into the city for a birthday celebration with his family. This is going to be the first time I meet his family. I know his family immigrated to the U.S. from Taiwan. What I didn't realize is that they are incredibly wealthy! We pull up to his family's house, and it's a full-on mansion with a gigantic fountain at the front yard behind the iron gate. Apparently, they own a second mansion as well that acts as a vacation home near a park, overlooking a serene pond. Francis's parents divorced a few years ago, and his father remarried a younger woman and has new children. His grandfather lives with them and owns the largest Asian investment firm in town, and his mother owns a major chain of Chinese restaurants that has three different locations. Francis often went home on the weekends to help out his mother at the restaurants. Grandfather looks serious, but his mother is rather friendly and cooks up an amazing birthday dinner for us.

In meeting his family, I feel ashamed of my own background. They are so successful that it's hard to relate to them. I do my best to stay quiet so that they will not find out who my grandmother is and the shameful stories I have about my family. I'm also afraid they'll find out how old I am. I am one year older than Francis, and being older than the man you're with is looked down upon in Chinese culture. I'm hoping they have enough tact not to ask me my age.

They don't ask my age, and they treat me nice enough that day! After meeting them, Francis brings me home with him on weekends and holiday breaks so that we can both work in his mother's restaurants. His mother is quickly pleased with how big of help I am since I've had experience working in restaurants before. She praises me constantly, but she is constantly yelling at Francis, calling him stupid, slow, and useless.

He never seems bothered by it, but it irks me endlessly. Though I hate to admit it, it lessens my view of him and makes him look weak. He never once stands up for himself, and I can't understand why he would let her walk all over him like a doormat. It hurts my heart that Francis doesn't realize how badly their toxic relationship impacts me.

I want my boyfriend, my man, to be respected, smart, and strong. I need him to have confidence in himself and a plan for his own future, instead of just obeying his mother's orders all the time. I'm worried his self-image is being damaged by his mother's yelling and deprecating nature and that he doesn't have sufficient time to focus on his schoolwork and career because he always puts his mother's needs first.

His mother seems to only care about her restaurant's business. This saddens me, but I keep trying to please his mother because I know that matters to Francis.

One day, as I am helping out at the restaurant, his mother asks me to go with her to drop off some supplies to another restaurant in Midtown Manhattan, which is directly next door to a fashion manufacturing office. When we arrive, the fashion manager, who is a frequent visitor, dines for lunch there, and he gushes all over me, begging me to be their model. An Asian woman with my height and build was too rare for him to pass up.

"You are exactly who I envision wearing these clothes. There is an exotic beauty about you that these clothes were created for. You must model them for us!"

The manager offers me a tour in his office and leads me into a spacious room where a modeling shoot is in progress. I am captivated as I watch the graceful movements of the models. For the first time, there is a curiosity inside me. Could I really be as elegant as these women?

It is like the room read my mind because the next thing I know, the manager's crew members flock to me, make-up tools in hand. They begin doing my hair and make-up as if it is the natural thing to do when a woman enters their presence.

When they are done, they bring out a long, modern, designer black dress with a low cut in the front. I go behind a curtain to change into it, and when I walk out, the crew members *oooh* and *ahhh* over me.

The manager sees me, and dramatically, his mouth drops open. It's not an attractive look. "I knew it! I'm a genius! You are perfection! Go stand over there in front of the canvas and do some poses."

I tentatively walk toward the area where I'd seen the other models posing. A photographer sees me, takes hold of my shoulders, and leads me to a spot in front of the canvas backdrop. Another photographer walks up, and together, they start taking pictures with their gigantic cameras. I've never seen cameras so big. For a moment, I think of Father and his love of photography. What would he think of these cameras? My wondering is quickly interrupted as the photographers begin shouting commands at me.

"Okay, pretty lady, let's do this thing! Show me what you got." I feel awkward, but make a pose with my hand on my hip like I'd seen one of the models do. The camera flashes.

"Turn to the left. Yes, right there. Chin up a little." *Flash.* "Now flip your hair slowly." *Flash.*

"Now turn to the right." *Flash.* "Smile." *Flash.*

"Be serious." *Flash.* "Pout." *Flash. Flash. Flash.*

They stop taking pictures and give each other sly smiles. "Am I done?" I ask.

"Yeah, you're done. You want to take a look?"

They gesture for me to come over to see the monitor connected to their cameras. I take in an image of the most stunningly beautiful woman on the monitor. She looks strong and fierce and undeniably gorgeous. Wow. Then my brain registers that it's me! I can't believe this is me.

Wow. What some makeup and the right outfit can do! It's magical. The manager notices me entranced by the photos. "See? You're fabulous! You must model for us!"

I return to reality and know that I must decline. "Oh, I'm so sorry, but I can't. And I have to return to work now. But thank you. This was an incredible experience." I quickly change out of the dress, put my normal clothes back on, and jet out of the studio.

For weeks after, the manager contacts the restaurant, asking for me and offering me tons of money to model. He even tells me if I become a model for him, he will sponsor a permanent resident visa for me. With this type of visa, I could work legally anywhere.

I am wildly uncomfortable about this, though, and I immediately think of my parents who would never approve of such a thing. I am focused on getting through college, the perfect plan of the future, and I don't need any distractions. Plus, his desperation gives me a bad feeling about his intentions toward me. I get the same dirty old man vibes that I got from Professor Wong, and I know that no opportunity would be worth that feeling of fear. Francis's mother doesn't seem to encourage the idea either!

The next time I go to drop the photographer's takeout orders off at his office, he tries again to convince me, and I firmly tell him, "I am not interested. I am not a model. Please stop asking."

With that, he throws a fit and asks me to take an entire rack of outfits home with me because they are for no one else. I'm shocked and say I can't accept them. He won't stop insisting, so I leave his office with ten outfits in tow. They are incredible!

Despite my discomfort with Francis's relationship with his mom, I do enjoy being with him. He is tender and loving. He adores me. He is so different from most of the people I know who are putting all their energy into schoolwork, focused solely on their future career advancement and success. On the contrary, Francis enjoys day-to-day life to the fullest and values spending time with me.

When I was struggling in a chemistry class, he decided to sit in my class to find out the professor's expectations of the students so he could help me. On top of teaching me the tricks of bowling, he also teaches me how to play racquetball. We go to see movies and spend time hiking in the park on school holidays. A few times, we harvest oysters and mussels by the beach and bring them home to make a seafood feast. It feels like magic!

Seven months into our relationship, my birthday arrives. I'm turning twenty-one and it's hard to believe I've been living here in the United States for a little more than two years now. This birthday feels like a celebration of finally feeling at peace in this country so far away from my parents.

Francis takes me to the huge music hall in the center of the school with a performance stage and plays on the grand piano the Happy Birthday song. He adds a few Beethoven symphonies like a professional performer. I never knew he is so musically talented!

Upon returning to my suite, he brings out a chocolate birthday cake with pink icing roses that he made. My jaw is wide open with delight, as it is my first ever birthday cake! I feel so special! In China, my parents dyed eggs the color red for my birthday, kind of like Easter eggs, but red is for good fortune. I like this new tradition just as much, maybe even more.

While we are cutting the cake with two of my suitemates together, the door cracks open, and I see Uncle George poke his head in. What a nice surprise! He comes after a business meeting nearby. I am excited to see him for the first time since I moved to Albany and to introduce him to Francis. After he eats a piece of cake, he is on his way to drive home. I am anxious about what he thinks and will tell Aunt Katie about Francis. I hope they like him. Although his unannounced visit without Aunt Katie leaves me with an unsettled feeling.

To my delight, Francis's mother also insists on celebrating my birthday. She takes me to Bloomingdale's in Manhattan and asks me to pick out my favorite outfit because she wants to buy it as a gift for me. I walk through the racks of clothes, feeling them as I pass, but am stopped by a beautiful pink silk shirt with lace. The material feels so soft in my fingers, and it thrills me. She buys it for me as well as an ornate musical jewelry box she picks.

After this, she takes me to an upscale restaurant for lunch, where there is nothing on the menu I can afford. As we sit down, I'm feeling thankful that she is taking the time to make me feel special. We order, and then she leans forward and throws me for a loop.

"Ying-Ying, there is something I must discuss with you."

"Okay. What is it?"

She looks calm and direct as always. "I've known for quite some time that you are not right for Francis. He is much too young and immature for a woman with the qualifications you have. You can easily find and marry a lawyer or a doctor, which is what you deserve. I want you to break up with Francis."

My stomach drops. When my tuna fish sandwich and mushroom soup are brought to our table, I can barely take a bite.

A few days later, Francis says he wants to take me out to dinner. I'm incredibly nervous because I'm sure his mother has told him to break up with me as well. The idea of not being with Francis hurts my heart.

He takes me to an amazing seafood restaurant in Long Island, overlooking the ocean. It's so sweet of him to treat me to one last incredible meal before he breaks up with me. We order, and while we wait for our food, I watch him, expecting him to act nervous, but he doesn't. Instead, he says, "Ying-Ying, I am so grateful that my mother likes you so much. She gave me extra money to take you to this beautiful seafood dinner tonight. She said you deserved to be treated well. My mother doesn't like just anyone, but she can see what I see in you, and it makes me really happy."

I am shocked.

"Francis, I don't know if she really likes me all that much."

"No, she does. She talks to me about your future and wants to do everything she can to help you succeed. She believes in you."

I honestly have no idea how I can tell him that his mother just asked me to break up with him. I don't want to be the one to make him hate his mother, or worse, I worry if I do say something, he won't even believe me. I'm fuming at how she could tell us such different narratives. It's entirely unfair. I'm not breaking up with him, but I also feel a distance between us now as I hold onto this secret.

From then on, I anticipate that every time I see him, he is going to tell me goodbye. It makes it almost impossible for me to be intimate with him, and I put up a wall to protect my own heart from what I feel is coming. Francis detects my change and asks me about it a few times. I usually respond to him with a "nothing." The distance continues to grow as a few weeks later, the school year ends, and

Francis reveals to me that he will not be returning to Albany in the fall. Instead, he is transferring to Columbia University located in the city. "My mother needs me to help in the restaurants, and I can do that and go to school if I am in the city."

I burst into tears as soon as I am back in my room after hearing this news. This is all part of his mother's awful plan to break us up! He is definitely going to end things with me at any moment. She is controlling and will stop at nothing to have her way.

My heart feels off. It has grown attached to Francis, but at the same time, there are so many worries I have about our relationship. I think of my own mother and her disastrous relationship with my grandmother, a woman who kidnapped her own granddaughter. I don't want that kind of life.

I don't want a mother-in-law who will stop at nothing to destroy my relationship. I also have doubts about Francis. I don't believe that he will have it in him to stand up for himself, let alone me, to his mother. Will he truly be able to put our relationship first if he finds out his mother disapproves?

I go back to Albany without Francis for my senior year, and school is more intense than ever. I have to take a psychology class to complete the graduation requirements. The professor, who is the head of the psychology department, is blind due to some health issues. He tells our class that his wife recently divorced him, and he lives in a motel by himself. Due to his blindness, he requires all of our homework, including term papers, to be turned in via tape recording. This is incredibly difficult for me as I have trouble pronouncing many of the psychological terms in English. He constantly rejects my homework and papers, making me perfect them for him over and over again until he finds them good enough. I often feel that he is taking his anger out on me!

I have four other full-credit classes, and on the weekend, I am working at a local restaurant. Francis and I barely ever get to talk. We don't have time to visit each other, and we can't afford long-distance phone calls. I have trouble expressing my feelings in written English, so we don't even write letters to each other. I feel like I'm losing him.

With all my studying, my back pain is flaring up again. The pain is so excruciating, I'm having trouble studying. A friend of mine says she knows an older student who is a self-taught chiropractor from Mainland China. She brings me to him, and he interlocks his arms with mine and lifts me up so that my back is laying on top of his back. My face is up toward the ceiling. Then he asks two girls to each grip one of my legs, Pulling them straight. He wiggles around a little, and then I hear a *pop* in my back.

"That should do the trick! I'll follow up with you in a couple weeks and see how you're doing."

After that I feel so much better, and a month later, I realize I haven't had any back pain since that incident. It is a miracle! When I tell another friend who is studying to be a doctor about it, she says I was lucky I wasn't paralyzed by this nonprofessional treatment.

In my crazy psychology class, I meet a very handsome Chinese student, Henry, who also lives downstairs in my dorm building. We connect as we complain and help each other with the psychology homework. He is highly intelligent and gentle. I can tell he is interested in me, but I try to keep my distance because of Francis.

One night, however, I give in and agree to study together. While we are reading through our notes, he starts doing impressions of our terrible professor, and they are so spot on that I laugh until I cry. He laughs too, and as we calm down, he grabs my hand. I quickly take it away.

"Oh, I'm sorry, Henry. I have a boyfriend."

"You do? I had no idea!"

"He goes to Columbia University, which is why you haven't seen him around, and honestly, we've barely talked the past month."

"Oh. Well, I'm sorry I grabbed your hand. Friends?"

"Friends."

I'm relieved he is okay with that because Henry is a wonderful friend. He talks with such thoughtfulness, and I feel like I could sit all day and listen to his ideas. He also shows up when I need him. One day, my eyes are extremely red and swollen from allergies. He volunteers to accompany me to the hospital, and he even cooks dinner for me afterward.

It takes real intention for me not to fall for Henry, but I am determined not to complicate anything else in my life. We are good as friends. Plus, I know there are countless girls who are interested in him. Even if I broke up with Francis and dated Henry, I am not confident that it would last.

I don't think I'm good enough for him, and I'm sure that if he finds out about my crazy family, he would no longer like me. He is almost too perfect, and I believe another girl could snatch him at any moment. But I do enjoy that he doesn't seem to pay attention to any other girl.

My life continues to grow more and more difficult. One night as I am studying in the library, I hear my name being called. I look up and see four young men, wearing black leather jackets, staring at me. I can tell immediately that they are part of a gang I've seen around the streets of Chinatown and on the news. I'm confused and petrified with fear.

"Yes? What do you want from me?"

One of the men steps forward and flashes open his jacket to reveal a gun. "How much money did you steal from your great-granduncle Sui Hong?"

"What? I never stole any money from him!"

"If I were you, I'd tell the truth, or there will be consequences. He's not your family, you know. He has his own child to think about."

"I'm telling the truth, and I can prove it to you. I have a bank statement in my room that I can show you. And I work at a restaurant on the weekends to be able to afford to live. Why would I do that if I'd stolen money from him?" I figure their son who never visits them is behind all of this. It seems like all he cares about is their money.

"Show us this bank statement."

I don't want to lead them to my dorm room, but I can think of no other way to prove myself. When they enter my room, they see how little I own. There is nothing that hints at money. When I show them the meager amount I have in my checking account and that I don't have any savings, they let up.

"You better be telling the truth. If we find out differently, we'll kill you. From here on out you aren't allowed to ever see or contact Sui Hong or Ling again. You are done with them."

They leave, and I collapse on my bed, taking in heaps of breath. After they're gone, I think of the day Sui Hong told me to keep that $40,000 check for myself, and I'm so grateful I never took it. Refusing that has saved my life! It terrifies me to know that these gangsters know where I live, and my heart feels the loss that I can never go back to Chinatown and visit Sui Hong and Ling.

A few weeks later, I'm studying in my room when there's a knock on my door that startles me. I'm not expecting anyone, and I'm still jumpy since the gangster incident. I slowly open up the door, and am surprised to see Uncle George. I'm so excited to see him! Since they live a couple hours away, it's so hard to visit them. I think it's been six months since I've been able to spend time with him, Aunt Katie, and the girls, and I miss them terribly.

"Uncle George! Hi! Come on in!"

"Good to see you, Ying-Ying."

"Good to see you too. What are you doing here? Is Aunt Katie here?"

"I was just in the area for work. No, Aunt Katie isn't here."

"Oh, okay. This is a nice surprise. How is everyone?"

Uncle George doesn't answer. Instead, he grabs me, pushes me up against the wall, and starts undressing me. I'm in total shock, and I try to push him off of me but he holds me tighter, and I can't move. He gets my clothes off and is undoing his belt as he holds his hand over my mouth. I can't believe this is happening. He takes his pants off, and then shouts out, "Oh, oh, oh!" He lets go of me and rushes into the bathroom.

I realize he's finished his business and already came at just the thought of what he was about to do. I quickly put my clothes back on, and grab my keys in case he tries anything else. When he comes out of the bathroom, I stand in control, my voice calm and strong.

"If you leave right now and promise never to show your face here again, I won't tell Aunt Katie."

"Uh, yes, okay." With that, he puts his pants back on and hustles out of my room.

My first reaction is that I feel so sorry for Aunt Katie. I love her too much to tell her about this. It could break up their marriage. It would devastate her, and she might even blame me for this happening. It grieves me, but I know that I can't go back to her home and visit her ever again. I just couldn't face her with this unpleasant secret between us! First Sui Hong and Ling, and now Aunt Katie. My heart breaks. In one short month, I've lost the only family support I have here. I know I will never see any of these relatives again.

I begin to lose every ounce of confidence in men. How many times could a man try to hurt me? Do good men even exist? How could George do this to my sweet, faithful, aunt after all she has done and sacrificed for their family? What is love anyway if it could be thrown away so easily?

12

Dylan

My parents' immigration code arrives in Shenzhen. The bad news is that in order to process their visas, the original practitioner, my aunt, needs to file the paperwork. Since she has cut us off entirely, the only other person who can sign off on the paperwork is Grandmother. She tells Father she'll only sign it if he divorces my mother, but he refuses. Their situation looks bleak.

I go to Emily for advice. She lets me know that my parents' only hope is if I become an American citizen or marry one in order to sponsor their visa. My other option is to obtain a working permit, the H-1 visa, like the one the fashion company offered me before, after I graduate and am hired by a corporation. With the H-1 visa, I can stay in the U.S. myself, but it will take at least five years to become a citizen and get the badge needed so I can then apply for my parents.

A failed attempt to move to the U.S. doesn't bode well for them in China. Luckily, they are able to keep their jobs, but any future promotions are put on hold because of their visa application.

What's scarier is that if another revolution were to break out in China, my parents could be jailed, or worse, for their attempt to get to America. The only thing working in their favor is that they live in Shenzhen where people are more accepting.

My parents are also worried about my sister. She teaches corporate law in China but is unmarried. At twenty-seven years old, ninety-nine percent of her peers are already married. My parents constantly write, asking me to find a boyfriend with a U.S. citizenship for her. This is the last bit of stress I need, and I honestly have no idea where to magically summon a man for a sister to whom I hardly speak.

On my winter break, I go to visit Francis in the city and take an afternoon to see Emily as well. When I get to her office, she is chatting with a beautiful and tall Asian woman I've not seen before.

"Ying-Ying, this is my friend Annie. We were college roommates back in the day!"

"Nice to meet you, Ying-Ying!"

"Nice to meet you, too."

We all go out to lunch and have a wonderful time together! Annie is full of life, is a business owner of a travel agency, and has the most adventurous stories! I love hearing Emily and Annie reminisce about their college days. Annie seems to adore me. She tells me how beautiful and incredibly smart I am. Even better, she doesn't care that I'm from Mainland China, which is refreshing, as it's always an insecurity of mine.

"Ying-Ying, you are absolutely darling!" Annie tells me. "I'm amazed you're going to graduate from the electrical engineering program at Albany. I hear that the program is extremely tough. You know, I'm looking for a woman for my brother Dylan. He is a very accomplished, brilliant oncologist and a researcher at University of New York Grossman School of Medicine. Would you be interested in meeting him?"

"You're so kind Annie, and I'm flattered, but I have a boyfriend. However, I have a sister in China who is a law professor and still single and would be very interested!"

"Darn! Well, maybe we can find a time to tell Dylan about your sister."

After our luncheon, on the way back to Emily's place, Emily tells me that Dylan was married to his medical schoolmate for two years, and they have been divorced for three years. There are many other women going after him. But he has never wanted to date any of them.

That weekend, I receive a card from Annie with a check for my next semester's tuition. Inside the card she writes in a beautiful, flowy script:

"Dear Ying-Ying: I'm impressed with how hard you are working to achieve your goals. This is a loan so that you can focus solely on your last semester studies and no longer have to work on the weekends. I'm looking forward to seeing you again soon. Cheers, Annie."

I'm floored with gratitude! How could a woman I just met be so generous? After twirling with joy, and taking in the shock of it all, I immediately call the restaurant and put in my two weeks' notice.

Three weeks later, Annie invites Emily and me to her house in Brooklyn for a weekend brunch. When we arrive, I discover that Emily and I aren't the only ones invited, however. A fit Chinese man is laughing with Annie as we walk in.

"Emily! Ying-Ying! I'm so glad you're here! Ying-Ying, this is my brother Dylan, the doctor I told you about," Annie gushes.

"Nice to meet you," Dylan remarks as he comes over and shakes my hand.

"Nice to meet you too, Doctor Dang," I say.

We all chat vivaciously over brunch, and I find Dylan a comforting presence. I love hearing his stories about the clinic at NYU, and I imagine walking that campus someday.

"Ying-Ying, where are you from in China?"

"Originally from Beijing but spent my middle and high school years in Shenzhen, where my family still lives now."

"Oh, that's great! I'm actually going to Shenzhen University next week to give a lecture."

"Really? Then you have to meet my sister who is a law professor at Shenzhen University!" The wheels are turning. This is my opportunity to show my parents I was trying to help. I take out a picture from my wallet that is of my family, and point her out to him.

"That's great. I would love to meet her and your parents."

"That's such good news!" I give him my parents' address and let him know how to contact them when he arrives. I leave Annie's house that day full of life and ease as I feel like I'm helping accomplish a major wish of my parents. I'm sure they will love Dylan, and I hope he feels the same about them.

A few weeks later, Dylan calls me to tell me he is going to interview a few fellows in Albany and would like to meet with me for dinner. I'm eager to find out about how the meeting with my sister went, so I agree with delight. After dinner, he takes me to the grocery store and loads a shopping cart with so much incredible food for me that I normally could never afford. We then go to the lake for a sunset walk. He asks me thoughtful questions about my studies and goals, and I feel comfortable around him. I'm thinking that he'll be such a wonderful brother-in-law when I realize he hasn't mentioned anything about meeting my sister.

"Doctor Dang, you haven't mentioned my sister at all. How did the meeting go?"

"I'm sorry, Ying-Ying, but I didn't meet up with your sister. But I did meet up with your parents for lunch. I really like them, and if I'm honest, I am interested in *you*."

This is not what I expected. "Oh, Doctor Dang, I have a boyfriend. He goes to Columbia University."

"Ah, I see. How serious is the relationship?"

"It's serious. We've been together for about two years. It has been hard since he transferred to Columbia. I haven't seen him in months, so I'm not sure where his head is, honestly. But I hope we're okay."

"Well, it sounds like there's still hope for me yet. You aren't married, so don't be surprised if I keep pursuing you, Ying-Ying. I tend to be relentless in my pursuit of what I want."

I blush at his words. From what I know of him, I know his words are true, and honestly, I'm flattered that such a successful man would be interested in me. I pause for a moment and take him in. I admire that, although he was born and raised in Singapore, he doesn't mind my being from Mainland China. I'm not attracted to him physically, but do like that he is a rather handsome man with an average height and only slightly balding. He also doesn't seem to mind my own height, which Mother always criticized.

More than anything, I am impressed by his reliability and drive. He received his doctoral degree at only twenty-five years old, and is a resident fellow at the prestigious NYU hospital, leading a cancer research project at the medical school clinic. He is determined to be a clinic director before turning forty. He's not had a serious girlfriend since his divorce three years ago. He instead focused on his career, and that puts me at ease for some reason. He's finally ready to find the woman who can walk alongside him in life.

There is a safety about him that I yearn for. Perhaps it's because he is seven years older than me and he exudes a level of maturity I feel I can trust. I haven't seen my parents in four years, and I am longing for a safe home, for the eradication of my loneliness, for family and a true sense of belonging. I'm exhausted and tired of the constant fight to hurdle obstacle after obstacle. I'm overworked, still fearful the gangsters might show up again, worried about money for tuition, food, and shelter, and constantly feeling, still, like I must hide who I am and where I come from.

I am not going to be unfaithful to Francis, but I sense my deep respect for Dylan. "I'm flattered, Doctor Dang, but I still am committed to my boyfriend."

"Of course you are. Well, Ying-Ying, I don't want this night with you to end, but I do have an early flight to Paris tomorrow. Let me take you back home."

I appreciate his politeness, and I am taken by surprise when a week later, I receive a card from him and a box of chocolates straight from Paris. I never imagined such a distinguished scholar like himself to be so romantic!

Francis somehow learns how to break into his grandfather's computer and uses it to call a few times a week. Each time he must be quick and sneaky because the calls charge his grandfather, and he could be caught. After a couple of months, his grandfather finds out what he is doing but allows him to use the home phone to make long distance calls occasionally.

Unfortunately, I usually miss Francis's calls since I'm either in the computer labs running computer programs or studying late in the library until it closes. On one successful phone call, we plan to meet for Memorial Day weekend in NYC while dropping a shipment for his mother. He picks me up from my dorm, and as we drive back into the pulsing heart of the city, we are stuck in bumper-to-bumper holiday traffic.

"Ying-Ying, I've been thinking." He takes a deep breath as he stares straight ahead. "Yes?"

"Let's get married."

My mouth nearly falls open. "What?"

"Today, after we drop off this shipment, let's go straight to the courthouse and get a marriage license!"

"We can't just do that! Your family doesn't approve of me!"

"What are you talking about? They adore you!"

"No, they don't. Your mother doesn't think we're right for each other." I hate having to tell him his mother asked me to break up with him months ago at my birthday luncheon. But he's asking me to marry him, and he's left no other choice.

"What? Why would she think that? You must have misunderstood her!"

"She doesn't think we belong together. And I don't want to come in between you and your family."

"No, I don't care. If they don't agree with this marriage, I will move out, and we can get an apartment on our own. I choose you!"

"Francis, I can't do this right now. I am so stressed with finals and school. My brain is frazzled. Can I please give you a decision after things settle down?"

"Sure. Of course," he says, his hands gripping the steering wheel tighter. "I understand."

Our lips are still for the rest of the car ride, but our brains are not. A frantic energy fills the space. It is time to make decisions.

For the next couple of weeks, my head spins with questions about my relationship with Francis. Do I really love him? I still have not experienced that same spark I'd felt with Wei Chang all those years ago. Is this just a temporary infatuation Francis has for me? Will he get tired of me as I get older and be unfaithful to me like Uncle George is to Aunt Katie? Will his family ever approve of me? Is marrying him inhibiting him from growing into the man his family wants him to be, from the chance to marry a Taiwanese woman, like I know they want him to?

Two weeks before the end of the semester, Annie invites me to go out for "girly time" as she calls it. Girly time means shopping in New Jersey, where there's no sales tax. I should be studying but honestly could use a little happiness and distraction for a night.

While out shopping, she tells me, "Today is special, Ying-Ying. You are about to be done with college, and I want to celebrate you in style. Let's have you try on some elegant evening dresses!"

"But Annie, I can't afford a fancy dress."

"Rubbish! You have an occasion tonight! You can wear it to the banquet we're going to. Just try some on for fun. You have a model body, and it would make me so happy to see you in them!"

"Annie, what banquet?"

"Oh, Dylan's clinic has a special banquet tonight, celebrating him! He's won the Harrison Prize, which is a significant award for those studying cancer. Only one proposal is selected each year nationwide, and he won this year! I am invited, along with one guest. Please come with me, I don't want to go alone!"

I'm shocked she wants me to go to Dylan's banquet, but I concede. "Okay, I'll go."

That's exactly what she's been waiting to hear, and she has a line of dresses for me to try on. I must admit I'm having fun pretending I have important events to go to that would require such an outfit. I try on a deep, rose-colored two-piece evening dress. In the mirror, I look like a princess, and Annie sighs with me at the sight, and then we giggle with happiness. There is one black, sparkly dress that is especially eye-catching on me. The next thing I know, Annie buys the black dress for me, and tells me it would be perfect for the banquet.

The evening comes, and the black dress adorning my body makes me feel like royalty. Dylan picks us up and drives straight to a banquet hall in Midtown where there are about a hundred people attending to celebrate his achievement. I am amazed by what he's accomplished. I'm also in awe of the party. At the center round table, a giant ice sculpture in the shape of the letter "H" is surrounded with fresh flowers.

The dinner is incredible—lobster and steak, or "surf and turf" as one man called it, which made me smile. This is my first time eating lobster, and though I've heard about it, I know it's a delicacy that few partake in regularly. The minute it hits my lips, I think it's delicious! To top it off, there are so many drinks and desserts offered that I have a hard time deciding what to partake in.

The people themselves are glamorous. They are decked out in gorgeous clothing and enjoying themselves immensely. I find myself staring more than I should because I'm fascinated with this society life I've never been a part of before. Many people, including Dylan's clinic director, ask how I know Dylan and seem disappointed when my response is merely, "I'm just his sister's friend."

After the dinner banquet, Dylan asks me to see a Broadway show at the theater across the street. "I already have the tickets. Please help me to celebrate tonight?" This is not at all what I had in mind, but I can't really refuse. Annie must rush back home because her son's babysitter only agreed to work until eight.

I'm honored he would ask me to be his date for the evening, so I agree to come along.

The play is beautiful, and I feel like royalty. Afterward, Dylan takes me on a romantic carriage ride through Central Park. I'm nearly twenty-two years old now. It's been more than four years since I arrived in the U.S., and I feel like I'm living someone else's life, getting to enjoy all the privileges of a class far beyond my own.

It's almost too good to be true. I'm clad in a stunning gown, accompanied by an intriguing, renowned doctor and his tenderness. I've been to an awe-inspiring dinner banquet and seen the stars in glittering lights on Broadway.

The night screams of romance.

The moon gleams above us, and I can't help but think of Francis. I miss him, and I'm still his, after all, but I shake him from my head so that I allow myself to enjoy this. This is a moment of reprieve from all the worry, from all the work, from all the constant exhaustion, from the answer I have yet to give him. Tonight is a celebration!

Two weeks fly by, and it's the end of June, which means the day I've worked incredibly hard for my entire life has arrived. I am graduating college from SUNY Albany with a major in electrical engineering and with full intention to obtain a master's degree in electrical engineering.

As I place my cap and gown to participate in the graduation ceremony, I think of my parents. We have communicated primarily through letters, which take ten days each way to arrive. They don't have a phone, but they call me from work every so often and leave messages for me at my school's office. I often miss seeing them, but today it almost feels unbearable. I'm so proud that I've accomplished a college degree, but my heart craves their presence. After years of work and hope, we should've been able to celebrate this together.

Dylan wanted to attend, but I declined. This is because Francis was meant to attend, but he arrives over an hour late, missing the entire ceremony. He blames it on traffic, but I'm disappointed in his neglect.

Afterward, he meets me at my dorm and helps me move out my meager belongings. My friend Henry comes to bid me farewell. When he finds out Francis is driving me back to NYC with him, he asks for a ride. We say yes, and the three of us make the one-and-a-half hours trek to the city.

I'm quiet on the drive. The exhaustion of the day's activities hits me. This semester was brutal, my finals so intense, and all of this was made harder by my wondering what I should do about my relationship with Francis. I realize that I have a future ahead of me still full of lofty dreams and goals. I don't know if Francis is part of those. Either way, I can't keep standing in limbo. I have to give him an answer.

We arrive in the city and say goodbye to Henry. This is the last time I ever see him.

Francis then drops me off at Emily's condo near the city where I'll be staying for the next few days. I stumble into Emily's guest room, exhausted, overwhelmed by the past few months and, honestly, the past few years. I fall asleep as soon as my head hits the pillow.

The sleep is the best I've had in months. I awaken the next morning with the clarity of mind to know that it would be selfish to marry Francis. I remember a vow I made to myself that I would rather set a man free than be trapped between his mother and him. I can't be responsible for tearing his family apart. I worry about how he would feel years from now. Would he resent me?

Or would he resent himself more for choosing a woman his family disapproved of? I can't risk such unhappiness for him.

My mind reels about his future and his happiness, and I don't even realize I'm not asking myself how I feel. I call and ask Francis to meet me at one of our favorite parks. I see him from a distance as I arrive, and it kills me to know I'm going to disappoint those kind eyes of his. But I've made my choice. It's time to do what I've been dreading for months.

He spots me approaching, and walks to me, wrapping me in a big hug.

"Good morning, beautiful," he says. I don't let go of his embrace. I stay there, staring at my feet. "Ying-Ying, are you okay?"

"Francis—" The tears start flowing from my eyes.

"Ying-Ying, what is it?"

"I can't marry you."

He lets go of me and looks at me as if I have punched him straight in the face. "What? Why?"

I recite the speech I've played out in my head all morning. "I don't see us having a future together. I know you can meet someone soon your family accepts who will love you, and whom your family will love, someone you can truly have a future with. I am not her."

"I don't want anyone else. I love you. Don't you love me?"

I don't want to answer this question.

He is oddly quiet, only a pained expression on his face. I expect him to say something, to fight for us, but he turns around abruptly and takes off away from me. I let him go. I walk around the park for countless hours, unaware of just how rapidly time is passing as my mind replays everything. My brain hits me with flashbacks of all the good times at first, until I will it to talk sense into me. I go over the facts and see the moments where he disappointed me, where I had a gut feeling we weren't meant to be together. I keep walking until I remember why I decided he wasn't the man for me, and I return to Emily's just as the sun is setting.

Emily has dinner made when I get back to her place. She takes one look at my face and then wraps me up in a hug. "You broke up with him, didn't you?"

I nod my head and bite my lip to keep from bursting into tears.

"Well, I have dinner for us, grilled salmon and a bottle of wine we can open."

As we eat and clink our wine glasses with a cheers to "new beginnings," Emily gets an idea.

"Ying-Ying, I think you need a vacation."

I nod in thought. Annie could get a great deal on tickets through her travel agency, and I did have a little bit of savings set aside. Maybe she was right.

"In the past four years all you've done is work and hustle and struggle. You just graduated from an amazing program and broke up with your boyfriend. The world is full of possibilities, but you need to get the hell out of town!"

I laugh, which feels remarkably good. "But where would I go?"

"Didn't you tell me you have a cousin in San Francisco who's been asking you to come visit?"

"Oh, yes. Susanna."

"Think about it. You need to do something for you!"

"Okay, I'll think about it."

Dinner with Emily makes me feel better, but once I head to bed, the weight of everything comes at me, and I cry myself to sleep.

The next morning, my swollen eyes stir open as I hear a woman outside my window calling my name. I get up and look out, seeing Francis's mother on the street below me. Since I don't have a car, she had dropped me off at Emily's whenever I helped her in the restaurants after work in the evenings, so it's no wonder she knows where I am. Why she is here, I have no idea, but I rush down to see her so she'll stop causing a ruckus.

"Why are you here?"

"Ying-Ying, I'm here to beg you to marry Francis."

"What? This is what you wanted. This is what you told me to do."

"Please. I will transfer the title of our vacation home to you both, and you can own and manage two of my restaurants. I will make sure you are well-supported financially."

"I can't do that."

"Please take some time and consider. It is a good offer. You would be foolish to turn it down."

She leaves abruptly after that, and I am furious. How dare she come back and bribe me to marry her son? I'm disgusted she thinks I am after Francis's money and that money alone is enough to make me marry him. If anything, this affirms my decision to end the relationship. If she'd come over and told me she would now accept me because she sees how Francis loves me, I might've considered going back to Francis, but now I see how she thinks of me. I'm not one to be bribed or controlled. I will marry freely.

In her, I see my grandmother's shadow. I see myself turning into my mother, sadness overwhelming me as I become a thorn between mother and son. I don't want to lead Francis to a life of pain, nor do I want it for myself. Though it hurts, I'm better off walking away now. For Francis's sake as well as my own.

This finality makes New York City feel claustrophobic, and all I want is to escape. I think seriously of my cousin Susanna's offer to visit her in San Francisco and know Emily is right. Now is the perfect time to go. I call Susanna and say I'm coming immediately. Annie helps me book a plane ticket for the following day. She mentions that Dylan is attending a two-week-long doctor's conference as a keynote speaker at Stanford University and is hoping to see me when I'm there. I can't think of seeing any man right now, but I politely tell her I'll get in touch with him.

Francis comes to see me the next day as I'm preparing to head to the airport. When I tell him of my trip, he asks if he can send me off. The entire ride to the airport, he begs me not to go, to stay and work things out with him. I am weak and sad, and seeing him makes me question everything, but I have made my decision.

"Francis, I've made up my mind, and I think this is the right choice for both of us." Tears well in my eyes, and I hurry out of his car when we arrive. I can't look at him as I say goodbye.

When I take my seat on the plane, the tears break loose and gush down my face. I wonder if I actually love Francis more than I realize. Maybe our relationship means something deeper than I'm willing to admit, and we do belong together. Maybe we just needed to overcome these obstacles. Maybe there is a way to create peace with his family. As the plane flies farther and farther from the east coast, my heart wishes it would do an about-face and fly back to New York. But no, I know it's too late. Francis must hate me for breaking up with him. At this, more tears come. A man sitting next to me keeps handing me tissues. I'm such a mess that I never even see his face, just his hand, as he places tissue after tissue in front of me.

As we approach our destination, I still don't know what my heart is telling me, but I decide for the duration of this trip, I will forfeit my need to know. An adventure in a new city sounds like the healing I need.

We land in San Francisco, and I make my way to the baggage claim area to meet Susanna who says she'll be waiting for me there. I met my cousin a couple years ago when she had a summer internship in New York. She's only two years older than me, and we get along great. I know time with her in a new place is exactly what I need.

The baggage claim area is packed with people from all over the world, arriving in bright and sunny California. I do my best to get out of the way of people hustling around me so that I can try and spot Susanna.

As my eyes scan the area, I see a familiar face, but it is not Susanna. I have to do a double take, but I'd recognize him anywhere. His slightly overweight stance, fairly good-looking face, and a pair of modern frame glasses resting on the bridge of his nose with a curious look in his eyes. It's Dylan!

Right as I see him, I hear Susanna call my name. "Ying-Ying!"

I turn around before catching Dylan's eye. There she is with her big smile and fit figure, waving hello. I wave back and go toward her, but Dylan beats me there. Susanna looks confused as this man she does not know is suddenly standing next to her.

"Doctor Dang? What are you doing here?" I ask.

"I heard you were coming to San Francisco, so I came to greet you!"

My cheeks turn redden at this. In Chinese culture at this time, an educated doctor stands at the top of the social food chain. Any woman from my community would feel lucky to date him. The fact that he is making such a big effort to see me is a huge honor. While I wish it was Francis standing here instead of Dylan, I can't help but feel flattered. Dating a man like this would make my parents so happy.

"That was kind of you to come here today. Susanna, this is Doctor Dang. Doctor Dang, this is my cousin Susanna who is so graciously hosting me this week."

"It is nice to meet you, Susanna! I'm sorry I didn't contact you myself, but would it be okay if I stole Ying-Ying away for the evening? I have some things I wanted to surprise her with. I promise to have her home at a decent hour."

Susanna looks at me and gives me a slight wink. My cheeks must now be a full-blown red. "Oh sure. If that's okay with you, Ying-Ying?"

"Oh yeah, that's okay." I feel obligated to say yes, but I'm also a little curious about what he has planned.

"Great. Ying-Ying, I'll go look for your bag at the carousel."

"Thank you." I smile. "I have one bright red piece of luggage."

As he walks away, Susanna turns to me. "Is that him?" I have mentioned Dylan to Susanna before over the phone.

"Yes! He's the prominent doctor from NYU medical school I told you about. But I had no idea he would be here. I'm sorry if this inconvenienced you."

"No, I'm just happy to see my cousin being pursued by such a distinguished man. Have fun tonight! I'll see you when you get home."

I tell her goodbye and help Dylan find my bag. He then leads me to his rental car, which is soon cruising north up Highway 101 toward Oakland. I'm wondering what Dylan has in mind for the day.

As if he could read my thoughts, Dylan asks, "Are you hungry?"

"Yes, a little."

"Great! My parents live in Oakland and were hoping to have me over for dinner. Would you mind going to meet them?"

"You want me to meet your parents?"

"Yes, Ying-Ying. I've told them so much about you, and they keep pestering me to meet you."

I feel honored that his parents are making time for me. "Sure, we can go meet them. I just wish you would've given me a heads up. I could've changed into something nicer."

He looks at my jeans and t-shirt and says in a kind voice, "You look perfect."

The next thing I know, we are knocking on the red wooden door of a small house. I'm nervous but greatly comforted when I notice a giant fig tree full of big, juicy, purple figs shading a well-manicured front lawn. The sight of the tree so similar to the one at my childhood home puts a smile on my face. I can do this!

I am introduced to his parents, who are a joy. They seem to be kind and gentle although his father is extremely quiet. His mother makes us an incredible Chinese meal, and as we eat and talk, I feel understood by her. I learn that Dylan's dad was handicapped in a car accident when Dylan was only nine, and his mother raised all four children, mostly on her own meager income. There's a strong quality of compassion in her that puts me at ease. We like each other immediately, but spending time with them makes me realize just how much I miss my own parents.

When it's time to leave, she takes out a twenty-four-carat gold necklace and gives it to me as a gift. I am taken aback and delighted that she likes me this much.

"Please come visit us again soon, my dear," she exclaims with a big smile on her face.

Dylan then drives toward the ocean at Golden Gate Park and takes me for a walk on the beach next to a boardwalk. I notice many families laughing and playing in the water or building sandcastles on the beach. There is a sacred sweetness to this summer night.

"Wow, that went even better than expected," he tells me. "My parents, especially my mother, love you!"

"Well, I loved her too. She is so kind, and her cooking is divine."

"Yeah," he stares off at the water. "I've never found a cook like my mother."

As we approach a bench, Dylan asks, "Would you like to sit down for a bit?"

"Sure." I say, though a part of me still secretly yearns for Francis.

We sit in silence for a moment as we watch waves crash against the sand. The ocean air rustles my hair. Sun beams warming my skin and the smell of salt water distract me from everything that brought me to this place. I feel relaxed, more at ease than I have in months.

"It is so beautiful here," I say to Dylan.

"It is." He is fumbling with something in his pocket. "Ying-Ying, today went better than I could've imagined. It affirms everything I've been thinking since I met you that you are the woman I want to marry."

"What?!"

He opens a box with a diamond ring in it, and I can't believe this is happening.

"Dylan, I—"

My mind spins. I still miss Francis. I barely know Dylan. And yet, Dylan is making me feel so valued, so special. After all of the horrible men I have met who have tried to hurt me, and knowing my parents may never get their visas without my help, I wonder if this is for the best. Maybe getting married to this kind, successful man is exactly what I need right now.

"I've already arranged everything. I have friends and family coming in for a wedding at the end of next week, some even from Singapore. Everyone is so excited!"

This is happening so fast. "I don't know if—"

"Ying-Ying, I want to take care of you. The money Annie gave you for your last semester of school was from me. I knew you were the woman I wanted to support. Also, I know of the situation with your parents. The sooner we get married the sooner I can be the petitioner of your parents' visas. When I heard you broke up with that guy from school, it led me to hope with fervor. You're who I want Ying-Ying. Don't make me look like a fool. Please accept my proposal."

"What? I don't even have a dress!"

"No worries! Annie bought you a rose-colored dress already. She said you love it and look great in it!"

The dress is not my big concern, but it felt like a last-ditch effort to make him think twice about rushing into this. Only days ago, I got out of my relationship with Francis, and now this famous doctor has planned a secret wedding for me that is to take place *next week*. I am touched by his intentions, by the way he secretly gave me the money for school, and that he is pursuing me with vigor. What I don't like is how my parents' visas are being used as a bargaining chip. Even if the thought also occurred to me, it feels manipulative for him to bring it up.

At the same time, I feel a strong pull on my spirit, a voice so loud that I can't ignore it, put there by my upbringing and the teachings of Confucius. For Confucius, one of the most important values is that of filial piety. This is not merely a showing of respect to one's parents but an inward attitude and belief system that we must repay the burden of being born and raised by one's parents, even if it means to sacrifice one's own happiness. It is my duty to take care of them at all costs.

I know that Dylan is everything my parents ever wanted for me. And I'm so tired of running, hiding from men who try to harm me, and trying to figure out my life on my own. This could be the step I need to be okay here in America, to really live the life I've wanted to, to make this my home in a way that feels right. There are so many pros and cons that my brain dissects this decision like the ultimate equation. Thankfully, I've always been good at math.

The Pros:

1. Dylan is confident and is already fighting for this marriage.
2. This would be a marriage my parents would be proud of.
3. I love his mom. The mother-in-law is deemed one of the most important aspects in finding a husband, and she is the kind of mother-in-law my mother insisted I find.
4. He can help with my parents' visa situation, so I can fulfill my duty and filial piety as a daughter.
5. Dylan has never made inappropriate advances toward me. He feels like a safe shelter for me from other men who would wish me harm.
6. He is successful, and I can be proud of who he is and what he does. We can have a legacy that my father will be proud of.
7. I will be taken care of and able to stay in the U.S. easily, with no more struggling.
8. I will not have to work illegal, odd jobs.
9. He is well-educated and will support me furthering my education.
10. He has not had a girlfriend in the three years since his divorce and is not the womanizer type who will be unfaithful.

The Cons:

1. I have a lack of romantic feelings toward Dylan.
2. This is all happening so fast.
3. I still miss Francis.
4. I don't know if I'm ready for marriage.

Though the pros outweigh the cons in my head, I know this could be deceiving. What if the cons hold more impact than the pros? I dreamed of a knock-your-socks-off kind of love, and I didn't have that with Dylan.

Would I be giving up on that possibility by marrying him? From what I saw with Uncle George, I didn't know if fairytale romances even existed. It seems more likely that relationships fade over time.

I do like Dylan, I admire his ambition, and I hear that the feelings I'm looking for can develop over time. He does score points for never attempting to have sex with me even when we've been alone. He's a gentleman. If I say yes, I know that I am determined enough to put my brain power and my heart to work on becoming the best wife in the world. I like the idea of this commitment; I know I'll be good with Dylan.

Thus, the next word I hear coming out of my mouth is, "Okay."

"Ying-Ying, are you saying—?" He looks so excited.

"Yes."

He wraps me in a hug, and holds my face as he kisses me on my cheek. I don't feel sparks, but I feel relief, and I can't help but match the smile he's giving me. He holds my ring finger to put on the ring, but it is at least one size too small to fit my finger.

13

Marriage

I'm getting married. One burdening question of my life is now answered. Dylan drives me straight to Susanna's after the proposal, and I fall asleep as soon as I lie down, not having the energy to process what just happened.

I call Aunt Katie the next morning to tell her the news. Though I have avoided seeing her in person much the past year since Uncle George's assault, we still talk on the phone once in a while. She is family to me. I wish things were different, as I've missed our time together, but I never want to see Uncle George again, and the memory of him attacking me in my dorm room would be hard to get out of my head if I saw Aunt Katie in person.

That being said, she was the first person I wanted to tell I am getting married. My parents still don't have a phone, and I know I'm not in love with Dylan. Aunt Katie is the perfect person to talk to.

As I recount the previous evening's festivities, I wait for a huge congratulatory response on the other end of the phone.

Instead, she says, "Ying-Ying, please do not invite me to your wedding."

Her statement feels like a knife diving straight into my stomach.

"Why, Aunt Katie?"

"It is clear you've let this doctor manipulate you into such a quick commitment. This isn't love. God calls us to marry for love. This is his will for us declared in the Bible. I just can't support this. But it sounds like you've made up your mind on what you're going to do."

Instead of acknowledging some of the truth in what she says, I am furious. I want to tell her how little she knows about love. She thinks she's in a godly marriage, but little does she know her husband's actions behind her back! That isn't love! I want to tell her, "Who cares what the Bible says?" I memorized every single word in Chairman Mao's Red Book full of lies, double standards, and manipulation. In the Red Book it prohibits dating, but Mao slept with countless women. It is a tool to control. Why should I think this Christian Bible would be any different?

But I don't say any of that. Instead, I reply, "Yes, I have made my decision. I'm sorry it displeases you," and then I hang up the phone, my stomach still in knots.

Moments later, the phone rings. It's Emily. She congratulates me with such excitement about my marriage, and it feels good, but since she is one of my closest friends, I can't hide from her.

"Emily, I'm not sure if this is the right decision," I tell her.

"Don't be silly and second guess this. Women are jumping for Dylan. Annie told me that many women have been interested, and he's disregarded all of them, one-by-one, not even going on a date with them. He wants you, Ying-Ying, and no one else. I always wished he'd be interested in me, but he isn't. You are the lucky one!"

"But Emily, I still miss Francis."

"You'll get over that soon. Since I've known you, I've wished you would break up with Francis. He is too young and doesn't have a career plan. Plus, his family doesn't treat you right, and you will never be happy with him if you're always dealing with a controlling mother like that!"

She can tell that I'm still hesitant, so she adds, "Dylan is your best choice in your situation, especially with your parents depending on you. And don't worry. In case it doesn't work out, you can always get a divorce. Look at me, I've divorced twice now!"

Her words weigh more heavily than I realize. She has always been a friend I look up to for so many things. I know she and Annie have been helping plot this marriage as Dylan knows so much more about my situation than I ever told him. But I trust Emily and know that she wants the best for me.

A few days later, Aunt Katie calls me back. I hope she's changed her mind and is calling to apologize. "Ying-Ying, I thought you should know that Francis has been calling me looking for you. He is very miserable and wants to make up with you. I haven't told him anything. I just could not bring myself to mention anything about your marriage. But I did say that he needs to move on with his life without you—that you aren't looking to take him back."

"Oh, thank you, Aunt Katie." As I hang up the phone, my eyes well with tears. The finality of my time with Francis ending is painful, but I know that Aunt Katie did the right thing. I hope this will give us both closure.

My cousin Susanna is incredibly happy for me as well. For the little she knows about Dylan, all she sees is how much he wants me to be his wife and how this could put an end to the struggles I have been through in the city. She tells me she heard from her family in China that my father has already told my relatives with great excitement that I am marrying a famous doctor in America.

The week flies by in preparations, and there it is—my wedding day—greeting me in the early morning. I have such mixed emotions about it all. I toss and turn all the night before in anxious anticipation, still wishing I could see Francis and tell him in person about this marriage. When the sun beams in, I get out of bed and start journaling, trying to get all of my jumbled thoughts out and focus on what is ahead of me.

Today I leave my old identity and become one with another. Today I step into the great adventure of marriage. This was unpredictable, and yet I feel the blessing it can be. I will do whatever it takes to make this the greatest marriage ever. I will be a joy to Dylan and I will love him through my commitment to our life together. I'm excited and nervous, but that's the way I think it's supposed to be. No great road ever rides smoothly. I am ready. We will be great together.

As I put down the period in my last sentence, Susanna bursts into my room without warning. "Happy wedding day, cousin! It is time to get you ready!"

She does my make-up and hair—pink blush shimmering on my cheeks, red lipstick making my lips pop, and my hair pulled half up with loose curls falling onto the tops of my shoulders. She then carefully helps me step into a big white wedding dress we found in the San Francisco fashion district that fits well enough without needing alterations. A long, sheer veil is placed on top of my head, lying elegantly against my back, and last but not least, I pull on some lace gloves that I love.

Before we leave, Susanna hands me a small box. "This is from Dylan." I open it, and a stunning ruby necklace is inside. She helps me place it around my neck, and it is the perfect touch to my ensemble. I look at myself in the mirror and am amazed by how beautiful and bridal I appear.

"You are gorgeous, cousin. Let's go get you married!" Susanna drives me to the courthouse where Dylan is waiting for me.

Dylan opens my car door as we arrive. He looks nice in his black suit and red tie. "You look beautiful, Ying-Ying." He smiles.

I feel like a queen, certain I am making the right choice. We get married in the San Francisco courthouse with just a few witnesses—Susanna, her husband, and Dylan's Parents. As we exchange our vows, a feeling of peace washes over me. I have found my safe harbor, just like my butterfly kite that rests in its fabric box when it is not set for flying! This man, who treats me with such tenderness, will be a great husband.

After we take our vows and he kisses me gently on the cheek, we walk to a nearby park where a photographer captures wedding pictures of us. It is a beautiful, sunny day!

Next, we head to the famous May Flower Chinese banquet hall in San Jose for the reception, where nearly a hundred people are waiting for us. I quickly change into the rose-colored dress Annie bought and sent over. We have a delicious twelve-course traditional wedding dinner banquet, but I barely eat as I'm introduced to all of Dylan's family and friends. The only people there for me are Susanna and her husband, which if I had time to think, would make me a little sad. But there's no time to dwell. The entire reception is such a blur of congratulations and toasts, as each guest comes to us and presents us with a red envelope filled with money. Before I know it, the banquet is wrapping up, and it is time to head out to the Marriott Dylan booked for our wedding night.

Dylan drives us there, and we're both nearly silent on the thirty-minute drive. I wonder if he's as nervous as I am to be intimate for the first time. I'm on my period, and I wonder if I should bring that up before we have sex. We haven't talked about so many things, and I realize there's so much I don't know about him. I'm curious what kind of lover he is although I have no expectations.

We step into our hotel room. There are candles lit, fresh flowers, and a bottle of wine chilling in an ice bucket. "This is beautiful," I say. Dylan doesn't answer and seems distracted by something, looking around the room.

"What's wrong?" I ask him.

He searches his briefcase. "Our airline tickets for the honeymoon trip! I can't find them! Where did you misplace them?"

"I didn't. I've never seen them."

"Don't lie to me!" He stares me down, his face turning red with anger. "I don't know where else they could've gone. Our first night married and you are already deceiving me!" He's yelling and his eyes burn with an anger I've never seen in them.

"What? Why would I even have them?"

His eyes narrow. "Don't question me!"

"What are you saying? Please don't ruin our wedding night. We can call the travel agent tomorrow if you still can't find them." I touch his hand to calm him. "We'll figure it out. Let's enjoy tonight."

He rips his hand away. "Don't you dare tell me I'm ruining tonight. How ungrateful you are! I'm paying for this room."

"I didn't mean to disrespect you. I just want tonight to be special."

"Isn't this room special enough? You are so greedy."

"Dylan, Why are you acting like this?" I ask, feeling confused and angry. "You're behaving so differently than I've ever seen you. What's wrong?"

"Of course I am, Ying-Ying. Before I was courting you, but today you are my wife."

I start crying as my shock kicks in, and I go lie face-down on the bed. How could this be the same man who cherished me for all these months?

He waits half an hour before joining me on the bed. I think he's going to comfort me now that he's cooled down, but instead it's about him. Without saying anything, he begins to undress himself. Once he's completely naked, he undresses me as well. I'm not in the mood, but I know it's my duty as a wife so I just lay there as he rushes to take my undergarments off. I'm expecting him to kiss me or touch me. Instead, he just quickly thrusts himself into me.

It is so unexpected and, since there is no lubrication, it is excruciatingly painful. I scream for him to stop, and a moment later he finishes and quickly pulls himself out of me. As the gratitude that he is no longer inside of me swells, the realization that he did not use a condom hits me.

"You didn't use protection?"

"No, but don't worry. I can't have children. My ex-wife and I tried for two years, and the doctor told me my sperm count is too low." He drops that bomb on me and then immediately goes into the bathroom before I can respond.

He doesn't say anything more to me before he goes to bed. I cry silent tears the entire night, unable to sleep as I know I've made a horrible mistake, and I don't see any way out of this. What's worst of all is the fact that he cannot give me children. I can't believe he would let me marry him without divulging that crucial piece of information. I'd always imagined someday being a mother. In fact, it was a secret dream of mine to have four kids. I wanted a houseful of children. I wanted to raise strong, beautiful humans who would have the opportunity to be whatever they wanted here in America. They would each have their own interests, questions, struggles and triumphs, and I would be there to support all of it. My heart shatters as these imaginary children disappear from my reality.

He finds the tickets at his office the next morning but does not apologize to me for the accusations of the night before. He is too busy packing for our honeymoon, which will be a week-long tour of Hawaii.

Even though he never holds my hand or kisses me, I love traveling and seeing such beautiful spots. It's like a movie as we drive along the island, and I'm overtaken by the glorious beauty of Hawaii. My awe is interrupted occasionally as Dylan takes every single opportunity to remind me how lucky I am to be vacationing in this paradise on his account. But I block out his comments as I lose myself in the island magic. As the car takes on miles, my mind floats back in time and reminisces of travels I had with my parents as a child. I recognize a similar feeling I had back then: My soul refreshes itself when taking in new places.

After the tour, we fly back to Dylan's condo in New Jersey. I'd hoped the vacation would ease my sadness that I will never have children of my own, but on the flight home the despair creeps in again when I see a family with two adorable girls seated in front.

Thankfully, I get a distraction as the next day there is a forwarded envelope waiting for me, informing me I've passed the Graduate Record Examination (GRE), which I took a month earlier. I'm thrilled I can now apply to graduate school and am excited to have something else to focus on other than wondering if I made the wrong decision marrying Dylan. The excitement soon turns into anxiety, though, as I realize most application deadlines are in two weeks.

When I tell Dylan the news, he presses me to apply for medical school instead. With his reputation in the field, he can conveniently help me with future career advancement, but I have my mind set on studying electrical engineering. I tell him this, to which he responds, "I know the real reason you won't apply to med school. Laziness. You know it'll be too much work, and you are just a small person without any real ambitions in life! Plus, to be honest, you're probably not intelligent enough to be a doctor. How pitiful!"

For the rest of the week, he continues to bring up medical school, and each time I tell him I'm not interested, he becomes angrier. His temper and irritation are my constant companions whenever he's in the room with me. Because of this, he keeps a great physical distance between us, which, as sad as I am by the lack of intimacy, is a relief.

One night as I'm working on my grad school applications, Dylan barges into our apartment after work and throws some unexpected information at me. He has just been hired as a lead physician and researcher at The University of Texas Harrison Cancer Center in Austin, Texas, which is a great honor because the center is recognized as one of the best research-oriented medical facilities for cancer treatment in the nation.

"You should consider yourself lucky to be married to such a successful doctor. It's remarkable you got me to marry you," he sneers.

He then informs me that after he returns from a three-week-long research series at Freie Universität in Berlin, Germany, we will prepare to move to Texas.

I'm shocked that I'll be moving once again to a place I've never stepped foot in and furious that Dylan never once told me this was a possibility or asked for my opinion on the matter. But the truth is, I have no choice. My husband just landed his dream job, and I'm forced to be the flexible one. Besides, The University of Texas has a good electrical engineering program I can apply to.

Dylan leaves for Europe two days after dropping the news of our move on me, and I am so grateful for the space to breathe while he is gone. I take this time at home to work on my graduate school applications. During my study breaks, I think about Francis. I wonder if he would take me back if he found out about the giant mess I've gotten myself into.

I also receive a quite extraordinary surprise while Dylan is gone. My cousin Esther, Aunt Danielle's second daughter, who was attending Yale University when I first arrived in the U.S., albeit briefly, rings me up. She says she's heard I've just been married and would like to take me to lunch.

The next day, I go to town and meet her at a famous New York bakery near Aunt Danielle's original condo. I have not seen or heard from her since I left her mother's condo five years ago. She is now married to her Yale schoolmate and has a beautiful daughter. She greets me with warm smiles and kind words.

"Ying-Ying, I'm so happy you're doing well in both your career and marriage. Your parents must be so proud you're married to a famous doctor."

"Thank you, Esther. I believe they are."

"I wanted to have lunch for a couple of reasons. First off, it's never sat right with me how my parents treated you. When I realized Mother had kicked you out, I thought you must've done something terrible, but as I got older, I realized you probably hadn't done anything at all. You see, Mother suffered from bipolar depression, on top of numerous other health conditions, which is why she would often have erratic spells or make rash choices like she did. I want to apologize to you for her."

"Oh, thank you. I always wondered what I did to upset her so much."

"Who knows? And it doesn't do any good to dwell on it any longer."

"How is she now? And Uncle Richard?"

"Well, they have both passed. Mother died only a year after you left, and Rick had a heart attack shortly after."

"Oh, I'm so sorry to hear that."

"Thank you, Ying-Ying. Now, my second reason for meeting with you is to give you something." She pulls out a red duffle bag. "I found this when I was clearing out things after my parents passed. I believe these are your belongings."

My heart begins to beat louder in my chest as I wonder what could possibly be in here.

"Thank you, Esther! I can't believe you've kept this all these years."

"I felt it was the least I could do, and it's not like it took up much space."

We chat for a little while longer, and I feel such comfort in knowing that my Aunt's treatment of me had not been my fault. Pieces are coming together, and I feel the possibility of forgiveness resting in me. I also can't wait to open the duffle bag. As we go our separate ways,

I thank Esther profusely for her kindness in meeting with me and returning my things to my possession.

I hurry home as fast as possible, waiting until I get into my bedroom to open the duffle. As I do, a thousand memories come swirling in of the girl I'd been when I first stepped foot in New York. The bag mostly has some clothes, the old pair of blue shoes uncle Richard took me to buy, a TOEFL study book, and some childhood photos, including the one of me catching butterflies at the park. And then, there it is. Folded up gently in the thin fabric box is my butterfly kite. I unfold it gently and realize I'm shaking with my ache for home.

As I feel the silk between my fingers, I sense how deeply I am not the girl I was. Transformation has taken place, and I'm emerging into the woman I was meant to be. I am determined to make both my marriage and my career a success. I've made too many sacrifices not to give myself that.

I feel a sense of hope when Dylan returns the following Friday night. He is a few days early, which I think is because he knows my birthday is the next day. Maybe he does care about me! He's exhausted from his travels and goes straight to bed, but I can't blame him for that.

I wake up the next morning on my first married birthday. I quietly get out of bed and go to the living room to take in a few moments alone. I allow myself to feel expectant that good things are coming my way. I'm hoping that the few weeks apart gave both Dylan and me clarity on how to make our marriage work for both of us. I'm excited to spend the day together.

My excitement soon turns to despair as Dylan sleeps all morning and into the late afternoon. When he finally stumbles into the living room, there is no "Happy Birthday, Ying-Ying," no gifts, no dinner plans, nothing. I remember how he had sent me all those gifts from Paris when he was pursuing me, and yet this time he did not even have one token to give me. My birthday passes by incognito—without a trace of celebration.

We begin our move to a part of the country I've never seen. As we settle into our new apartment, something is not right with me. I feel sick almost every day. When this doesn't get better after a couple of weeks, I find my way to see a doctor. At the doctor's office they have me do a couple of small tests. After the tests, I stay in a treatment room by myself for what feels like an hour. The entire time, I worry about my life. My only consolation is that Dylan has been very on top of taking care of the paperwork to get my parents their visas, and I just found out I've been accepted into The University of Texas's electrical engineering graduate program with a full scholarship. I hope to see my parents again sometime soon, and I can't wait to get back into school. I will be able to focus on my studies and not on the hardships at home.

I daydream about being successful and about working on the latest computer technology that will impact the world, making communication across the globe easier than ever, advancing every industry, including medicine. As I sit in the treatment room, I wonder what technological developments would improve the work of a doctor.

I'm shaken out of my thoughts as an older nurse dressed in purple scrubs comes in with a much too large smile on her face.

"I have some amazing news! You're pregnant! Congratulations!" she says to me.

It takes me a beat to register what she says, and then I use my words to counter her declaration. "That is impossible! You have made a serious mistake. I am not pregnant. You must've switched my test with someone else's. Learn how to do your job!" I can hear myself screaming at this woman at the top of my lungs and can't recognize myself in this. When I notice the look of horror on her face, though, I know I must be hysterical.

A doctor rushes in, and he sits me down. "Please calm down. We can double check the test. Please just take some deep breaths. You are going to be okay."

I sit down, but my body is shaking. This cannot be happening. On our wedding night, Dylan and I had sex, and he came instantly. I had been on my period, and though I didn't have time to grab any birth control, I didn't feel anything. There was also Dylan's condition. I thought I'd be safe. This cannot be possible. How could a flash of a moment result in a pregnancy?

The doctor returns and confirms that I am indeed pregnant. I don't cry, I don't smile, and I don't yell this time. I just feel numb as my mind tries to wrap around this inevitable fact I never expected to encounter.

On my way home, I come to the conclusion that I must get an abortion. I have my whole life ahead of me! I am going to conquer graduate school and make an ambitious career for myself, and I need to get my marriage on track. How can I bring up a baby with Dylan when our marriage is truly horrible? No, this cannot happen. But I know I need to tell Dylan and make this decision with him. It is his child too, and as much as I dread what his response might be, I know it is the right thing to do.

When I get home, Dylan is reading intensely at the kitchen table. I debate whether or not to interrupt him and stand in our entry way longer than normal, messing with my purse and trying to control my nerves.

"What are you doing? Why are you fidgeting?"

I'm surprised he even notices me. "I just came back from the doctor and I have something I need to tell you."

"What is it now?"

"Well, I . . . I, uh—"

"Ying-Ying, you are an adult woman. Use your words like one."

I fight back tears, as I say the words I'm terrified of. "I'm pregnant."

I wait for the yelling or look of disgust or even apathy from him, but instead, a softness overcomes him. He sets down the book and immediately jumps up. He holds me for the first time since our wedding.

"This is a miracle, Ying-Ying! It's magnificent! We are having a baby! I can be the father that I have always wanted! I want it to be a boy! Let's celebrate!"

He grabs his coat, takes my hand, and whisks me away outside as we head to dinner at his favorite Chinese restaurant. At dinner he talks to me animatedly, and I start to wonder if this baby could be the thing that draws us together. I know I cannot have an abortion. It would destroy Dylan and our marriage. And I know that he will have trouble conceiving again. This is most likely his one chance to be a father.

I can do this. I've done so many hard things, and I know that I have more in me. I'll have this baby, and I'll find a way to still complete grad school.

14

Pregnancy

Sadly, it doesn't take long until Dylan is keeping his distance from me once again. The only "caring" he does for my pregnancy is to force me to drink twelve ounces of milk a few times a day. It makes my stomach ache, which I find out later is because I'm lactose intolerant, but he's heard it is good for the baby to develop strong bones so he presents me with the glass of milk every day and yells at me to drink it. He doesn't stop yelling until I've finished the glass. The yelling makes the taste of milk sour, and I hate it. I vow that when this pregnancy is over, I'll never drink milk again.

To prepare for the addition to our family, we look for a single-family home to purchase. He sends me to work with a real estate agent, and after two months of searching, the agent and I find a home Dylan approves of. We have a closing date in three weeks, and I start to plan for the decoration of the nursery.

Two days before the closing, Dylan tells me over dinner that we must breach the closing contract and that we cannot buy this home.

"Why? We are so close to it being done. Why call it off now?"

"My mother called earlier, and their bank is threatening to evict them because they haven't been able to pay their mortgage. Apparently, my father has been gambling their money away. They're in a mountain of debt, and it's up to me to help them."

I see then his loyalty. Being the only son, Dylan has the sole obligation to rescue his parents so they can stay in their house at their old age. I know there is no arguing here. We must help them. My dream of a beautiful house for our baby will have to wait.

Though I understand, I'm bitter about the house falling through, and that doesn't ease as I am exhausted during pregnancy and yet still expected to do all the house chores without any help or gratitude. Instead, Dylan loves to critique.

His biggest complaint is my cooking; he constantly criticizes whatever I make since it is different from his mother's meals. I take cooking lessons and collect cookbooks, but it is never up to his standards. After he eats, he leaves his plate on the table and then goes straight back to his study. Never once has he offered to do the dishes. I often wonder as I wash them why he is the way he is and how I found myself in this position.

On top of all of it, there is a rift in our intimacy. Since our honeymoon, Dylan has still never touched me physically in the bedroom. I often think that sleeping next to him isn't that different from sleeping next to a big, cold rock. I feel so empty, alone, and unwanted. This loneliness scares me, like I am lost in a totally strange and dark space where wild animals could jump out from anywhere at any time, right at me, and no one is there to help me. Sometimes I find myself shaking with fear. How can I be married, with my husband in my bed, and yet feel like no one is for me? To calm down, I tell myself it must be because of my pregnancy. Dylan doesn't want to take any chances in case it could hurt the baby.

My one saving grace is that seven months into my pregnancy, my parents arrive in America with the help of Dylan's sponsorship. When I pick them up from the airport and see their faces again my eyes well up with tears. I have to take a few deep breaths before going up to them. I've dreamed of this moment for so long.

"Mother! Father!" I call out as I walk toward them. There are so many people hustling around us, but as our eyes connect and they see me, I feel for a moment that time freezes. I wonder if they even recognize me. I'm such a different woman than the girl they saw leave for New York five years ago. Do my hardships appear on my face? Am I still their brave, brilliant daughter, or do they see in my eyes the pain of the life I find myself in? I want to run up to them and hug them and cry for hours, but instead I put on a giant smile. This moment isn't supposed to be about me. I know how hard this is going to be for them. They've left everything they've ever known, and nothing about this place will feel familiar for years. It is my duty to put them at ease.

I take them back to our two-bedroom bi-level apartment, which has the master bedroom on the top level. They will stay with us and be able to help when the baby is born. I am incredibly grateful they will be here, but it is an interesting middle-ground for myself to be in. I feel stuck between who I was—the daughter they knew—and the wife I am now asked to be. Neither identity feels like who I truly am or who I want to be. It is a strange dance to be who everyone expects you to be instead of being yourself.

On the following Mother's Day, I take my parents to visit Grandmother in New York per my father's wish. My father hasn't seen her in fifteen years since the day she dropped off Ying-Hong. When she opens her apartment door and sees my parents and me standing in the hallway, she looks directly toward my mother and yells out, "How can you become so fat, so dark, and so old now?" The culture worships fair skin tones, so to say a woman is "dark" is highly insulting. It doesn't get any better from there. The rest of the visit is dragging and unpleasant as we endure an earful of her condescending monologue. I'm grateful when we are finally able to leave.

At home, I am both surprised by and grateful for how much Dylan treats my parents with a high level of respect. He is always on his good side around them, speaking in a calm voice and being polite and overly accommodating. My mother makes him tea and brings it to his desk while he studies at home. It is a treat that they all get along well and one less thing to worry about.

In private, though, Dylan either ignores me or acts like I'm the worst thing to have happened to him. I've learned that the research clinic is a highly competitive environment and everyone is battling to prove they can publish the most research papers, get awarded the largest grants for the clinic, and have the most prestigious speaking engagements. Faculty members are constantly forming secret alliances and participating in cutthroat politics. It's a circus, but Dylan is always ahead of the game.

He works every day including holidays, and aside from eating and sleeping, he is almost always seated firmly at his desk when he is home. He brings in an incredible amount of grant money for the clinic and has a plethora of fellow students who work underneath him, constantly producing research papers for him, and even checking and responding to his emails for him. Fueling his work ethic is the fact that the clinic director is planning to retire in six months. Dylan tries to impress him so that he'll be nominated for the position. Because of this, he constantly loves to host people as part of the plan. Unfortunately, he always asks me to play the perfect hostess when he does this, which doesn't let up during my pregnancy.

At eight and a half months pregnant, I feel terrible, especially with my history of back pain, and I know that, at any minute, I could pop this baby out. It's hard for me to get in any comfortable position to sleep, but one morning I'm actually asleep, dreaming of myself as a child in China. There are jumping fish and dancing and butterflies . . . and peace.

"Ying-Ying! Wake up! Now!" The peace evaporates as my husband's yelling takes me back to reality.

"What's wrong?" I mumble.

"Ying-Ying, I need you to listen to me."

"I'm awake."

"Sit up now."

It takes more energy and strength to sit up than he will ever know, but I do it anyway. "What?"

"I've decided we need to host a banquet for my clinic before this baby is born. I want to do this the day after tomorrow. I've invited thirty people over. I need you to make sure the apartment is spotless, and you need to make appetizers, multiple main courses, desserts, and a couple special cocktails."

"Dylan, I'm so tired. Can we make it smaller at least?"

"No, absolutely not. This is important for my career advancement. I need the whole clinic here to impress the director. They are coming over Thursday at six."

He then abruptly leaves the room before I can counter with any rationality. Thus, my duty as his wife.

The next forty-eight hours are pure insanity. Dylan leaves out a list of the kinds of food and drink he wants me to make from scratch. Each item is more complicated than the last. I'm cleaning and organizing everything and then shopping around at multiple stores to find all the ingredients I need.

I have to start prepping and cooking the day before, and I don't stop, not even to sleep, before the guests arrive. My parents are so new to this country, they depend on me for most things. They don't know how to drive a car or use any of the kitchen equipment, including the microwave and stove, so they can only help to clean vegetables and do other small tasks. Dylan does nothing to help, and he goes into the bedroom to take a nap before the guests arrive.

My feet are throbbing, my back is aching, and I have an excruciating headache, yet Dylan tells me I must serve each guest each course and make sure nobody's glass is ever empty. For thirty people there is never a moment to stop and sit. I think at any moment I might pass out.

They leave at ten o'clock, and I've never been so happy to see people go home. I resent how Dylan had such a relaxing and fun evening, laughing with his colleagues as he never laughs with me. I'm hoping for a thank you or some sort of acknowledgement that I had a hand in making the night go well.

"Ying-Ying, you looked sad all night. You need to learn how to be a better hostess. People want to see smiles and pleasantness. You embarrassed me."

I've never felt such anger. "Dylan, I was so exhausted and my whole body is in so much pain from this pregnancy. I've been working non-stop to make this night for you with little notice. And tonight I have the worst headache of my life."

"Pregnancy is not an excuse, Ying-Ying. My mother had four children. How can it be a big deal to have *one*? Women do this all the time."

How I wish I had a gun. If I did, I would shoot him right there.

A week later I am climbing, or more like waddling, up the stairs with the laundry basket, when a contraction stops me in my tracks. I lean against the wall and take some deep breaths as it passes. I continue up the stairs, when a few minutes later another one hits, this one even more painful. I sit on the bed and keep taking deep breaths. I'm not sure if this is what labor feels like or when I should go into the hospital. Another contraction hits, and this one makes me yell out in pain.

My parents are already asleep, but thankfully Dylan is home, and when he sees my condition, takes me straight to the hospital where I go into the most horrendous labor. My back is in excruciating pain that feels unbearable paired with the pain of childbirth. I keep screaming.

The doctor offers me an epidural to ease the pain, and before I can say yes, Dylan cuts in. "No, she will not take an epidural. I will not take any chance of hurting our baby. My mother had four children without one, so you should be able to do this easily, Ying-Ying."

I'm in too much pain to argue.

The labor is long and arduous, and by the time I'm supposed to push the baby out, it's been fifty hours, and I'm too exhausted from all the pain. I do my best, but our baby is still not coming. They bring out giant forceps that are supposed to help grab her and pull her out, but they are unsuccessful. They are considering wheeling me into the operation room to do a C- Section when the doctor suggests one last attempt that involves vacuum-sucking the baby out.

This works, and after fifty-two hours of labor, a baby girl is now outside of my body.

Isabella, named by Dylan, is a big baby, born at eight pounds nine ounces and nineteen inches long. The combination of vacuum and forceps procedures made a grapefruit sized lump on her head and red marks on her face that make her look like an alien, but I don't care. The moment the doctor places her in my arms, I look into her sweet, innocent face, and my heart overwhelms me. I understand in an instant the powerful maternal instinct that can overtake a woman's heart. It has now kicked on like a roaring faucet.

My dear Isabella, I will do whatever it takes. I will make whatever sacrifice is needed to protect you and to give you the best life you deserve. You have my whole heart. What a transformational love this is!

15

Hope

I have to stay in a double room at the hospital for an extra few days. The woman in the bed next to me is allowed to go home after one day and is ecstatic to get home with her own baby. I can't relate. This special treatment I have at the hospital is wonderful. The nurses are extremely attentive and helpful.

All parts of my body, especially my back and wrists, are in so much pain that I can't even stand in the shower. One of the nurses says she'll help me, and she holds me up so that I can get a quick shower in. They bring me food and drinks but don't force me to eat anything I don't like. Dylan visits me every so often with the special soup my mother made for me, and it is a nice reprieve.

If my insurance didn't limit it, I would stay here as long as I could!

When it is time for me to return home, Dylan comes and picks the baby and me up. Luckily, I secured the car seat weeks ago, so I don't have to worry about that. On our drive home, I look out and take in the view. Only a week earlier, we were in winter, but now spring has sprung! The sun is shining and flowers are popping up everywhere. Mother Nature seems to be mirroring my own transition as I step into a new season, my baby sleeping safely in a car seat behind me.

Unfortunately, I've injured both of my wrists from gripping the bed railing so hard and for so long that I can't pick up Isabella on my own. I have to rely on my mother or whoever is around to help me breastfeed. I can't even bathe her myself.

Dylan adores Isabella, thankfully, but his joy does not translate to helping with the work of a baby. He holds her at times but never changes her diaper, feeds her, or rocks her to sleep when she is awake crying at night. It takes seven months for my wrists to heal, but I am insanely relieved when I notice the change. I was so afraid they would never regain their strength.

With my wrists recovered, I am motivated to clean and organize the house in between caring for Isabella. Luckily, baby Isabella is a deep sleeper, sleeping at least five or six hours straight at night ever since she was five weeks old. This gives me enough rest to start a busy day fresh.

One night while I am organizing the bathroom, I find a few *Playboy* magazines hiding between the pile of Dylan's research materials. I'm shocked. We still haven't had sex since our wedding night, and part of me had begun to assume he doesn't have a sex drive. Seeing these magazines shows me that isn't true. He just doesn't want to have sex with me. I realize then that this strange noise I hear occasionally from the bathroom isn't from him being constipated but from him masturbating.

I confront him about the magazines that night, but he just turns red and won't answer me. That's when I have an idea. I remember during one of the faculty dinner parties, a colleague of Dylan's mentioned a renowned psychologist, Dr. Edward Wheat, who specializes in helping couples with their intimacy issues. He even published a bestselling book titled, *Intended for Pleasure*.

"Dylan, I think we should go see Dr. Wheat to work on our intimacy issues. We can work it out together and get our marriage on track. Doctor Jones says he's amazing at what he does and is very well-respected. His office is only thirty minutes away."

"I don't have a problem, Ying-Ying! I'm just not attracted to you because you refused my advice and didn't go to med school. You disrespected me, and I don't think I can have sex with a wife who does not respect me."

I decide to surrender this fight. Right now, I cannot imagine being intimate with such a husband either.

In September of that year, I begin my graduate school program. School is great. I meet many new friends, but as I sit in the classroom, my mind is often daydreaming about Isabella. I wonder what she is doing with my mother and what cute new development is taking place as I sit here listening to a lecture. As I look at my professor's face, it is replaced with the sweet, innocent face of Isabella. I find myself trapped between school and motherhood. As she gets older, every time I leave for school in the morning, she grabs me and cries for me to stay. It breaks my heart to see her tears and makes me doubt if I should continue with my studies. I want so much to stay home to hold her and play with her!

When I am home, though, I'm all hers! I love to cuddle her on my lap and read books to her. Even though Isabella is a baby, Dylan brings home children's books that tell of our Chinese history, which I read to her. I appreciate this more than he knows since so much Chinese literature and history was omitted from my textbooks in China growing up. Reading to Isabella reminds me of the strong and beautiful parts of our heritage.

Dylan and I are both captivated by Confucianism. He encourages me to memorize the teachings from a book called *Three-Character Classic*, which shares Confucian ideals in storybook form, so I can teach the principles to Isabella as she grows up. Two of the most important lessons I take to heart are "What you do not want done to yourself, do not do to others" and "A great man is hard on himself and a small man is hard on others." These words become my guiding compass in hoping to achieve a happy and peaceful life.

My time at home is limited because part of my scholarship requires me to serve as a teaching assistant in the department. I have to conduct study lectures and provide office hours to help undergraduate students and grade homework for the professor. On top of work, I have to study with rigor and take care of the baby and my parents, who still barely speak English. I also must be the optimal wife to my husband who continues to believe the wife should do all of the housework so that he can go on to achieve his career ambitions. He brings over many of his doctor peers from all over the world, whom I must entertain and dote on when I am home. I sometimes leave the laundry basket of clean clothes by the stairs to the second floor until I'm already heading that way. Dylan jumps over the basket as he heads up to the bedroom rather than carrying the basket himself.

On average, I am sleeping two hours a day in order to complete my studies and domestic duties. A few days a week I have to stay in the computer lab to run programs until midnight or later. I walk, in the dark, to my car in the parking lot and then drive home. The area near school is famously unsafe, but I have no choice. When I arrive home, the house is quiet. Everyone is asleep, and Dylan is snoring away.

One night as I leave the computer lab to head to my car, a student—a tall, brunette man with pretty blue eyes—stops me.

"What are you doing?"

"I'm going home."

"It's one in the morning, and you're walking to your car?"

"Yep."

"Do you always do that?"

"I have no other option."

"Well, I can't stand by and let that happen. This area is dangerous, and a woman walking by herself is unacceptable. I'm walking you to your car."

He introduces himself as Dan, and I cannot help but feel grateful for his presence. I feel much safer.

After that night, if Dan is in the computer lab when I leave, he always walks me to my car. One cold January night, we each work in the lab until dawn. As he walks me to my car, he asks me to have breakfast with him.

"Ying-Ying, I really find you extraordinary. Would you want to go out to breakfast with me right now?"

My throat catches at his kindness. I want to accept but know that it would not be appropriate.

"Oh, thank you, but I'm married." I hold up my left hand, adorned with a golden wedding band on my fourth finger.

"You're *married*? What kind of husband would let his wife walk by herself at night? That's outrageous!"

I couldn't argue with him. Self-pity was my constant companion, and I felt helpless against the ever-growing sadness that resided within me. Even after I reject his offer, he still walks me to my car like the guardian angel he is. After that semester though, we aren't in class together, and I never see him again.

It brings me to tears when I think about how I will go through my life without physical intimacy or any romance of my own. I crave a spiritual connection with the whole of my being. I cry often, overwhelmed by the impossible task of pleasing my husband. No matter what I do, it is never good enough, and I am always anxious around him.

I try to connect with him and tell him I would like to be intimate, but every time I do, he tells me I have a dirty mind. He tells me sex for pleasure is bad, and it would drain one's qi, or energy. He insists that the distraction of sex makes one weak and sick and gives one a shorter life.

He thinks nature walks, outings, or really any other forms of entertainment are a waste of time. He believes that every waking minute should be used for work. I am triggered regularly by seeing passionate lovers in the park or on the street. Even a romantic movie poster can bring me to tears.

I daydream about a hero popping into my life and rescuing me from this soul-draining hole I find myself in. The hero often looks like Francis. I miss him every day, and think about him constantly, but I never consider contacting him. I can't imagine facing him and telling him about this life I lead. I know, in my current state, that if Francis asked me to come back to him, I would, and I can't chance that. I can't do that to my family. Divorce is shameful, and I can't bring shame to my family and baby Isabella. Even worse would be finding out that Francis no longer loves me and is with someone new. Such a discovery would crush my daydreams. Imagining what it would be like to be with Francis again is what gets me through my reality. I can't tell anyone about these urges, so I take to writing them down.

One particularly lonely night when Dylan is deeply asleep, I go to the living room and look out the window. It is the Chinese Moon Festival night where the moon is at its most round and brightest of the year. Moved and overwhelmed by the romantic Chinese legend of the Moon Festival, I grab my notebook and begin writing to Francis.

Dear Francis,

In the quiet night, the bright round moon in the clear night sky made me think of you. How I wish you could ride the wind to fly near me. My brain transports me to the days we were together when you charmed me with bagels and bowling. I stay in these joyful thoughts until baby Isabella cries my name and I am flung back to reality. You are only ever allowed to be a memory, and we can only share the beauty of the moon from far apart places.

Your darling,
Ying-Ying

It feels good to put my thoughts to paper, and from then on, I journal whenever I miss Francis, soaking up the small doses of relief. At the same time though, I feel pangs of guilt that my most internal thoughts and desires involve a man who is not my husband. I know my marriage isn't what it should be, but I am committed to it. I could never leave Dylan for what it would do to Isabella or to my parents. Plus, I am grateful Dylan provides well for us, gives us a stable home, and is kind to my family. I rarely bring up Dylan to any of my classmates I meet in school. Because of this, many of the men express interest, but I never reciprocate. The only other man I'd want would be Francis. And I know I cannot have him.

The next school term, though, I have a new officemate. The first time I meet him, I am stunned by how much his physical appearance resembles Francis. A virtual carbon copy! His name is Kaito, and he has just finished his PhD courses and has been hired as an instructor while completing his thesis. I ask him questions about my homework almost every day, and he is so patient and intelligent as he answers and explains things to me.

We talk often as we work side by side, and I learn that he got engaged a couple months ago to a woman he'd never met before from his hometown in a small seashore village of Japan. His mother arranged the marriage, and his future wife is still in Japan, waiting for him to go back at the end of the school year in a couple months to have the wedding. He listens intently as I vent about my life, share my dreams for the future, and fill him in on the latest developments baby Isabella is displaying at home. He tells me often I look beautiful, and I feel such chemistry, enjoying the way he looks at me. It reminds me of how Francis once had.

On Mother's Day, Kaito asks if I want to go for a walk after we've finished our work. We've gone on walks before around campus, but this time he drives me to the botanical garden, which is beautiful and peaceful. We don't see anyone else in the garden. It is just the two of us. I'm so taken by the elegant nature of this place. There are dragonflies, birds, and butterflies in the air around us. I feel like a kid again at the sight of the butterflies. Just like when I was a little girl in China getting my picture taken chasing a butterfly, still I'm captivated by their free movements and a beloved dance they seem to perform as they fly about.

This is the first time I've enjoyed any nature since I moved to Austin two years ago, and I feel a lightness inside me I haven't felt in years. The air around me is aromatic. Sweet, colorful flowers permeate my senses. We approach a small lake, and everything is incredibly serene. As we walk around the lake, his hand brushes mine. I act as though I don't notice, but inside my heart flutters. It feels so nice just to have that slight physical touch.

It happens again a moment later, and I can't help but smile. He then grabs my hand, intertwining his fingers with mine, and we continue walking, our hands clasped together. It feels so sweet and romantic. I have never held my husband's hand this way.

We stop at one point, and Kaito turns to me. I feel like I can't breathe. The next thing I know, he wraps me in the most glorious hug, tight and strong, and I release any tension that was inside me. It feels so incredible to be held! I don't ever want him to let go. The sky's the perfect shade of blue. A slight breeze cools the warmth of the sunshine. Everything is perfect.

But after a while, he releases me. I'm disappointed, until he grabs my face in his hands and kisses me with all the passion I've ever wanted. The kisses multiply. Neither of us seem to be able to help it. We want more, and it feels like nothing we do can satisfy all we desire. As we continue to kiss, he pulls me behind a giant tree. In a blur, we begin to make love, and it feels like heaven has opened up for me.

When it is over, we walk silently back to his car. Still, we hold hands. I know I should feel bad about this, especially because deep down I know this won't be the last time, but I don't. I'm ecstatic to finally know that I don't have a problem in the area of intimacy, and after so many years of suffering, a little happiness, a little hope, is necessary.

The semester comes to an end one month later. Sadly, that isn't the only thing that ends. As our graduation and Kaito's wedding date approach, I know I will have to give him up. The day before I accept my master's degree, he puts a beautiful Akoya pearl necklace from his home town on my neck as we say a tearful goodbye. He is getting married and has accepted a job offer to be an associate professor at the University of California, Irvine.

One of my professors has offered me a full scholarship for the PhD program in electrical engineering. The professor also offers me a position to manage the computer lab in his stead, which pays well and is an incredible opportunity.

Though I am honored, I don't think it is the best option for me. I am exhausted, and I know the intense doctoral studies, paired with working at the lab, would continue the cycle of barely being able to spend time with my daughter. She is already two years old, and I've barely had time to play with her! I crave time with her, reading and playing. I am tired of missing who she is becoming. I also need the income to buy a house with more space for baby Isabella to grow up in. I want her to have her own bedroom.

I turn down the offer, much to my professor's dismay. He tells me if I ever change my mind, the offer will always be there in the future. I then apply to a plethora of corporate jobs. I figure that if I just work for a corporation, I will make good money *and* have more time for my family. Multiple job offers begin piling in, but I decide to take one with *Motorola, Inc.* They are considered one of the most prestigious

American corporations and nearly have a monopoly on the telecommunications industry worldwide.

I am excited to venture into corporate America and am amazed when I receive my first paycheck. It is a substantial amount of money in comparison to anything I've ever made. I now have my own money to buy clothes and my own car so that I can finally take my parents out to see the world around them, which I haven't yet been able to do. I call my real estate agent and tell her I am ready to look for a house again and a condo for my parents.

A few months later, we purchase a modest but beautiful house, which will be ready to move into in two months. My parents move into their condo near the city as well. I am finally living the American Dream of home ownership! I am making this happen.

Even though I'm bringing in a great income, Dylan is furious I gave up the PhD program. When I first tell him I decided to take the job, he tells me, "*Motorola* is going to go bankrupt soon if they hire employees like you who are too dumb and lazy to put in the work to get a PhD."

His words sting, and he makes it a point to bring up my laziness and his disapproval at every opportunity. As much as I try to disregard his comments, they echo in my head while I work, and I wonder if I'm actually competent enough to have this position. The majority of the company staff is male, most of whom are much older than me and have PhDs.

I'm a young, Asian woman without a doctorate degree. A few times I was even assumed to be a summer intern because of my youthful looks. I feel like I will never measure up! I can tell it is difficult to gain respect based on my demographics, so I put in countless hours to show my worth to the company. I want to prove all the stereotypes wrong.

I look for ways to improve my self-esteem and find Zig Ziglar's book, *See You at the Top*. The point that sticks out to me most is one where Ziglar describes the discovery of the Sukhothai Traimit Golden Buddha in Thailand. This golden Buddha, the world's largest, weighs 5.5 tons and measures at 15.5 feet tall. It is believed to have been created sometime between the 13th and 14th centuries, but during the 18th century, the statue was secretly covered with a layer of stucco plaster and colorful glass to conceal it from an enemy army invading Thailand. 200 years later, the gold Buddha was still hidden underneath the stucco. In 1954, a new building was constructed to house the statue. During the move to its new home, in an attempt to lift the statue from its pedestal, the moving ropes broke, and the statue fell hard to the ground. The construction team had underestimated the weight, thinking it was only stucco. When it fell, some of the plaster coating chipped off, allowing the gold surface from underneath to be seen. Shocked, the team paused the move and carefully removed all of the plaster, revealing the fully gold statue. They also realized that the gold Buddha was built in nine parts that fit together seamlessly and was accompanied by a key found at its base, which could be used to disassemble the statue, allowing for easier transportation. What a discovery!

Zig Ziglar uses this story to illustrate the message that "We must *believe* we are born with valuable gifts waiting to be discovered." Reading about this miraculous story motivates me to march forward, knowing that my inner potential is ready to be seen.

Urging my self-esteem journey forward is the best boss in the world. His name is Alex, and he is incredibly intelligent, having received a PhD from Stanford. He is a gentle, caring man who also happens to be gay. This helps me put my guard down because I am not worried that he has ulterior motives when he's nice to me or when he compliments my work.

I'm typically very quiet in work meetings. One afternoon though,

Alex asks me into his office. In his hand, I see a report that I've written. I'm worried that I must've done something wrong.

"Ying-Ying, I've just read your report."

"Yes?"

"And it's good. It's really good. What you've proposed was a brilliant idea."

"Oh good. Thank you."

"I'm just wondering why you never mention any good ideas like this in our meetings."

"Oh."

"We could use more brain power like this. I'd like for you to speak up more if you're comfortable."

"I appreciate that, Alex. I'm just insecure about my accent. English is my second language, and I'm worried you won't understand me or I won't sound as intelligent as others."

"Sometimes I do have to listen extra intently to understand what you're saying, but Ying-Ying, do you know what I usually think when I hear your accent?"

"No, I don't."

"Your accent tells me that you've had a richer life than most, definitely one richer than mine. And that you have many experiences that I can learn and grow from. Please don't ever think that your accent holds you back. What your accent represents is what's going to keep pushing you forward."

I leave his office feeling so believed in. I realize in my day-to-day I am always apologizing for who I am not rather than celebrating and promoting all that I am. After our conversation, I do my best to speak up in meetings, and I thrive under Alex's leadership. He constantly looks for opportunities for me to grow, giving me extra responsibilities and multiple promotions. I feel excited to go to work, and I'm grateful something in my life is on an upward track.

While work improves, my home life remains a mess. My parents deal with their new lives very differently. My mother is having an easier time adopting the new culture, accepting any job she can manage. She helps me with Isabella and takes care of a couple of my friends' children as well, being paid good money to do so.

My father, though, is mourning the loss of his career and the personal goals he'd had before the move here. His hearing has declined since his time in China, making the challenge of learning to speak English almost insurmountable. He can read and write in English, but holding a conversation continues to prove difficult. His identity has taken a hit, and as he tries to reinvent himself here, a great sadness bursts forth.

When his leave of absence from his university in China is about to expire, he has to decide whether or not to return to China and resume his position. He makes a sacrificing decision to stay since my sister and her family's visas depend on his U.S. citizenship. If he stays in the U.S. for five full years, he can then apply for them.

He finds a few odd jobs, none of which stimulate him in the way he wishes, but eventually, he lands a teaching position at the newly open Confucius Institute at the university, which keeps him content. On the side, he is hired to be the chief editor who translates English into Chinese for a Chinese trading company. These purposes give him drive and help to lift his spirits.

16

$\mathcal{D}arkness$

Because we have extra money now, I decide it would be nice to have a break and accompany Dylan to some of his speaking engagements around the world. I am especially excited to join him on a trip to Italy as it's a country I've always dreamed of seeing. I know Dylan will be busy working, so I am looking forward to exploring on my own.

When we go to check into our American Airlines flight, a giant line precedes the counter. Dylan complains about the long wait. When it is finally our turn, he requests an aisle seat since that will make it easier to get up and walk around during the long flight.

"I'm sorry, sir, but all the aisle seats have already been taken," the ticket agent says politely to him.

"Do you know who I am?" He flails his hands. "I am a famous doctor who is traveling to Italy for some extremely important engagements that are life or death. I need an aisle seat."

"I understand, but there's simply nothing I can do."

I feel awful for this young girl just trying to do her job. There is no way she can see what's about to happen.

"This is discrimination because I am a minority! I will sue American Airlines for this!" He screams so loud people all around us can hear, "This is unacceptable!" Everyone is looking at us, and I wish I could disappear.

The ticket agent's manager rushes over to defuse the situation. He ends up upgrading us to first class, free of charge.

As we leave the ticket counter, Dylan whispers to me, "See, you just have to fight for every good thing in life and then it will be given to you."

I'm unable to enjoy my first-class seat. I feel ashamed the entire flight that we were given these seats unrightfully. I decide that if I can help it, I'm never going on another trip with Dylan.

When we arrive in Rome, things only become worse. On our first full day there, we are scheduled to go on a wine country tour in Tuscany, set up for us by the clinic rep, Maria. Unfortunately, Dylan wakes with a sore throat. He insists on seeing a doctor immediately, and we must cancel our wine tour.

An Italian doctor comes to see us and determines Dylan simply has a cold. Dylan doesn't believe this and demands to see a Chinese doctor. The Chinese doctor gives him a special herb brew to drink for the next few days. Sadly, the symptoms don't subside.

"It must be throat cancer." He says to me on our fifth night there.

The next morning, he demands X-rays, MRIs, and a biopsy. The next couple of weeks are full of examinations. I spend the entire time in Italy accompanying Dylan to doctors' appointments. Each time the doctors find no sign of anything serious, Dylan believes they are incompetent.

"Italy just doesn't have the advanced technology we do in the U.S."

It isn't until he sees specialists in America who confirm he doesn't have cancer that his paranoia finally subsides. That is when his mood completely shifts. As soon as he knows he's in the clear, he becomes obsessed with having another baby. After weeks of him constantly pressuring me about it, I snap at him.

"Are you insane?! We can't have another baby right now. We're a mess! We need to fix our intimacy issues before we can even think about another baby."

"It's your fault we have intimacy issues. If you cared about how you look and worked on losing the extra fifteen pounds you gained from having Isabella, I would be more attracted to you."

I have no words in response. The idea that it's solely my fault we have issues is the most ridiculous thing I've heard. It's impossible to have a conversation with him, and at this moment I don't want to share even the same air as him so I leave the room.

But things continue to be on the up for Dylan. He is promoted to the director position that he always wanted. He immediately sets his next goal: Within the next five years, he will set up a new international cancer research center named "Dang Clinic."

The celebration of Dylan's promotion is an elaborate banquet, well-attended by renowned cancer doctors from all over the world. Also in attendance are local news stations, and even a reporter from *The New York Times*, which publishes an article on the event the next day.

Dylan and I, as his wife, are in the spotlight. Though I'm proud of this remarkable achievement, I'm horribly uncomfortable with being the center of attention, especially next to Dylan. Dylan seems made for this spectacle of academia elite. He remembers the names of every person who comes up to congratulate him and has a well-conceived vision when asked about his plans for the clinic. I mostly stand silent next to him, smiling and listening to him repeat the same brilliant thoughts over and over.

He is asked to make a speech in the middle of the event, and though it is well-spoken, highlighting his ambitious goals for the future, I'm disappointed he never mentions my name or the support I've given him these past few years. I blink back tears, and if anyone were to look at me, they would see only a proud wife, emotional over the accomplishments of her husband. They would have no idea that those tears represent the surrender and realization that I'll forever be second to his career.

His promotion comes around the time of our third wedding anniversary. He books us a room at the beautiful Lake Austin Resort. This is the first time he's done anything to celebrate our anniversary, and he goes all out. At an amazing dinner overlooking the lake, he presents me with a Tiffany's diamond necklace. It's stunning and calls to mind our romantic night in New York before we were married. When he wants to, he *can* be romantic, I remind myself. He is sweet and tender to me all evening, and I wonder if now that he's achieved a major career goal, he might be more focused on our marriage and family. When we get back to our room after dinner he asks if we can have sex.

"Now is the perfect time to try for a boy, Ying-Ying. Since I'm the only son in my family, I want a son to carry on our family's name and give Isabella a little brother."

I'm concerned about our intimacy issues, still wishing we would go see Dr. Wheat, and I'm not ready to have another child with Dylan when we have so much to resolve. But I'm sure the chances of getting pregnant with his low sperm count are meager. Last time was most likely a fluke. And overall, I don't want to ruin the best night we've had in our marriage, so I agree to sex. This will be the first time since our wedding night.

There is still no foreplay. He lays me on the bed and puts himself straight inside of me. It isn't as aggressive as before so the pain is manageable, but it is over in only a few minutes. I don't experience any pleasure, and it is far from my sexual daydreams, but I hope this is a step toward more intimacy between us.

A miracle happens again! I miss my next period and take a pregnancy test, and it comes back positive! Two months later, we have our first ultrasound.

"Looks like you're having a boy," the doctor announces.

Dylan is there with me. He gets so excited by the news that he actually hugs me, and I laugh out loud at the shock of feeling his touch. A boy! I imagine what he will look and be like. It is my turn to name our baby since Dylan named Isabella, and secretly I know I want to name him "Noah." The name means "rest" and "comfort" in Hebrew, and it's time to receive some comfort. I'm excited for what's to come!

Two weeks later, though, I'm woken up in the middle of the night by the worst abdominal pain. The cramps are so painful I can barely get up, but I somehow manage to stumble to the bathroom. That's when I notice I'm bleeding profusely. I'm terrified and feel that I might pass out.

"Dylan, I need a doctor!" I scream, and luckily as I keep screaming, he hurries to my side, looks at me in horror, and rushes me to the hospital. That night, the doctors do all sorts of tests and keep talking with Dylan. I'm largely left out of the loop and feel out of it, but every time a nurse comes by, I say, "Is my baby okay?"

Hours go by before they tell me, "You've had a miscarriage." And though I normally don't like to cry in public, I begin to sob. All I feel is failure until that failure turns into overwhelming grief and the harsh reality I have to face. My Noah, who I already loved so deeply, who I was so excited to hold and teach and watch grow, has been taken from me before he could meet the light on this side of the universe.

I go home the next day, and on the drive home, Dylan blames me for the loss. "You were not careful. You should've eaten better, drank more milk, and rested more. You worked too hard. You hurt our baby."

Tears silently stream down my face, and I know he is disgusted with me. I know we'll probably never recover from this.

My mother comes over one day to check on Isabella and catches me crying. I've been determined not to burden my parents with my personal struggles, and I don't want to tell them of the problems with our marriage—how Dylan won't even look at me let alone touch me, or how I'm still grieving the loss of Baby Noah. I also have a feeling that if I say something, their sympathy will be meager. Anytime I complain about anything, they lecture me on how I need to appreciate the fortunes of my life, and that any sadness I am experiencing is the fault of my own skewed perspective.

But when my mother catches me crying uncontrollably, she stops what she is doing and sits next to me.

"Ying-Ying, what is it that makes you so sad?"

I know I could make up a million excuses on the spot, but I decide it's time I tell her the truth about my marriage. When I'm done, her response surprises me.

"Oh, Ying-Ying, the answer is simple. You just need to find a boyfriend to have on the side for some fun. Dylan is traveling so often it should be easy to keep that kind of relationship hidden from him. Have some fun!"

This wasn't the answer I was looking for. I've already had a short affair, and it didn't fix my main problem. It also overwhelmed me with guilt. No matter my unhappiness, I never felt that being unfaithful was okay.

Dylan's mother also had thoughts on the matter. She calls us often to catch up. She and I always get along, and I often talk with her for a while. Unfortunately, Dylan would often make me cry right before one of her phone calls. His mother could always detect that on the phone with me.

"What's wrong, Ying-Ying? Why have you been crying?"

"Oh, it's nothing."

"Please tell me. I want to help."

"Ask your son. Maybe he will tell you."

"Fine, give him the phone."

"It's your mother," I would say as I handed him the phone and walked out of the room.

Unfortunately, I could still hear him talking with her.

"Mother, it's nothing. She is always emotional. I am happy; we are good, but I think she needs to go on antidepressant medication. She is always acting crazy."

This cycle continues until, finally, I believe her to be sincere a couple years later. I tell her that Dylan won't touch me since I lost the baby and how, even before then, his frequent masturbation prevented him from being intimate with me. I tell her about Dr. Wheat and how he could help improve our intimacy.

"You see, in Dr. Wheat's book, he points out how most of the physical pain the wife experiences is caused by mental separation from the husband. He says there are ways to learn and resolve intimacy difficulties from both the psychological and the physical perspectives. But Dylan prefers to avoid our issues," I confide to her.

"Ah, I see. I had no idea about this situation. You should have told me much earlier. It sounds easy enough to fix. Let me plan a trip to visit you, and I will convince him in person to go to see Dr. Wheat. Please make the appointment, and book a ticket for me. I will help make things right." I immediately book the earliest appointment available.

I know she means what she says, and I feel it is possible she could convince him. If Dylan will listen to anyone, it's her. There is a trickle of hope in me as I think about us being healed and being able to have intimacy. It leads me to want to be honest with him and to fix our emotional issues as well. I want to tell him that when I'm normal, in love, and lubricated, I don't suffer with pains! But I can't yet risk that. I clearly know that if I want to be intimate with him both physically and emotionally, I'll need to confess to him I had an affair, hoping for a chance to rekindle our marriage.

Sadly, only one week after his mother's visit, even before our appointment to see Dr. Wheat, she is diagnosed with late-stage dementia. All of my dreams of bettering our marriage are put on hold as his mother needs to be the priority. To try and ask for anything more would be selfish, considering all she and Dylan are going through. Dylan and I take turns traveling back and forth to be with her, to make sure she gets the treatment she needs. We are heartbroken when, after two years of battle, she passes away.

After the passing of Dylan's mother, I go to see my doctor for a routine checkup. The doctor detects a sizable lump in my left breast. It's terrifying, but I go through a series of medical procedures. The doctor needs to perform a lumpectomy and then biopsy the tissue of the lump to determine whether it's cancerous. Before the surgery, I tell Dylan that I want to get my own apartment and live by myself to recover if the test results turn out to be positive for cancer because I couldn't heal with all of his complaints. Luckily, it is a benign tumor. A few months later, I have another surgery to remove some hemorrhoids that are causing severe constipation.

My body is going through the ringer, but I'm not the only one suffering. At the same time, Isabella is experiencing intense migraine headaches. She consistently holds her head and rolls around on the floor in pain. I take her to all sorts of doctors, and after dozens of tests, no one is able to diagnose her. The fifth doctor I take her to suggests that the pain may be triggered by the stresses of her home environment.

Dylan and I argue often and heatedly about how to raise Isabella. Dylan is constantly saying that I'm not doing enough to push Isabella. Though she is barely in kindergarten, Dylan buys third-grade math workbooks in Chinese and urges me to teach Isabella this level of math at home. I try to refuse, thinking it will only stress her out and cause confusion at such a young age, but I never hear the end of it. Dylan then forces me to sign her up for piano lessons, which Isabella has no interest in. If I go a day without making her practice, Dylan berates me, saying our daughter will be a failure if I don't force her to practice for hours every day. I don't have the energy to force Isabella to do something she hates, and eventually, the piano teacher tells us we should stop forcing her to take lessons because we are just wasting our money.

Dylan critiques the way I discipline. "You should use a stick and hit her over the hand if she doesn't work hard enough," he tells me.

Yet I am the one always buying groceries, always cooking, always seeing to the needs of Isabella and everyone else. I'm the one who notices Isabella's moods and the one who talks to her about her day.

For Halloween, I stay up late for days to make Isabella's costume. I want her to be proud of her unique costume at the annual school parade. Each year, I put in so much thought and work into arranging all the special details of her birthday parties. I never want her to feel forgotten on her birthday. I want her to be celebrated for the joy she brings the world. I fight for what I think is best for Isabella, but this always escalates into yelling matches and often tears on my end.

Isabella must hear all of this. The doctor's prediction makes sense.

That being said, though I want to put the blame on Dylan for Isabella's stresses, I can't help but know that I'm part of the equation. It's one thing to know that I am struggling, but to know my child struggles as well spirals me to a dark place where I feel like I can't do anything right. I think about my marriage, my unborn baby, Noah, and feel shame for having had an affair during grad school. I've told no one, and I carry the burden of it daily. I blame myself for our problems even though I know it's not all my fault. The thought that I can't do anything right plagues me. At first, I know it isn't all true, but the more it pops up, the more I believe it.

My only comfort is my time with Isabella. I carefully record the first step she takes, the first word she says—every little moment feels huge. Her two big, shining, round eyes and most innocent sweet smiles warm my heart and give me the purpose to function in life every day.

The more Dylan criticizes, the harder I work to be perfect. Perfection feels like the sun I'm aspiring to as I hope to earn his acceptance and affection this way subconsciously. After a long while without seeing improvement, my hope is diminishing. I don't see the possibility of making him happy. I am exhausted both mentally and physically. Still, most people praise how wonderful Dylan is and say that I am the luckiest woman to be his wife. All around me women beam with envy. Out of respect for Dylan, I don't want to go around and talk about my marriage struggles. Meanwhile, because I have discovered Dylan's masturbation habit, he doesn't even bother to cover when he is doing it. He has yet to be intimate with me since the miscarriage, and each time I find him pleasuring himself, it feels like an unbelievably painful rejection.

Dylan comes back in two weeks from a conference in China and seems especially irritated with me for an entire month after. I'm used to his temper, but this is bad even in comparison. I wrack my brain, trying to figure out what is bothering him. I press him and press him, hoping for a clue, until one night he finally bursts. "Of course I'm angry with you. Your boyfriend signed for my package from a doctor in China while I was gone."

"What?! I don't have a boyfriend! And I never received a package from China." Then I add, "Besides, if I did have a boyfriend hiding from you, I wouldn't be stupid enough to have him sign for something." With a slight smirk, I head to the kitchen to make dinner, feeling elated that I said exactly what was on my mind.

"Lying doesn't suit you," he states, following me, his tone cold. "I checked with the post office. They have proof that a man signed for it."

"What is the name of this man?"

"You should know. His name is Ken Moore!"

"Why have you never asked me about it?"

I am confused, though determined to find an answer to this. *Moore*? I don't know anyone named Moore, and I spend the next week poring over any person around me that could be named Moore until it hits me. We have a new neighbor! Can their name be Moore?

The next day, I knock on the door of the new neighbor who moved in two months ago. A middle-aged man answers with a quizzical look in his eye. I feel like I'm about to be interrogated.

"Hello?" he says gruffly. "May I help you?"

"My name is Ying-Ying. I live next door."

"Oh, hi there!" His tone changes immediately. "I'm Ken Moore!" He reaches out and shakes my hand firmly.

I can't help but smile. Ken Moore. The culprit.

"Maybe you can help me settle something with my husband. Did you happen to sign for a package of his about a month ago? The name would be Doctor Dang."

"Hmm . . . you know what, I do remember I signed for someone's mail! One second."

I watch him go back to his mudroom and look under a mountain of mail and old newspapers.

"Dr. Dang you said?"

"Yes."

"Ah, I got it right here. I'm sorry, I totally forgot about it."

"Oh, thank you. I really needed this."

I smile as I leave, exhilarated that I finally have proof Dylan is wrong. I come back to our place, and Dylan is at the kitchen table. I set the unopened package with his name on it in front of him.

"Our new neighbor is named Ken Moore."

"Huh."

He doesn't even look up at me, and there is no apology issued. I'm disappointed and frustrated by the lack of communication and trust from Dylan. I'm sick and tired of being thrown accusations and forced to prove my innocence on an almost daily basis.

I believe there is not a single soul in this world that understands my disappointments, exhaustion, and hopelessness. I assume both Francis and Kaito are married and have their own children now. I don't want to burden them. Plus, they must hate me: I am the one who broke up with them. I even start to think I am a horrible human being, unworthy of any happiness.

Soon I think of suicide, and the negative ideas come without reprieve. Life is too hard. I'm such an imperfect person, and I *deserve* an awful marriage. This overwhelming pain is also impacting my child. I have little happiness in my life and nothing I'm looking forward to. The American Dream I've worked so hard for isn't enough. I am extremely depressed, and my hope is so nonexistent that I just want it all to end. I research methods of suicide and ruminate over which way I should go about it.

One night, I'm determined to do it. I decide I'll try to overdose on pills. I scour all of our medicine cabinets and have my pill cocktail all ready to take before I go to bed. Dylan is working late downstairs in his office, but he'll be up later, and I want it to be him who finds me and has to explain this to everyone. When it's time to go to bed, I burst into tears. I sit on the bathroom floor, my face soaked and my body shaking as I talk myself into believing the commitment for what I've decided is the only answer for my future. There is no other. It's terrible. I see no way out of the life I've buried myself in, and I tell myself that if I do this, everyone else will be better off too. No one wants such an empty and sinful person around.

Yes, that's it.

I stand on shaky limbs. I fill up a cup with water that will help me swallow the handfuls of pills I've laid out. I watch the cup fill until my eyes are blurry and it begins to overflow in the sink. I never imagined this. I never thought my end would happen in such a manner. I never understood why someone would do this, but now I do. I thought death was the worst thing that could happen to a person, but now I know better. Suffering without any hope of a way out—that is worse.

I take a deep breath and feel peace that soon this will all be over. I grab the first pill and take it. I grab the second pill and take it. I grab a third pill and take it. I grab the fourth . . . but I hear Isabella. She is crying and calling for me. I can't ignore her, and it's probably best I say goodbye, take one last look at her.

I go into her room and immediately take her into my arms, soothing her and telling her all the words I wish someone would say to me.

"It's okay, my darling. It's all going to be okay. You are safe. You are loved. I love you."

She's had a nightmare, and tears have wet her face like they have mine. I stroke her hair and take in her face as she calms. As her breathing settles and she starts to fall back asleep, a smile creeps onto her lips. The sweetness of the moment makes me smile as well. I watch her sleep and take in her room. Hanging on the wall is my butterfly kite. I hung it in her room when we moved into this house but had forgotten it was there. I stare at it and remember what it feels like to look back and see how far I've come. Though I'm ashamed of so much of my life, perhaps it shouldn't be over yet. Perhaps, I'll get stronger. Perhaps something more is out there for me. This thought is enough of a pull that when I go back to my room, I throw the rest of the pills away. For today, I want to be able to see Isabella's smile tomorrow. I can't miss that just yet. Deep down, I'm terrified one day I will lose control again and let this episode repeat.

I cannot do this to my darling Isabella.

17

Fixing

On top of my mental and physical health issues, work is escalating. I was promoted to be the team manager in the new year, working under a director named Mark, who is pleasant enough. He seems to trust me to get the work done and thus, doesn't check in too much, which I appreciate. I am currently leading a major project, which is keeping me working an average of sixty hours a week. It hurts to know that Isabella has to take the school bus home to an empty house, and even after I get home, I usually can't spend time with her because I have to continue working remotely just to keep up.

I know my physical and mental health are struggling. Work, with its demanding nature, once served as a distraction from everything else. But lately, work dynamics have become more complicated. Not only am I leading a project but also, I am figuring out how to navigate many different personality types and a rising culture of cutthroat office politics. The daily struggles leave me exhausted. Tension greets me in every room I enter, and a break never surfaces.

A few doors down from my office is a company-hired counselor. I pass by her office every day on my way to and from the elevator, but I have never thought about going in. One Friday, as I'm getting ready to head home from work, I notice the door is cracked open. I pause and see the counselor sitting at her desk by herself. Something in me knows this is my chance. I need help, but I've never stopped to get it. Still, I am curious about her, so I watch her for a moment. I intend to leave without catching her attention, but she looks up and spots me.

"Hello! What can I do for you?"

"Hello. My name is Ying-Ying." I hesitate, unsure for a moment what I am doing in her doorway. "I think I could use your services."

"Of course! To do that, we just need to set up an appointment. How does Monday at one sound?"

On Monday, I open up to her about my consistent suicidal thoughts. She listens intently and at the end of the session gives me an assignment. "Ying-Ying, let's see if we can find any triggers that might be causing these thoughts. Let's have a session once a week over the next few weeks. But in the meantime, I want you to keep a journal of when these thoughts happen. Every time you have one of these thoughts, write down when and where it takes place."

After a few weeks, she notices a pattern. "Ying-Ying, it appears that most of these thoughts begin around Friday at noon and continue through the rest of the day. This leads me to believe that what is causing these thoughts is not work-related but home-related. My job here is just to work with clients who are having work-related issues, but I have some recommendations for therapists who work on marriage and family-related stresses."

The moment I leave her office, I breathe with an enormous sense of hope, and with the source of my problem pinpointed, I now can eliminate work issues as the cause and find a clear direction to follow.

That night I go home and tell Dylan what I've found out, and I beg him to work things out together. I suggest we go to counseling sessions as a couple.

"You are the unhappy and problematic one; therefore, you should go alone to get cured. I have no complaints. If you have a problem with me, then why haven't you asked for a divorce yet?" he tells me.

I've been determined for so many years not to get divorced. I know I would feel shame, and I don't want to disrupt or harm Isabella. I've heard children of divorced parents have a more difficult time than others.

At the graduation for my master's program, when Kaito put the precious pearl necklace around my neck, he asked me if I wanted to get divorced and be with him instead. Though I knew I'd be happier with him, I just couldn't do that to Isabella. I also remember thinking that I couldn't do that to Dylan. I vowed to stay with Dylan for better and worse at the court. I still believe one should marry only once in a lifetime and divorce is shameful. It is my obligation not to bring shame to my family and the little sweet and beloved Isabella.

Still, I daydream about seeing Francis and of running off to be with him instead. But I know it is all a dream. I'm the kind of woman who makes a commitment and sticks to it no matter how hard it is. Thus, if Dylan won't go to counseling, I will, and I will find ways to fix my unhappiness and hope that it will make our family life better.

The first therapist I see tells me to find a divorce lawyer about thirty minutes into the first session. That isn't why I'm there, so I seek out a second therapist. He wants to prescribe me a heavy dose of antidepressant medications and says I'll probably need to take them for the rest of my life. That doesn't sit well with me either. Right off the bat I'm zero for two.

I head back to work highly discouraged after my meeting with the second therapist. I'm exhausted and wonder if I'll ever not feel this way. I go into the break room to grab some coffee and run into a tall Asian woman I've never met before.

"Hi there!" she says upon seeing me. "I just have to say you are beautiful. I love your suit." Her compliment takes me off guard. I can't remember ever being complimented in such a way by another woman. I take her in and am amazed to meet another woman who works here and who is just as tall as me.

"Thank you! You are so beautiful too."

She laughs, and her laugh is infectious. I can't help but laugh with her. "I'm Joyce."

"I'm Ying-Ying. It's nice to meet you."

"Nice to meet you too. How's your Tuesday going?"

Normally, I would've just said, "Fine," but Joyce is so warm and inviting I can't help but be completely transparent.

"Oh, it's been rough."

"Really? Why is that?"

"I just started going to therapy, and the second therapist I tried earlier was even worse than the first."

She smiles knowingly. "Oh, I totally understand. I have two kids and just got divorced and we're still negotiating the custody battle. If I didn't have an amazing therapist, I don't know where I'd be!"

"Really?"

"Yes! He's the most wonderful therapist! He's been such a blessing to me throughout all of this. I can give you his card if you'd like."

I am hesitant, but I hear that American phrase, *third time's the charm,* in my head. "Sure, I'll take his card."

"Why are you here, Ying-Ying, and what are you looking to gain from me?" Gary, Joyce's therapist, asks me at the beginning of our first session.

"I want to be happier in my marriage."

"If you want to be happier in your marriage, why isn't your husband here with you?"

"He doesn't think he's the one who needs counseling. He thinks I'm the only one with problems."

"Okay, well, I'll be honest, I can't work on your marriage without him. But I can work on you. How does that sound?"

"I think that sounds like a good start."

Gary isn't in a rush to get results. He realizes I need time to come to my own conclusions. I feel heard and understood in our sessions, and I keep them up once a week. In our time together, I realize that having multiple health issues at twenty-eight years old is a red flag that something is wrong emotionally.

"Ying-Ying, it seems like your physical body can't keep up with all the unhappiness and stress that is taking place internally. Also, I know you want to stay in this marriage for Isabella, but it sounds like this family stress could be what's causing her physical distress as well."

It made sense, but I still didn't think the answer was divorce. I thought I needed to find an answer, to find peace outside of my marriage that could improve it.

Joyce and I go out to lunch or dinner once a week after our encounter in the break room. She's so encouraging and an amazing listener. I tell her about Francis one day and find myself bringing him up more and more as we get to know each other. She tells me I need to get closure with him sometime.

As I tell her about my life, my fears, my struggles, and my doubts, she always makes sure to tell me how strong, amazing, and capable I am. I find myself calling her quite often, and every time I do, she speaks softly and tells me there is a God who loves me, who sees me, and who has a beautiful future set out for me. She tells me that whenever I doubt that, I should pray. Her words comfort me. I don't know if I believe in "God," but learning to pray is helpful so I listen to her advice and pray to a god I hope I believe in someday.

It's hard to take Joyce's compliments at first. For many years the loudest voice in my head has been Dylan's, which screams the opposite. But as time goes on and my friendship with Joyce builds, I begin to believe her words are true. I begin to see myself in the kind of light I've always wanted to.

I've been going to see Gary for more than two years. Isabella is eight years old when Gary gives me an assignment that wakes me up. He gives me a paper full of questions that are supposed to evaluate my marriage with a score at the end. I get almost zero on the result. I couldn't say yes to ninety-nine percent of what qualifies as a healthy marriage.

I'm a math and science person. I see the number. I see the big zero. That undeniable number is my alarm clock. I know what I must do.

"Gary, the next time I'm here, I want you to work on helping me and Isabella get through this divorce."

The next night, Dylan comes home around nine at night and finds me sitting at our kitchen table reading. He barely acknowledges me though I know he sees me, and he starts to head upstairs when I stop him.

"Dylan, I need to talk to you." I set down my book.

"I am tired and am going to bed," he responds.

"This cannot wait."

He turns around and comes toward me. "What is it?"

I take a deep breath, and a sense of calm washes over me as I look into his eyes, and say, "I have decided I want a divorce. I need you to please be home tomorrow morning to receive the divorce documents."

Dylan scoffs and glares at me with such condescension. "I don't believe you actually mean it. I'll believe your words when I see the documents."

I don't say anything else and go upstairs to bed. He'll believe me soon enough.

The next morning, I am getting Isabella ready for school when I hear the doorbell. I refuse to answer it because I want Dylan to do it. I want him to be handed the envelope. I want him to open it himself. I want him to have the sinking realization that I meant every word from last night.

Isabella and I rush downstairs so that she can catch the school bus. Out of the corner of my eye, I see Dylan at the table, looking at the documents. When I come back inside after Isabella leaves, I see a defeat in Dylan I've never seen before. I know he wasn't expecting this. His eye twitches as he stares at the divorce papers.

"Ying-Ying, I can't believe this. No. I don't want this. I'll do anything. Please change your mind! Please!"

There is a desperation in his voice that surprises me. It helps me to remember he is human also, and I wonder if this is the catalyst he needed all along.

"Come with me to counseling. Let's see if that can help."

"Okay, I will. Just tell me when."

I book a session the following week, hopeful that this can help us and that we can confess all of our wrongdoings in the past and have a clean slate. Unfortunately, my hope proves futile.

Dylan is in common form, putting me down in front of the counselor, accusing me of being greedy and unreasonable.

"I am a famous doctor, a good provider. I'm a very good man, not one of those womanizers. What more could a woman want? She will not be able to find any man better than me, and she should be thankful. Her life would be so much worse without me. Every problem in this marriage is because of her selfishness."

It's hard for me to stay quiet. Besides wanting a husband who is actually kind and respectful, I imagine most women prefer a man who likes to have physical intimacy at least occasionally. We have only tried to be intimate less than a handful of times during our entire ten years of marriage.

We go to a couple more sessions anyway, but each time it is the very same. He can't see outside of his own delusions, and he isn't willing to change a thing. After the third session, all I want is to get out of this marriage. Thus, I reactivate the divorce process.

A few weeks into the divorce journey, Joyce comes to help me convert our guest bedroom into my own sanctuary. My lawyer suggests it won't look good if I move out right now.

As soon as Joyce comes over, Dylan lays into her. "You are not welcome here! Leave this house now!"

"This is Ying-Ying's house also, and she has invited me over. You have absolutely no right to tell me to leave without her consent."

"Fine, then I'm going to call the police on you."

"Go ahead." She says, hands on her hips, staring my soon-to-be ex-husband down.

I watch this interaction and am captivated by Joyce's strength. Just watching her elevates my own confidence.

Dylan does call the police, and two arrive within an hour.

"What seems to be the problem, sir?" one of the officers asks.

"This woman refuses to leave my house and I want her gone."

"Okay. Well, why is she here in the first place?"

I come forward. "I am his wife, and this is my very good friend Joyce, who I invited over to help me with a project, which she very kindly agreed to do. My husband just doesn't like me to have company over."

The police turn their attention back on Dylan. "Sir, do you understand what it means to be a husband?"

"I'm a famous doctor. Of course I do."

The burly policeman rubs his finger across his chin in disgust. "Then I am surprised that you would not give your wife equal privileges in this place she also calls home. If I were you, I'd take into consideration her needs too. If she wants to have a friend over to help her, there is no crime in that. It's a bigger crime that you would insult her for doing so by calling us. We have far more serious matters that this city needs us for. Please don't call us again, understand?"

The other policeman turns toward Isabella, who is hiding in a corner looking terrified, and comforts her. He then turns back to

Dylan. "Look how scared your daughter is now. Please don't do this again—for her sake."

The policemen turn to leave, and Dylan glares at them as they exit. I try not to laugh as he stares in our direction. He is furious. I'm afraid what he'll do next, but he just runs up the stairs, into the bedroom, and slams the door. Joyce and I look at each other and do a silent victory dance, covering our mouths as laughter pours out of us.

My husband doesn't know it, but Joyce shared with me in private that she is transgender. She was born a man and spent most of her life as a man. She understands how men think, and she isn't intimidated by my husband in any way. I love that she has such a unique perspective into both sexes. It is strength.

Later that night, Joyce urges me to find closure with Francis. Weeks later, I pick up the phone, my hands trembling, and dial his number. It rings and rings and right before I think no one is going to answer, I hear, "Hello?" Immediately, I recognize the tone of his voice. How I've missed the sound of him speaking.

"Francis. This is Ying-Ying."

There's a pause on the other end of the phone, and my stomach drops.

"Ying-Ying?! What took you so long to call?" He laughs infectiously, and my whole body tingles.

He seems surprisingly happy to hear from me. We talk for a few minutes, and I find out he went on to graduate school and works now at a successful business firm. He informs me that he got married just two weeks ago and is very much in love with his wife. He mentions that next month he is going to fly into Austin from New York for a business meeting and would love to catch up if I have time. I tell him yes, and on a Thursday three weeks later, we meet at my parent's house and head to a nearby restaurant to catch up on the past ten years.

I'm amazed how easy it is to just pick up where we left off. Hours fly by, and I'm shocked when I realize it's midnight and the restaurant is closing. We both agree we need to get some rest. Before he leaves, though, he says, "You know Ying-Ying, when you left me, I couldn't get out of bed for weeks. I couldn't believe it was over. I loved you so much. I kept thinking any day now you would change your mind and come back. For years after, I imagined running into you accidentally and it being fate that would bring us back to each other. I thought you were the one for me."

"Francis, I'm sorry."

"Don't be sorry. It was you who taught my mother a lesson and paved the road for my wife. My family treats her so much nicer because they learned from what happened with you."

"That's good. Still, I'm sorry."

"It's okay, Ying-Ying. It's worked out for us. I found the woman I didn't know existed. I found the one who is right for me now. The next time you are in town, I'd love for you to meet her."

In our conversation, I find out the true reason for Francis's transfer to Columbia University. It was because he had ruined his GPA to the point Albany had to expel him. He was too embarrassed at the time to admit it to me, which caused my false assumption that it was his mother's plan to break us up. In a way, this clarification comforts me. She was better than I assumed.

However, he is surprised by my description of his mother's criticisms toward him while working at her restaurants. He felt he'd been praised highly by his mother at home since he was young. He says with certainty, "If I heard those words, I would be angry like you, and I would have stood up for myself immediately!"

Looking at him now, I don't doubt it.

He looks puzzled for a moment. "The only explanation could be that my mother said those words just for you to hear, thinking it would cause you to be disappointed and think less of me so you might decide to break up with me." We still do not know the absolute truth, but this theory does make sense for the time being.

We ended the night after hearing the miracle story of him meeting his wife and the exciting news that they are expecting their first baby. With the truth of the past finally revealed and cleared up, he hugs me goodbye and whispers in my ear, "I hope you will find your happiness soon." I savor the moment, the hug, and the hope. In fact, as I fall asleep that night, I savor the entire night's conversation. I savor the sweetness and the comfort and our ability to be open with one another. I still feel guilty for having caused Francis so much pain, but at least I know he is happy now and I didn't totally ruin his life. At the same time, I am sorry for myself that there is no open door for us to rekindle our relationship. Secretly, I was wishing for a romantic spark again. I hope someday I can find the type of love he has.

A few weeks later, Joyce and I must travel to New Jersey to attend a company conference. I ask her to come along with me to a dinner to meet Francis and his new wife. Before we meet them, we do some shopping to buy a gift for a newlywed couple we both know. We enter one store, and there is a truly kind owner who chats with us. The strangest thing is she looks just like me.

As we exit the store, Joyce yells out, "Did you notice that lady looked exactly like you?"

"You thought so too? Yes, it was the weirdest thing!"

We arrive at the restaurant an hour later, and there is Francis, waiting as he sits next to the store owner we'd just met! He introduces her as his wife, and we all burst out laughing, having just met an hour before. What a serendipitous moment! I adore his wife. I find out she is also from Beijing originally, and we have a lot in common. The dinner goes wonderfully, and from then on, I know Francis and I can be good friends again.

With Joyce's support to rely on, I file for joint custody of Isabella. Dylan hires a famous lawyer at triple what a standard divorce lawyer charges, one with a record of winning all custody cases for fathers. They contest for full custody. He also hires two other divorce consultants to assist him. From that point on, Dylan uses any strategy his lawyer, or whoever supports him, tells him to use, trying to tear me down and prove that I'm an unfit mother, unfit employee, and unfit citizen. Another goal of his is to drag out the divorce as long as possible because, as I age more, the chance for me to remarry will decrease. Dylan believes no man will marry an older woman, so Isabella will not need to live with another man.

First Dylan calls my director, Mark, at work, and asks him to testify that I am a terrible employee. Mark refuses, but this makes Dylan so angry that he finds the phone number of my director's wife and tells her that her husband and I are having an affair.

For weeks, Mark's wife tailgates me, looking for an ounce of evidence that this is true, but she cannot find anything. Whenever she sees me, though, she yells and accuses me of ruining her marriage and sleeping my way up the corporate ladder.

Because of the accusations, Mark thinks dating me is a brilliant idea. One night, as we are leaving work, he asks if I would consider exclusively dating him. He tells me that if I accept, he will divorce his wife and give me an immediate promotion. The last thing I want to do is break our company's rules and destroy another woman's marriage. I have no choice but to quit on the spot.

Dylan also asks Will, one of the fellow students in his clinic, and his wife, Tina, to testify that I was an unfit mother, urging them that if they don't, he will not let him graduate! They tell him straight out that from the little they'd seen of me, they'd only seen me as a good mother. They tell Dylan that they are Christians and will not lie, even if it means forgoing his doctorate.

This is huge because I know this couple have had to overcome so many hurdles to get Will to his degree. The husband worked with a different doctor advisor on a thesis for five years only to find out that once it was completed, a similar thesis had already been published by someone else. Thus, this student found Dylan and has been working with him for the past three years on a new thesis. I overhear the entire conversation, and for the first time I am extremely moved by Christian principles. The integrity of this couple standing up for a woman they barely know when they're in a vulnerable position sticks with me, and I am extremely grateful.

Dylan's antics continue, though. He is restless in his attempts to win custody. He accuses me of having a sexual relationship with Joyce. Then he asks one of his students to scoop poop into Isabella's underwear so there will be evidence that I am neglecting her and not changing her underpants. He then tries to gather evidence that my father is a spy for the Chinese Communist party. He bribes Isabella with rewards, intending to make her tell the court she'd rather stay only with him.

Dylan, Isabella, and I are each interviewed and evaluated multiple times by the court-appointed psychologist. The divorce proceedings drag on for more than two years, and my lawyer insists I need to live in the same home as him the entire time. On December 12, 1996, the judge reaches his final verdict and awards me full custody! What a relief! Now, Dylan will move out, and I can focus on building the life I genuinely want for my daughter.

As soon as I leave the courtroom that day, I'm hit with the memory of the butterfly kite soaring high in the gray-blue sky. After twelve years of marriage, I feel as though I finally have the freedom to soar too.

18

Freedom

Life is peaceful without the constant criticism and beratements from Dylan hovering around us. I can make decisions about Isabella without putting on battle armor and enjoy time with my daughter. She is growing fast and thriving. After work, I drive her around to her cheerleading lessons and competitions, study sessions, and social outings. Her health immediately improves, and the horrible headache vanishes. I love that she feels better, I am less distracted, and I can focus on witnessing the amazing woman she is becoming.

Life is finally falling into place. My sister and her family are granted citizenship. My parents are feeling more and more comfortable with their new lives in this country, and my work is going smoothly.

Will eventually graduates to become a doctor at a local hospital. We keep in touch as good friends. Jeremy, his first little boy with his wife Tina, was born after two years of infertility treatments. Tina announces the exciting news to me: "Ying-Ying, I am reserving the spot for Jeremy to be your future wedding ring-bearer now!"

"Well, you better have a more reliable back-up," I say, flattered by her confidence. "I don't even have a boyfriend yet!"

I continue to be given more and more responsibility at work. My new director, Pamela, goes out of her way to intentionally discover the potential in me that I usually hide unknowingly. At the first performance review meeting with her, she concludes with confidence, "Ying-Ying, you have outstanding skill sets that are rare to our company. I must create opportunities for you to use them and let them shine."

I resist my rising tears. I am in disbelief that I actually have female friends who are not intimidated and jealous!

My heart full, I go home that night, and I recite the lullaby I used to sing to Isabella,

"This little light of mine, I'm going to let it shine, let it shine, let it shine . . ."

I become more comfortable in being myself. I no longer need to feel guilty for my talents or for being a beautiful woman! I start to see I'm a worthy and valuable person. Pamela nominates me to head a project in Tokyo for two years. I am then recruited to the job by the vice president of the company. I'm floored by the honor of this opportunity but have to decline for Isabella's sake. Though the vice president says he can easily arrange a prestigious international school for Isabella to attend in Tokyo, I know I can't take her away from her father completely. The vice president is disappointed, and part of me is too, but I finally have some peace, and I want to keep it that way.

I'm grateful my work life and home life are both going well for the first time. I take Isabella to museums and on hikes, and we bake and do crafts together. I attend a local community choir with Joyce, practicing once a week to perform on major holidays. Joyce and I take ballroom dance lessons and go dancing on the weekends whenever I have time. It is a fulfilling and pleasant life.

Both Isabella and I continue to see Gary. Gary encourages me to find a meaningful relationship when I tell him that my plan is to wait until after Isabella has gone to college. Gary insists that a good relationship with another man will be beneficial for Isabella to experience.

With this insight, I want to find a partner I can have an intimate life with. Dylan remarries only a few months after the divorce, which surprises me at first but is honestly a relief. Dylan and his new wife adopt a set of twins, a boy and a girl from the Philippines, to complete their wish of having a family together. The happier Dylan is, the less I must deal with him. I know it'll be harder to date at this stage in life where most men are already married, and I have Isabella to think of. I've defied the odds time and time again as an immigrant who knew no English but who now has a master's degree and is accelerating up the American corporate ladder. If I put that same kind of determination and brain power into my love life, I'm sure I can find my person.

I go out to bars sometimes with Joyce, who is also looking for a new romantic relationship, and though I hate the process, I think it's good for me to put myself out there. Plus, I don't know how else I'm going to meet a man! As a single woman out on the town, I feel more like prey than the hunter I long to be. Who decided on these rules anyway? As a woman, you are expected to get all dolled up and then casually sit at the bar with your girlfriends while you wait patiently for a man to approach you. The man may be poorly dressed and might give you a line you know he has used countless times before, but you're expected to smile and act like you think it's cute. If the conversation takes off, then you're expected to go back to his place, which is conveniently just down the block. Without even knowing each other's last names, there's an anticipation that sex is bound to happen, and somehow, in that one encounter, you're supposed to know whether or not you have a connection that could lead to lifelong happiness!

I play the game to a point, but I don't sleep with the men on the first date, and this usually does not go over well. The way they ask me to come back to their place with a greedy look in their eye is disconcerting. One time I even tell a man after his offer, "Thank you for the invitation, but I find sleeping with a man I barely know, who I might never see again, disgusting." He doesn't like that and goes on to say I must suffer from sexual inhibition and other mental illnesses and should go see a psychologist. Oh, how fragile the egos of men are, and how strong we women have to be to simply say "no."

The bar scene provides disappointment after disappointment, but I'm determined to learn how to date successfully. I spend time thinking of and writing down what I want in a partner, and I become a student of healthy relationships. I go to the bookstore and scour every top-selling book on relationships. My favorite is *Men are From Mars, Women are From Venus* by John Gray. I learn that to be in a healthy relationship, it is helpful if you are in a healthy place yourself. This leads me down the never-ending portal of self-improvement.

I read ten of Deepak Chopra's books on spirituality and relationships and then go to one of his conferences to meet him. It's enlightening, and I find his words soothing.

I meet a woman at the conference who tells me her story of finding contentment through Buddhism. I'm intrigued and make the decision to study Buddhism for six months, but in the end, I find that it doesn't make sense to me. The theory of being perfect in life doesn't resonate with me. I am so broken and will never be perfect with my record of being divorced and having had an affair.

Will and Tina invite me to go to their Christian church on a few occasions, but I'm skeptical. The way they memorize the words of the Bible as truth reminds me too much of memorizing Mao's Red Book as a child. Mao was the biggest hypocrite, not following the words he himself had written, and I won't be led by such rhetoric again.

In spite of my quest for self-improvement, my luck in the dating game doesn't change much. I've given up on the bar scene, and I hope that I'll meet a man some other way.

There are a few men from work who have expressed interest, but none of them spark in me a desire to date them. A co-worker introduces me to Joseph, a Chinese-American who is a patent lawyer for our company, and we become friends. Sadly, his wife passed away recently.

One day, I tell him that my father is having legal issues with the publication of his book, and Joseph volunteers to come over and help him out. The next night, he comes to my parent's home with me and immediately bonds with my father while my mother prepares an amazing dinner in his honor. Joseph is tall, smart, and only two years older than me. I enjoy his company but haven't yet felt a spark of connection.

He and my father hit it off, though, and for months my father continues to invite him to family dinners that Isabella and I will be at. It is sweet but so obvious what my father's intentions are.

When I book a trip for my parents, Isabella, and myself to go to Europe, my father calls Joseph and invites him along. When I find out, I don't argue. Part of me is curious. Maybe, in the right circumstances, I could see another side to him that would interest me.

Joseph meets us in London. As we travel from England to Paris, the Netherlands, Switzerland, and Italy, my parents volunteer to watch Isabella so that Joseph and I can have alone time together. We go to dinners and walk the streets of Europe together, but things aren't clicking for me. On paper he is perfect. He is smart, successful, Chinese and has the approval of my parents. He tries to buy me a Rolex at one point, and at another he suggests buying me a diamond. It's generous, but I can't accept it. I know the truth: I don't enjoy his presence.

It doesn't take long until I'm wishing he hadn't come on our trip at all. He has all these opinions about what we should do and eat, and before I know it, it's day seven, and I am yelling at him that he shouldn't be on this trip at all and that he shouldn't tell me what he thinks. This is in front of my parents, and I avoid their eyes the rest of the day. The next week of travel feels awkward, and Joseph is quieter than usual. Our interests conflict with each other, and he is trying to lead the trip while totally ignoring my desires. I am saddened that it doesn't work out. When we return to the U.S., Joseph and I don't talk as much, but my father continues to invite him to family dinners.

Six years after my divorce, I am the lead manager on a project to develop a brand-new feature called "Short Message Service." This is a project that will be a game-changer for the telecommunications industry. We are using this breakthrough feature in unlimited ways: to create a heart monitor device for doctors to implant in the chests of people with cardiac problems. This device automatically sends an emergency signal to the hospital if the heart rate becomes abnormal, and an ambulance will be called to the location; to create a smart meter for gas companies to monitor readings remotely—and for vending machine companies to monitor inventories without sending a live person to check; to create digital street parking meters that can charge credit cards so people won't have to worry about carrying enough change; and to create a cell phone communication system that allows people to access the internet and send each other short written messages (this will later be referred to as a "text message").

My boss asks me to lead this project when it is a mere infant in its initial concept stages. There are little to no industrial standards for these features yet, and thus, we're developing the standards from scratch. Even with the blank slate I've been given, I'm excited as I can see the potential this project has for the future.

It takes a couple of years, but our team successfully sends the first ever text message in the entire world, and it transforms the global industry. It's incredible to see! I'm constantly in the throes of work, but on that day, I take a breath and look at the journey that brought our team here. It's amazing how dedicated teamwork can open up a whole new world in our industry. Little sparks of imagination are now a reality.

We start to get billion-dollar contracts from companies worldwide for this feature. Service providers like AT&T, Verizon, and T-Mobile begin to offer this feature to their subscribers across the globe. One of my responsibilities becomes to assist with software installation for our customers. In between two such meetings—with Samsung in Seoul, Korea, and SONY in Tokyo, Japan—I get a couple of free days. I make a diversion and stop in Bangkok, Thailand, to fulfill my dream of seeing the magnificent Golden Buddha with my own eyes.

As I approach the statue, I am ecstatic! Having read about the incredible feat it was to create this Buddha, I am enthralled and can't help but reflect on my journey to where I am now. I am so grateful that my team's project was successful and can't wait to see what else life has in store. As I travel back to the U.S. after Thailand, I'm filled with excitement and hope.

Another part of my job entails meeting with other tech companies in order to create international standards. About once a month, I am required to go to meetings with all the major players, including AT&T Bell Laboratories, Nortel, Samsung, and Qualcomm. These meetings are usually held in the U.S. or Europe, but can be anywhere.

In every meeting, each company submits their proposals for the meeting, and we review, discuss, and vote on them as a unit. Oftentimes, a long debate ensues where each company tries to get their proposals to be approved, and it feels like a rodeo. Each representative does their best to ride the bull until the other representatives throw them off.

In May, after a year into developing this feature, our meetings are held in Kauai. Four engineers from Nortel make a proposal, and I am the only one from my company, Motorola, to attend. I don't agree with their proposal, and I am vocal about debating with them.

The debate lasts all morning, and as we break for lunch, the representatives from Nortel invite me out to lunch. I think this is just a plea for me to agree to their proposal, but I accept since I am alone. I have a great time at the luncheon and find out two of them are from the Austin branch of Nortel.

One of the younger-looking reps is named Hank, and he is particularly friendly toward me. I take note of how tall he is, the blue in his eyes, and how sweet his smile is as we get into a passionate discussion about the architecture of Frank Lloyd Wright. We exchange business cards before going back to the meeting. Our conversation keeps me smiling throughout the rest of the day.

The next week, Hank calls and asks me to see an annual event of the Frank Lloyd Wright tour that is happening locally. I happily accept. I feel things I've never felt on that day. Hank is brilliant and funny and treats me with such intention and respect. He's six years younger than me, but has already filed thirty-six patents with his company. I'm impressed not only with his ambition but also with his deep sense of humility. He doesn't brag about what he's accomplished but only admits to the thirty-six patents after I badger him for the answer.

The one date multiplies, and soon we are going out at least twice a week. I am falling for him, and when he drops me off on our seventh date, he brings out a vase of multi-colored roses from his own garden. I ask him if he wants to come in. I know from him kissing me good night that I am deeply and passionately attracted to him, and over the past couple of weeks, I have often found myself daydreaming about what it would be like to make love with him.

When the time comes, he comes in tentatively, not assuming what will happen (although I'm sure he is hoping for it, as am I). He leads me to my bedroom, and he begins kissing me. I'm pushed against my own wall as he continues kissing and caressing me until my breath is gone. I want nothing more than to have him. He is so present and knowing, making this the most incredible physical act of love. It is beyond anything I've imagined, and I feel no guilt or shame afterward because I know I love him. I have a deep feeling that this could be it—the man I was always supposed to find.

That night we make it official, and the next year we are together is a blur of bliss! We travel together to most of our monthly business meetings, scheduling our flights so that we can sit together on the plane and stay in the same hotel. My favorite trip involves going to Nice in France. More than once, people ask us if we are on our honeymoon. It makes me giggle every time. Things are going so well that we begin to talk about the potential for marriage. This is what I've been looking for. This is the passionate type of love I always knew existed.

He takes Isabella and me on trips to Oregon to meet his parents and where his brother and sister are also present. I love his family, and they adore me as well. This relationship is beautiful and brings me so much happiness! I haven't yet introduced him to my parents, but I know the time is coming.

19

Uncertainty

Hank and I have been dating for a year when my cousin Susanna comes into town for a visit. It's been years since I've seen her, so we plan a special dinner with our parents. She calls me the afternoon before, begging me to bring Hank to the dinner so that she can meet him. Hank has been in Germany for work all week, but he will arrive home in the afternoon. I'm pretty sure he'll be too tired to take me up on the invitation, but I casually ask him when he arrives at the airport, and he agrees, much to my surprise. I don't have a chance to tell anyone that he is coming since not many people have cell phones yet. Even though I've met so many of his family members already, I've avoided introducing him to my father because I am worried he won't accept that I am dating an American, especially when he still hopes I will marry Joseph. Still, I feel hopeful tonight will go well, and I'm looking forward to having him finally meet my parents.

Hank arrives to dinner directly from the airport, bringing with him a beautiful bouquet of white hydrangeas for my family. He knows that I adore hydrangeas, especially the white ones, and I'm touched by the gesture. White flowers represent reverence, humility, peace, gentleness, and purity to me. Unfortunately, it occurs to me it may be the wrong color to bring to my parents since white blossoms are only appropriate for funerals in Asian Cultures because the color is associated with death. It is unlucky to give someone white flowers for other occasions.

When he enters, he immediately hands the flowers to my mother, and I try not to cringe as my parents give each other an uneasy look. I'm waiting for an ungracious reaction but am relieved they are tactful enough not to make any comments about it.

Thankfully, Susanna comes over to me and exuberantly introduces herself to Hank. "So, you must be the amazing boyfriend I've heard so much about!"

"I hope it's me. Otherwise, Ying-Ying has some explaining to do!" Susanna and I laugh, but as I turn to look at my parents, my father is glaring at me and my white boyfriend.

"I don't speak English!" He says to me as he rises out of his seat and leaves the room.

"Grandpa, you have just spoken English!" Isabella blurts out quickly.

Mother looks disapprovingly at me and stays quiet the entire dinner as Susanna does her best to be a mediator between us.

I knew this could be an issue, but I underestimated just how badly my parents still want me to be with someone Chinese. I guess part of me thought their move to America would make them less strict in their ideal partner for me, but I realize that was foolish to believe. Father is also horrified that I'm dating a younger man. He tells me the next morning, "The age difference and your cultural differences will break this relationship apart. It might be nice now in its beginning, but a man will always want a younger woman, so he won't stay!"

My father avoids eye contact with me the rest of the week. My heart is crushed because he is my role model, the type of man who set the standard for what I should look for in a husband. It's disappointing he doesn't approve of me dating Hank and that I can't share this part of my happiness with him. I've leaned on my father my entire life as a voice of wisdom and reason. He represents safety and a place to land if ever I need it.

I'm saddened by the loss of his approval, but I'm also angry at what I think is a ridiculous and old-fashioned standard to hold. American men are no less worthy than Chinese men. I originally married the type of man they approved of, and look how that turned out! I wish he'd be happy for and proud of me, but I can see that he won't be. Hank handles the situation well, saying he understands, but part of me knows he is hurt by the reaction too. My mom is working full-time now, and Isabella is in high school. I can look after herself after school. Isabella and I don't depend on my parents as much anymore, and they don't need me as much, either. I decide it's best to avoid seeing my parents for a while.

In the meantime, the dot-com companies in Silicon Valley, California, are blowing up and aggressively recruiting tech experts like Hank and me to move to the Bay Area. Due to my experience, I am getting two to three calls from recruiters every day. The offers are tempting. The salaries are double my current pay. Plus, they'll give me stock options that could potentially turn me into a millionaire. *Time* magazine writes an article that says due to the shortage of women engineers, a woman in Silicon Valley could easily get ten dates in one hour just by sitting at a bar. I love Hank, and am not looking for anything else, but it would be empowering to be one of the few women working in the up-and-coming Silicon Valley.

Hank is also heavily recruited and decides to hop on board and take one of the offers, begging me to come with him. Perhaps if I didn't have Isabella or my parents to think of, I would've joined him without a second thought. Instead, I tell him I need to think about it.

Isabella is now in high school, preparing to take the SAT and taking six AP classes at a time. She recently broke her arm from a cheerleading competition and had to have surgery, so she's out for the season. Dylan now has other children and is still constantly visiting clinics around the world, so he barely has any time for Isabella.

Isabella is also grieving the loss of her best friend since first grade who recently passed away from a drug overdose. I've heard other parents talk about how they've found their kids doing drugs, and that is a worry of mine as well. I don't want her to get into that kind of crowd. This is a fragile time for her, and like always, my priority is whatever is best for her. I call my lawyers to discuss custody issues, and I talk with a child psychologist about the potential impact of moving Isabella across the country during this time. The lawyers say moving Isabella out of the state could cause trouble if Dylan wanted to pursue a new custody battle. If I moved and left Isabella with Dylan, the child psychologist tells me that, due to the unique bond between mother and daughter, my leaving could feel like abandonment and could damage Isabella's confidence for the rest of her life. "She might feel like a second-tier priority and that she isn't enough to win the affections of her parents," the psychologist tells me.

Nothing about this move weighs in Isabella's favor, which means I have to turn it down. Once again, I'm stuck in the middle, torn amongst what everyone else needs from me. I hope Hank will understand. I call him and ask him to come over as we need to talk about California. I'm grateful that he arrives almost immediately.

Hank comes in with a weak smile, unsure what I'm going to tell him. He hugs and kisses me sweetly, and I savor the sensation, knowing I cannot take them for granted.

"So, what are you thinking, Ying-Ying?"

"As you know, this decision is complicated because I have to think of what is best for Isabella."

"Of course. But I also hope that you doing what is best for you can be best for Isabella as well."

"Maybe. But in this case, I don't think so. I conversed with both my lawyers and a child psychologist who knows Isabella. The lawyers said it'd be risky custody-wise to leave the state, and the psychologist said that if I move away from Isabella at this time in her life, it could be detrimental to her confidence. She is at such a malleable age."

"So, you're not coming to California?"

"No. Not until Isabella is done with high school. Then, I can evaluate."

"Damn it, Ying-Ying." He begins pacing around my living room.

"I know this is disappointing, but I'm still willing to make our relationship work long-distance. I love you Hank, and I don't want to give up on us."

He says nothing to this but stops pacing and stares at the wall across from him with eerie silence. I know he's processing everything. He didn't expect me to make this decision.

"No," he finally says.

"What?"

"I can't, Ying-Ying. I can't waste my life waiting for you to choose me first. If you're not coming with me, we have to break up."

"Break up? No! You would just throw away everything?"

"Long-distance never works. I'm just saving us from having to pretend that it will. I'm sorry. This hurts so bad, but goodbye, Ying-Ying."

He doesn't hug me before he leaves, which is probably for the best. I don't know if I could've let him go if he had. My entire body trembles with despair and shock. Never did I think he wouldn't want to work things out. He always spoke about how much he loved me, and about getting married someday. How could physical distance diminish all those promises?

I'm devastated. This is my first time falling in love and being in a committed relationship based on that love without any fear of visa issues or money, or even my parents' well-being. I'd been able to focus on us. Everything felt right, and I thought that I'd found it—the kind of once- in-a-lifetime love you're supposed to have.

Then, just like that, Hank gets a call from California, and in a cruel twist of fate, I'm considered an unworthy opponent to combat a Silicon Valley career opportunity. I feel blindsided more than ever, and I don't know if I can take it anymore. Why is my life one tragedy after the other?

The disappointment makes me sick, and I call out of work for the next week. I stay home in bed, not eating. Lying there in a numbness of emotion that is beyond sadness, I fall into hopelessness. This break up transforms any optimism I had into a fear of the impossibility of having a lasting relationship when my priority is being a mother. I don't want to lower my standards in the dating department. However, it seems too much to ask for a man to love me and make the sacrifices needed for Isabella. It took me six years, post-divorce to meet Hank, and with that timeline, I don't think there's a chance that I'll ever be in love again.

A few days after the breakup, Isabella knocks on my bedroom door and brings in some chicken noodle soup and my favorite almond cookies she'd made for me to eat. She stays next to me for a while. I still have no appetite, but my heart swells with her sweetness and thoughtfulness. I take a few spoonful of soup to appease her.

I'm proud of that girl.

The next day, Joyce stops by. We are still close friends, but because she's been living with her girlfriend and I've been so invested in Hank, we haven't spent much time together recently.

She must've heard we broke up, though, because she's been calling to check on me. I just couldn't bring myself to pick up the phone. Apparently, that encouraged her to show up at my door.

"Ying-Ying, we are getting you out of here and going out to

lunch," she booms as I open the door with trepidation.

"No, Joyce, I don't want to go out."

"Too bad. Get dressed."

"I'm not hungry."

"Fine, then we'll just go on a drive."

I throw on some clothes, and we hop into her white convertible BMW and take off. We don't talk much because I'm unwilling. When she blares classical music, I start to remember to live a little. She pulls up to a restaurant.

"You ready for some lunch?"

"No," is all I say as I shake my head.

"Okay, then."

She keeps driving another forty minutes until we arrive at Crown Seafood, one of my favorite restaurants. My head perks up a little, but we find out they aren't open for lunch. She drives another half hour until we are in front of Adam Restaurant atop Covert Park at Mount Bonnell. It is always a treat to come here, so when Joyce suggests we go up and have lunch, I nod my head yes. We go up to the open rooftop. As we are seated, I take in the breathtaking views of the Colorado River and the city in the distance. It is then that I realize I'm actually hungry.

The food and Joyce's exultant company help immensely, but the next day, I am back in a sea of sadness. Hurdle after hurdle has been thrown my direction, and I've always landed over them. This hurdle scares me, though, and I don't know if I can make it. My thirty-nine-year-old heart is heavy, and my hope for the future is dismal. For the first time in seven years, depression rears its ugly head again, and I think of the night I had prepared those pills.

An emptiness overwhelms me even still. I envy married couples around me and pity myself without a loving relationship. My depression leads me to find answers, and I again hope to find meaning in religion. I pick up Buddhism a second time, and while it gives me some relief, I still can't find practical answers to my real-life questions. I am a kind, hard-working, beautiful woman. I am over-qualified for the affections of any man not to be in a loving relationship. So why is my life so difficult? It just does not seem fair!

20

Forgiveness

I tell myself repeatedly that suicide isn't the answer and realize it would be a good idea to go back to seeing my therapist, Gary, so I schedule a few sessions with him. I'm grateful for the space to say exactly what I think and feel without guilt, which helps a little, but I'm still not functioning normally.

At the end of our third session, as I'm leaving his office, a flyer on his wall catches my eye. The flyer is colorful, with a picture of a giant, orange sun. It says, "Recovery Conference: Reconnect with The Hope You Were Created to Experience."

"Gary, what is this conference?" I ask.

"It's an event this Saturday put on by a local church for those recovering from depression, addiction, or really anything that is inhibiting their hope. It will be a day of encouragement. It could be good for you to go."

"I'll think about it. Thank you."

I do think about it, and when it comes time for the weekend, I can't imagine staying home alone. Isabella is at Dylan's for the weekend, and with Hank out of my life, I don't want to sit with only my loneliness as company. I decide to go to the conference.

I arrive at the church at eight in the morning, right on time along with two-hundred other people. I sit in the back corner, trying to be as far from the others as I can be. Most people look comfortable being there, but being in a church feels foreign to me.

They play worship music, and many of the people there close their eyes and raise their hands as they sing along. There is a desperate passion, a cry for more, and a beautiful emotional pull of hope from these people. I can feel it all around me—this crazy notion that perhaps by putting their hearts out there, they will have a connection with the creator of all. I tap my foot to the music, and there's a part of me that feels like dancing, but I resist. I don't want to do anything that will draw attention to myself, but part of me wishes I could feel the freedom I had as a young child, dancing around the park, chasing butterflies.

After the music, a pastor comes on stage and speaks a message on forgiveness. It hits my soul hard. "What can hold us down and trap us to our core is guilt and an inability to forgive. If there's anything you hear today, you must know that you are forgiven. Jesus Christ died a horrific death, not in vain, but so he could save you. On that cross he paid for all of our sins in order to abolish the barriers that kept us distant from God. Jesus gave of his life so that we could know freedom, so that you wouldn't have to carry with you the burden of failure each day. You are loved and your mistakes paid for. They carry no weight when you give them over to Jesus."

Hold on a minute. This Jesus paid the price for all our sins? Does this include the affair I had, which has always weighed heavily on my heart? Or the shame of rushing into my marriage with Dylan that devastated me and ended in a horrible divorce? Or even the guilt I've had from having a physical relationship with Hank before any marriage commitment? I can feel my normal pattern of spiraling into the rabbit hole of all my mistakes start to quake, but the words of the pastor stop me.

"You are forgiven. Plain and simple. So, you can now forgive others."

All this shame and guilt made me feel unworthy of any happiness, but this Christian God still forgives me and loves me? I'd never heard a religious message like this before. To not have to earn love, but to be given it freely is not covered in the sacred texts I was exposed to as a child. I feel for the first time that it might be possible for me to have a clean slate and potential for a promising future—and maybe even a newborn baby—unmarked by the bitterness of the world. I might cry with joy though I'm uncomfortable doing so in a room full of strangers.

The pastor further explains his thoughts on forgiveness: "When we harbor anger and resentment for those who treat us unjustly, it will make us become a slave to resentment and bitterness. Refusal to deal with resentment can destroy us and those we love the most. It allows pain and sorrow to continue affecting our well-being. For us, forgiveness is simply a mental decision, but for Jesus, it was life or death. Do you need any more reasons not to forgive?"

I'm listening, but this idea of letting the offender go freely is hard to swallow. Shouldn't they deserve to be in jail or suffering the consequences for what they did? As I think this, though, I'm immediately reminded of the horrible ending of a movie I saw recently, *The War of the Roses.* An extremely bitter married couple go through a divorce, and neither is willing to give up the elegant house they live in. They end up killing each other during the final fight of the movie. As I picture the devastating scene, I see that it came from the most damaging type of bondage that the pastor is talking about. I'm realizing I can't find peace and happiness until I forgive those who wronged me—and until I forgive myself.

In the middle of the day, we break for lunch and then meet in small groups to discuss the messages we were given in the morning. My small group leader, a woman who has more wrinkles than I've ever seen but a smile that overshadows them all, asks some questions to our group: "What does forgiveness look like in your life? What are the areas where you need to let more forgiveness in?"

There's an awkward pause as we wait for the first person to have the courage to speak up. I look down at the floor, trying to think of my inevitable answer.

A woman in her mid-thirties who exudes a strong maternal instinct speaks next. "For me forgiveness is freedom. When I withhold forgiveness, I'm digging myself a hole that gets harder and harder to climb out of the longer I go. You see, I was a drug addict for fifteen years and dropped out of med school after my high school sweetheart broke up with me. I felt like a failure for years, but God showed me how to accept that though I am not perfect, my story isn't over. When I trust God and choose forgiveness, the chains that were trapping me seem to evaporate. In the last four years, I have been drug-free, and I just completed medical school. I am even married and expecting a baby in six months."

Whoa. My mind is in shock. That's a pretty big turnaround from simply learning to forgive.

"Wow! What a great example of a fresh start that begins with accepting we are not perfect. God doesn't expect us to be perfect, and that's key in being able to forgive ourselves. That makes it easier to embrace a new life," our group leader says.

A man, a professor-type, remarks, "For me, forgiveness has to be a rhythm, a pattern that must be attended to frequently. I can find infinite grievances and block out others in my ill wishes toward them. But if I remember one of my rituals is forgiveness, I can combat those thoughts daily. I think we want forgiveness to be a one-time thing, but it's an everyday discipline to keep us free from the web of bitterness."

Everyone nods in agreement at his words, and the ruminations continue until I realize everyone else in the group has spoken. All eyes turn to me. This theme of forgiveness almost overwhelms me. I could think about all I need to forgive for days.

"Honestly, I barely know where to start," I blurt out. "First off, I've spent my whole life committed to achieving everything I ever wanted, striving to be perfect. Perfect student, perfect employee, perfect wife, perfect daughter, perfect mother, perfect friend. But my life has been miserable, and I haven't been perfect. I've been hurt by so many people in my life. Hearing today that only Jesus is perfect, well, it makes it possible to finally forgive and stop blaming myself for making the wrong choices, choices that put me in tough situations that led me to a life full of unhappiness. If Jesus can forgive me, then I can forgive my parents, my sister, my aunt, my grandmother, Francis's mother, my ex-husband, the leadership of China! I can also forgive Hank for leaving, and even my daughter, who I sometimes say is a burden, even though she's my greatest love. I've put my hope in so many others who let me down, and I blame them for the hardships of my life. I need to forgive myself too because I often only see the bad parts of my life and think that is my fate, and I don't believe things will get better."

They all listen intently to me, and I feel almost naked, having shared these details with people I've just met. But they cover me in grace and acceptance and a shared understanding. It seems we all struggle to forgive others, but we struggle more to forgive ourselves.

"Thank you, Ying-Ying, for your honesty and vulnerability," the group leader coos. I feel my shoulders relax, and only then do I realize just how tense I've been for who knows how long.

The day flies by, full of powerful messages, and I feel more encouraged by each passing minute. At the end of the day, the pastor presents the final statement: "Forgiveness is not blindly erasing our memory banks of those who treated us unjustly but waiting faithfully, believing God is keeping good records of the injustice in this world and is making them right."

Then he asks, "Whether you have been treated unfairly, are guilty of attempting revenge, or any other form of retribution, *are you now willing to turn the responsibility over to its rightful owner?*"

I have goosebumps all over my arms as I take in his words. I have been in school for so many years, worshiping knowledge and studying everything from the most state-of-the-art technologies to devouring every self-help book that could mend my interpersonal relationships and bring me a perfectly happy life. And yet this one fundamental piece of the puzzle was missing. I am already enough for this kind of love I've always wanted. I don't have to live my life in a state of perpetual shame from my mistakes. God has forgiven them and wants me just as I am. I can let it all go. I can give it to him.

I take a deep inhale, trying to prevent tears, as I realize this. I am stunned that today I finally found an answer in the Christian Bible, of all places, in words that I have been skeptical about all these years. I laugh out loud as the thought occurs to me: It seems I have found the perfect answer in my imperfect itself! God doesn't care that I don't have everything figured out. I just need to trust him, and know that I can lean on him. This doesn't make logical sense to me yet, but it feels right. And, at that moment, that is all that matters.

The music plays, and people all around me are singing. I'm still too in my head to join in, but I appreciate the beautiful rhythm around me. When the final note plays on the last song, I can't believe it's already five o'clock and the conference is over.

I walk out of the church, still in a daze, and the beauty of the sky hits me like a ton of bricks. I stop in my tracks and take in the picture before me. Bright orange and purple hues paint the sky with the boldness of a Van Gogh piece. The clouds are in shapes I've never seen before, almost as if they were trying to get my attention. The show-offs. My breath catches in my throat, and I think I might cry as peace overwhelms me. I feel as light as a feather, and as I close my eyes to soak in the moment, I feel like a breeze might sweep me up and make me fly straight into the clouds just like my silk butterfly kite. This peace is potent, vast. I sense a power like none I've experienced before. The burdens that had planted my feet to the ground in worry are now released, and I feel a freedom so unfamiliar that I think this must be the God they talked about at the conference today. I honestly have no idea how long I stay in this moment, but as the sky turns dark, I wake up to reality and decide I want to find a local church to attend. I'm curious about this God who claims he loves me regardless of my mistakes and imperfection. I desperately *need* this God, and I want to feel this freedom again!

My journey into faith is slow moving but consistent. I try out multiple churches on Sundays, usually sitting in the back row, and leaving right after the service is done. I find encouragement from the messages, and I love closing my eyes and listening to the worship music. I am given a Bible from one church but have a hard time reading it on my own. I'm still somewhat skeptical. Plus, many of the passages don't make all that much sense to me.

The biggest change, though, is the sense of peace I now have. Though my circumstances have not changed, I feel as though I can breathe deeper than I ever have before. I'm not constantly looking for the next opportunity or relationship to give me security, happiness, or hope. Instead, I am finding my peace in the knowledge that there is a God who sees and loves me. That is all I need, and I trust that God knows my needs and desires even more than I do. I trust that I am taken care of and so is Isabella.

One afternoon, my cousin calls and notifies us that my grandmother, now ninety-four, had a stroke and was taken to the hospital in critical condition. I immediately book the airline tickets to take my father to go to see her in New York. All the past years, she has never wanted to see my parents again after their initial visit.

My father's hearing loss has prevented him from talking on the phone easily. Plus, perhaps he may be tired of hearing the nonstop gaslighting centered on my mother. But he has written often to offer his help with anything she may need. Without any response from her, he has continued to send money on holidays from his meager pay, but she tears his checks into tiny pieces and returns them back to him.

My step-grandfather died nine years ago, and my grandmother has bonded closely with her granddaughter, Vicky, who has always lived nearby. Up until her stroke, Grandmother has been able to shop and cook for herself. In fact, she had prepared a meal for Vicky's birthday that evening. Vicky found her on the floor by the dining table chair when she arrived. On the dining table were Vicky's favorite dishes, still warm.

Grandma never awakens from the coma, and we stay in a hotel until after her funeral, which is arranged by Vicky according to grandma's own detailed plan. In the open casket, Grandmother looks peacefully asleep, with the custom, elegantly made light-blue suit covering the white silk-lace blouse that she prepared. She also wears a stunning set of diamond and pearl earrings and a necklace. She still looks incredibly young, with perfectly smooth skin and few wrinkles.

I am surprised to realize I don't hate her anymore.

21

New Beginnings

After a few months of being single, I am trying to be better about accepting social invitations from friends. A co-worker invites me to play tennis with her and a couple of our colleagues one afternoon, and I happily accept. I'm new to tennis but loving it so far and eager for any opportunity to play.

When I arrive at the court, I notice a tall, brunette man amongst our group of four. I find out his name is Owen, and he also works for our company. We play doubles, and Owen is my partner to start. We are a mediocre team, but my abs are sore from laughter. This is exactly the kind of release I need. I am immediately comfortable around him and find him to be not only attractive and well-dressed but also well-mannered and funny. He never gets upset when I make a mistake, but I definitely tease him when he shows frustration over his own mistakes. He reminds me of my favorite boss, Alex, which makes me think he might be gay.

When we finish our match and are about to leave, Owen tells me he loves to dance. "In fact, a few of my friends and I are going dancing this Friday night. Would you care to join?"

Yep, definitely gay. I tell him, though, that I have a business trip but would love to be invited to the next outing.

I get back from my business trip, and work is crazier than ever when I am given a new project to lead. Months fly by, and I don't have time for tennis or social events in general. I'm invested fully in making this project come to life. It's exhilarating, and my brain is going wild as we move forward with each baby step.

One day, we finally make a major breakthrough and complete the project. To take a breath, I wind up in the work cafeteria for lunch. I rarely go there because I'm always slammed with work and don't take a break until I leave at the end of the day, but today is a good day, and I deserve some lunch.

As I'm dishing up veggies at the salad bar, I hear a familiar voice. "Ying-Ying?!"

I look up, and directly across the salad bar from me is Owen. He wears a giant grin on his face, which catches me off-guard for a second. He has a great smile. We greet each other, and I explain I have been busy with work and haven't had time to socialize.

"I completely understand," he says. "But, hey, a few of us are going dancing again tonight. Would you want to come?"

I hesitate for a second, wary of Owen's intentions and my own limited capacity to let loose these days. But I deserve to have some fun and celebrate with work going so well! I am also still pretty sure Owen is gay, so I don't have to worry about the pressure of a one-night stand or anything in that department. It is a safe decision.

"Sure! I'm actually free tonight."

"Great, I'll see you there!" He fills me in on the details of when and where to meet.

I go straight to the dance studio after work (I've stayed later than I meant to), and thus, I show up in my business attire. Right away, I see a woman I recognize from work who smiles at me and tells me, "I'm so glad you're here! There are so many quality men to dance with. Have fun!"

I look around for Owen and spot him at the opposite side of the studio, swing dancing his heart out with another woman. I'm admiring how in-sync they are when an older man with graying hair and eager green eyes asks me to dance.

As we dance, he holds me closer than I'd like, and his breath is horrific. When the song ends, I thank him and do my best to walk away from him. Another man asks me for the next dance. I concede, but while we dance, this man keeps asking me about my race. When he finds out I'm Chinese, he asks me if I am a Communist.

During the next song, a younger man asks for a dance and grabs my ass at the end of the song. Another man has no idea how to hold me and keeps changing the position of his arms so obsessively that we barely move. The next man is incredibly nervous and keeps stepping on my feet and then apologizing.

I'm having a terrible time with these guys, and my work heels are killing my feet. I go sit in a dark corner, hoping that'll deter any more of these "quality" men from asking me to dance. I spot Owen again and admire the routine he and his partner are immersed in. Their movements are fluid, and you would think the woman weighed nothing the way Owen twirls her. The song ends, and suddenly Owen catches my eye from across the room. Next thing I know, he's coming straight toward me.

"Ying-Ying, why are you not dancing?"

"Oh, you know, I just had a flock of great dance partners who were incredibly impolite, had terrible breath, and stepped on my feet. I'm good."

"That sounds terrible."

"Yeah, but I'm all right. I was watching you, though. You and your partner have quite the rhythm!"

"Well, we're practicing for a competition we have coming up."

"Ah, that makes sense. You were so in-sync!"

"Would you care to dance with me, Ying-Ying?"

My feet plead with me to say no, but my spirit will have none of that. So, I respond, "Sure!"

As we dance, we chat, and I'm finally having fun! He moves gracefully, keeping his eyes on my own, and asks me questions.

"Do you like dancing, Ying-Ying?"

"I do actually, though I rarely do it. When I was a kid, I loved dancing until I was chosen to be in a dance academy that was so rigorous I strained my back."

"Sounds intense."

"I'm Chinese. We're intense about the things we commit to."

"Duly noted."

"I have a question for you."

"Okay, go ahead."

"Are you gay?"

His mouth falls open for just a second. "No! You thought I was gay?"

"Sorry! I just don't know that many men who like dancing."

"There are more than you think."

"Sorry."

"It's fine! I *was* married. We got a divorce a year ago."

"That's hard. I got divorced a few years ago."

His hand squeezes my hand just a tiny bit tighter. The pressure feels good. "So, you understand."

"At least to a point."

At that moment his dance partner comes over. "Owen, are you done fooling around? We've still got work to do!"

"Don't worry, Irene, we're solid. That last time was perfect. Let me have some fun!"

Irene crosses her arms and storms off but not before giving me the greatest death-glare I've ever received.

"Is something going on with you and your dance partner?" I ask.

"No, definitely not. We're just dance partners. We would kill each other if we ever tried to date. She drives me crazy."

I laugh, feeling an unexpected wave of relief.

"I hear that you're looking for a church," he says.

"I am. How do you know that?"

"I've been asking about you."

I smile. "Do you go to church?"

"I have been since the divorce. I was pretty low after that. I was seeing a therapist, and then a co-worker invited me to this men's Bible study he goes to. It's been amazing and has inspired me to dig deeper into the Bible. Last month I just finished it."

"Finished the entire Bible?"

"Yeah. I'm kind of that way. If I put my mind toward something, I go all in."

"That's amazing! I want to be better about reading it."

"It takes some discipline, but I think it's worth it. I'm also looking for a regular church to go to, though. Would you want to check out a church together this Sunday?"

"Yes, I would love that." The rest of the group comes over to say they're heading out, and we follow suit. While dancing with Owen, I forgot about everyone else. I never expected the night to go this way, but I'm looking forward to our Sunday date!

We have a great time at church. It's nice for me to sit with someone, and it's a first for me to go to church with a man. After the service, Owen walks me to my car. I notice we are walking extremely close together. I almost shiver when his hand accidentally brushes mine.

"Ying-Ying, can I take you on a date this Friday?"

Oh, how I wish I could say yes. "I can't. My sixteen-year-old daughter has a youth group on Fridays, and it's about an hour away. The youth leader takes her home, but it still takes me two hours round trip.

"What if I drove with you?"

"What?"

"Yeah, I can drive with you. We can have quality time in the car." I am both shocked and touched. Somehow, he knows how to give me the date I need, and I'm certain he will make suffering through Austin traffic much more enjoyable.

So, on Friday, Isabella, Owen, and I drive to the youth group, chatting constantly along the way. Owen and Isabella seem to be hitting it off already.

On the ride back, Owen and I talk, sharing information on our goals, our dreams, our pasts, and our present realities. I'm amazed how well he listens and how easily I am able to open up to him. The drive flies by in a blur.

"Someday, I want to move to California. I want sunny climates and easy access to the beach. I don't want to dread winter but want to learn how to surf, and when all my Austin friends are complaining about the Austin climate, I'll be paddling in the ocean."

I laugh at the idea. "That does sound nice. There are plenty of job offers in Silicon Valley for people like us. I considered it once, but I can't leave Isabella out here. Maybe when she's done with high school, I'll reconsider. But for now, I'm stuck with the brutal climate."

He returns my laugh. "Well, I'm in no rush anyhow. I'm a patient man."

The words are exactly what I'd hoped Hank would've said to me a year ago, but Owen and I are just getting started. I would hate to be the one to hold him back. If he stays, does he know how much he'll be giving up for us? If I were on my own, I would hop on these opportunities without hesitation, but Owen isn't in a rush. He has this quiet confidence that I love; it's as if he somehow knows everything is going to work out in the right, divine timing.

After that, Owen and I begin to date on the regular. He comes over occasionally and plays video games with Isabella. Funnily enough, I often overhear Isabella talking to Owen about her deepest thoughts. Owen listens and treats her like an adult. I always craved deep conversations like these with Isabella, and here she is opening up fully to Owen. Isabella begins asking, in the middle of the week, if Owen will be coming over on the weekend and is disappointed if I say no.

This connection between the two of them makes it hard to guard my heart from falling, but I have to. Owen told me in his last marriage that he was the one adamant about not having kids. That should definitely make him a terrible candidate to date a single mother, right? He's also the same age as Hank, six years younger than me. I'm forty and I don't want history to repeat itself. It seems to get harder and harder to recover. I still hear Father's words telling me a younger man will never want to stay with an older woman for long.

Since I reconnected with Francis, we catch up on the phone every few months. He is very happy in his marriage and is always hoping I'll find someone. He's always asking me if there's anyone I'm dating or interested in, so I tell him about Owen.

"Why are you so hesitant about him, Ying-Ying?"

"What do you mean?"

"I can tell by the way you're talking that you're hung up on something."

"Well, I think the biggest thing is that he's so much younger than me. I keep thinking he's going to change his mind the way Hank did."

"Ying-Ying, age doesn't matter if his character is quality. Look beyond the number, get your dad's voice out of your head, and let yourself be happy. This man sounds amazing. He could be the one for you, Ying-Ying. I have a feeling."

After my conversation with Francis, I give myself full permission to open my heart up to Owen. He is kind, caring, gentle, smart, fun, handsome, and *straight*! I can't believe I told him I thought he was gay! When we hug, I feel butterflies in my stomach and a sense of peace and safety in his arms. He is a very good listener just like Francis, and I find myself falling hard for him. We enjoy trying out different churches and cooking dinner together with Isabella. I begin to think Francis is right, and Owen could be my future.

After five months of dating, though, this thought is squashed. Owen tells me he needs a break from the relationship because he feels we are getting too close, and he is not sure if he can handle being responsible for Isabella's well-being as well as my own. I'm disappointed but hardly surprised. I honor his feelings and am grateful he is honest with me before things go any further. Plus, I love him enough to support whatever will be best for him. However, this just fuels my self-told narrative that I won't be able to find someone as a single mother. Love just isn't in the cards for me.

After we break up, I am okay, though, and I don't fall into the same type of depression I did when Hank broke up with me. This is progress. I miss Owen every day and crave his arms around me, but I know that God has me. I only want a relationship where the man is one-hundred percent dedicated to me and Isabella, and if he can't be, I would rather be on my own.

Two months pass, and I wish I could say I am over Owen, but I'm not. I often find myself thinking about him. One night, I am driving home from work in rush hour traffic, and my mind begins to daydream about our times together. How I wish I could run into him serendip-itously. I just need to be around his presence. I'm jarred from my thoughts by a loud *bang!* and the feeling of impact that throws me forward. It takes me a moment to realize I have just rear-ended the car in front of me—I've just had my first car accident while daydreaming about an ex- boyfriend! Ugh!

My car has to be in the shop for three days but is salvageable. When I pick it up, I'm determined to get over Owen. In order to function, I need to move on and forget about him completely.

As if on cue, when I get home, I receive a phone call.

"Ying-Ying, it's me Owen."

"Hi." There's a pause, and I'm desperate for him to speak again. "Why are you calling?"

"I have clarity. About us."

"Okay?"

"The time apart just confirmed how deeply I feel for you. I love you, Ying-Ying, and I want to take our relationship deeper toward finally making a commitment. I was so worried about hurting Isabella because I have such little experience with kids. I still feel that way, but I think I can work on it. I was wondering if there's any way you would take me back? And if so, if we could go see your therapist, Gary, together so that I can learn how to be a parent?"

I can't believe what I'm hearing. Not only does Owen, sweet, thoughtful Owen, want me back, but he's willing to do everything I tried to get Dylan to do. Here is a man I love initiating couple's therapy. I might collapse with happiness.

"Yes. Let's do it, Owen! I've missed you."

"I love you, Ying-Ying."

"I love you too, Owen."

I say those words to Owen with an ambivalent feeling, swinging between the joy of making up with Owen and the paranoia and fear of being hurt again. I know that to develop a deeper relationship with Owen this time means I am making a serious commitment to him, one that could lead to marriage. But I have concerns, and at the core of my concerns is my doubt that I can get along with his family.

Owen's father is a renowned heart surgeon and has been having an extramarital affair with one of his assistants. They even have a baby girl together while he is still married to Owen's mother, who is a wreck throughout all of this. It breaks my heart to see her in so much anguish, and it scares me that Owen seems to not be as discouraged by the situation as I am.

Owen takes me out for a romantic dinner that night, and though I'm immersed in his love over the candlelight and the piano music playing in the background, my mind is analyzing everything. He senses my worries, something I'm always amazed he can do, and when the dessert is served, asks me, "Ying-Ying, you seem distracted. Would you like to tell me about it?"

Part of me wishes I could just crawl into a hole, but the stronger part of me finds a way to give him the response I'm dreading. "I love you Owen, and I was so excited about the idea of us getting back together, but I'm afraid I cannot continue with this relationship."

I can barely get that sentence out because my heart is breaking apart. I look straight into Owen's eyes, which I'd been avoiding most of dinner, and see that his face is full of confusion. His confused face is always so endearing, and I can't believe I'm doing this.

After taking my words in and realizing I have nothing more to say, he speaks. "Why, Ying-Ying? I thought we love each other deeply and we are happy together. You must give me a reason."

"Please, I don't want to. I don't think you would like what I have to say."

"Try me, Ying-Ying!" Owen insists.

I am still reluctant, but I owe such a sincere man an explanation, and I do not want to repeat the mistake I made with Francis by not telling him the truth before breaking up. I take a big sigh and gear up to speak my mind.

"Truthfully, I don't like your father. I'm afraid I can't relate to your family well, and I'm worried about our happiness amongst these complicated relationships all mangled together. I'm afraid of being hurt again."

At this he grabs my hand and looks straight at me. The confused look is replaced with one of earnestness. "Ying-Ying, that makes two of us! I understand completely because I hate what my father is doing and what my family's situation is. Thank goodness! I thought you didn't love me anymore. We can work through this." His body language relaxes, and I can hear such relief in his voice when he makes a suggestion. "How about we discuss this with Gary? I think with the genuine love we have for each other, we can work things out and have a happy life together, regardless of my family drama. Give me ten sessions to see Gary together. If we have tried that, and at the end you still feel uncomfortable, I will honor your decision."

This is such a profound idea to my ears. How could I not be moved and accept his suggestion?

22

Peace

We start dating again and going to therapy regularly, with a tradition of having dinner afterward, and we even land on a church we both love.

With Gary's help, I start to realize I have trust issues. As Gary puts it, "Oftentimes, because of some extreme violence or trauma experienced early in life, one may find it hard to trust anyone or anything, even God."

Realizing I don't want to live with fear as my master, I decide now is the time for me to let go of the past hurts and take a leap of faith, putting my life in God's hands. Owen is worthy of my best efforts. Breaking up with him is no longer an option in my heart!

We attend the church for a few months before we decide to take the next step and get baptized together. The moment is so beautiful. Our pastor tells us that baptism is representative of our covenant with God. Much like a wedding is a public declaration of the commitment of two people to each other, baptism is a public declaration of our commitment to God. As I emerge from being submersed in the giant tub that's been placed in the church, I can't help but know that this is not only the next step in our relationship with God but also with each other.

Owen asks me one morning for Joyce's number. "I just have a question for her," he tells me. The next day I receive a call from Joyce.

"Guess what?!" She is squealing as I answer the phone.

"What is it, Joyce?"

"Owen and I just went ring shopping for you! I'm not supposed to tell you, but I figured you'd want a heads-up. I'm so excited for you, Ying-Ying! And don't worry, I have no idea when he's going to do it. But he has a gorgeous ring! Oh, but I have to go! Bye!"

With that, she hangs up, and a big smile makes its way across my face. I'm going to marry Owen.

It's September in Austin, one of my favorite months of the year. I love the tension between the end of summer and the beginning of fall—the best parts of the two seasons, combined. I'm sure Owen will propose this month. It would be perfect for any sort of outdoor proposal! Weeks have gone by since Joyce's call, though. I'm dying to know when it will happen. I wake up every morning, wondering, *Will today be the day?* I try to analyze his facial expressions and breathing to see if he seems anxious or like he's trying to hide something, but he doesn't. He always seems calm.

I'm thinking these thoughts as I walk into work early on September 11th, only to be greeted by chaos and horror.

"America has been attacked!"

"Planes just crashed into the World Trade Center!"

"They're reporting another crash at The Pentagon!"

"They could attack any city next!"

As I comprehend their cries and look at the television screens in our office, a sinking feeling comes over me. My colleagues and I go home early that day. No one can focus. Fear invades our hearts, and we all want to be with our families. I spend a lot of that day reflecting on my time in New York, hoping all my family and friends there are safe. I can picture so clearly walking past the Twin Towers, a symbol of the invincibility I felt in America. It's no wonder they were the pillars of strength the terrorists decided to knock down.

Owen comes over that evening, and we cuddle up as we watch the news with shock reverberating through every pore of our skin. The numbers keep pouring in of those who have died, those who are trapped under rubble, and the countless first responders sacrificing everything at the scene. Images I thought would only ever be present in an action film fill our television screen. On repeat we see planes crash straight into the Twin Towers. One impossible, tragic crash, followed shortly by another plane doing the same exact thing. It's hard to believe it's real.

The news cycles are already sharing heart-wrenching recordings of people leaving what they know to be their last voicemails for their loved ones. I cried earlier, but now I feel numb. Our whole world has changed right before our eyes.

"I was going to propose to you this weekend." Owen says this after we listen to one of the recordings—a husband calling his wife and daughter, telling them goodbye, that he loves them more than anything, and to be strong for each other.

"You were?" I can barely say the words. It feels strange to have disappointment for my own life when so many have lost theirs.

"Yes, I had it all planned out. I had a reservation to take you on a Horse Carriage tour around the Lady Bird Lake to propose to you and then dine at the Azul Rooftop Restaurant where we could celebrate with champagne. But it doesn't feel like the timing is right now. I don't even know if anything is going to be open."

"That was sweet of you, and don't worry. We'll figure out when the time is right."

Part of me is excited hearing his plan, and I know he's put great thought and intention into his proposal. Still, it hurts, knowing it cannot happen that way now. I wonder if God doesn't want me to marry again. Nothing seems to go right for me in that department.

On Saturday, a few weeks later, Owen and I are out to hike on the River Place all afternoon. It is our first time out since 9/11, and it feels both eerie and refreshing. Still in our hiking outfits, we drive to Oasis for dinner with a breathtaking view and the most spectacular sunsets I have ever lain eyes on. For dessert, the waitress brings out a slice of double chocolate cake with a sparkler candle on it. I laugh as the sparkler does its dramatic dance, and it isn't until it goes out that I notice a diamond ring on the plate. I look up at Owen, who stands up, walks over to me, and gets down on one knee.

"Ying-Ying, you are my forever. You are a woman unlike any other—brilliant, beautiful, compassionate, innovative, and resilient beyond any person I've met. Thank you for choosing me these past couple years. We've had some bumps in the road, but it's been remarkable smoothing them out with you. Please make me the happiest man in the world. Will you marry me?"

My eyes well with tears, and though I am not at all surprised by this, I'm overjoyed. The look in his eyes as he asks me to marry him will stick with me forever. That is how a man should look at the love of his life. I'm so honored to be the recipient of that look.

"Yes, Owen, yes. Of course!"

He stands up, and so do I. He wraps me in his arms, the arms I will get to have around me forever, and kisses me with such passion that I can think of nothing else. It is only after we break apart, that I realize the entire restaurant is cheering!

We decide we don't want to wait too long to be married, and we set a date at the courthouse in December with a plan for a large wedding in May when the weather is warmer. My dad, who learned from his mistake with my last boyfriend, accepts Owen with open arms. My parents, Owen's parents, Isabelle, and Joyce all attend our small wedding.

As we leave the courthouse, marriage license in hand, I feel giddy with happiness. I'm amazed at what God can do. As a schoolgirl in China, could I ever have imagined marrying a loving, white, American man at the downtown Austin courthouse? After everything I've been through, I'm so grateful to be living this story.

Two months later, on Valentine's Day, as I'm anticipating a wonderful date night with my *husband*, I receive an unexpected phone call. "Ying-Ying, it's Hank."

My stomach drops. Hank, who I have barely spoken to since he left us to go make it big in Silicon Valley, is calling me. But there's no mistaking it, even after everything. I recognize his voice as if I were still used to hearing its rhythms regularly.

"Hank? Why are you calling?"

"I'm going to be in Austin this Friday. Can I take you to dinner? I have some things I want to talk with you about."

My stomach drops, but my curiosity gets the better of me. "Of course. Just name the place, and I'll be there."

With my husband's reluctant blessing, I arrive at The Rainbow Lodge five minutes early so that I can have time to take a breath. I don't know how I'll feel seeing Hank again, and I have no idea what he wants to talk about. I don't even think he knows I'm married.

The hostess takes me to our table, where no one is sitting yet, and where a light-blue Tiffany's bag sits with a card with my name on it.

"I think you're supposed to open this right now," the hostess tells me. I start to feel hot, my cheeks likely turning bright pink as I open the card.

Ying-Ying,

I had a dream a few nights ago that I will forever lose you, and I could not bear the feeling. I have gone after my career first, and now I see that doesn't mean anything if you are not by my side for the rest of my life. I love you. I would like to marry you. I hope I'm not too late.

Love, Hank

Oh, no. This isn't good. I can feel all sorts of eyes staring at me as I open the bag and take out a Tiffany's box with the most enormous diamond ring I've ever lain eyes on. It must be about three carats. I know by how aware I am of everyone else that this isn't right.

"What do you think?" It's him. I look up and I see the blue eyes I'd fallen for years ago and the awkward smile on his face that always drew me in. I can't speak.

"I know you can't leave Isabella, and I respect that. I've had the time to really think things through and gain perspective, and I realize it was stupid to give up on us. We are great together. Everything made sense when we were together."

"Hank, I—"

"Also, I heard you're getting married in June. But I couldn't let you do that without trying to talk you out of it. I felt like it was better to do it now than to show up at your wedding and be the person to speak up when the pastor asks if anyone opposes the match!" He chuckles at this.

"How could you propose to me knowing I was going to marry someone else?"

"Well, I—"

"You're too late. We got married in December but are waiting to have the wedding in June. He treats me incredibly well and is the one for me. I've chosen him and it's done."

I'm trying to keep my voice down, but the restaurant is so small, I know we are providing the other tables with a healthy dose of entertainment. Hank looks like he's been hit by a bus. He didn't see this coming, and his eyes are beginning to well with tears. I don't know if the tears are from disappointment or embarrassment—probably a combination of both.

After a long silence, he simply says, "I screwed up, huh?"

"Hank, I loved you. I wanted to be with you, but it didn't work. We didn't choose each other. Now it's too late."

I stand up because there is no way I can be in this room for a second longer.

"Okay," he says. "Goodbye, Ying-Ying. I wish you the best."

"You too."

I rush outside, doing my best not to burst into tears. I stand there taking full breaths, part of me hoping Hank will come out after me. But I know he won't. His ego is too fragile for that.

I am confident Owen is the one God has chosen for me, but the timing of this return of Hank brings up all the memories I thought I'd buried and throws me into a cycle of varying emotion. I need to let Hank go, and though I thought I already had, I realize letting go is a process that sometimes you must ritualize. Reinforcing this end is painful. I was blindsided, and it feels like the initial breakup all over again. It's surprising how easy it is for my brain to go straight back to who I was in that season, someone unable to see a speck of hope. I remember that woman so clearly, and I can feel the temptation to stay right there, in that skin, mourning and pitying myself and my future.

But I don't. I don't stay in that place. That woman is no longer me. My future is full of so much hope now.

Epilogue

In June, Owen and I have our giant wedding, which is beyond all my expectations. We have two-hundred guests in attendance, and as I prepare to walk down the church aisle, I feel God's presence. This moment is completely opposite to that of my first wedding. I don't feel ignorance or anxiety about this choice. Instead, I feel content and confident. I am not looking to be taken care of. I am not looking to put everyone else's needs above my own. I'm allowing myself to be happy and whole.

Will and Tina's children are an important part of our wedding ceremony, and Tina's promise to me becomes reality. Jeremy, seven years old now, walks down the aisle, carrying the ring pillow with both hands in front of his chest. His little sister, Jamie, who is five years old, holds a white basket on her left arm while spreading red rose petals onto the walkway with her right hand. Both children are wearing their darling outfits and adorable smiles.

Isabella is one of the youngest bridesmaids, looking stunningly beautiful standing next to Joyce on the stage in line with other bridesmaids.

Father leads me to the altar, and I'm so grateful for our relationship, which has rekindled. I'm grateful for the ways he has welcomed Owen even though Owen isn't Chinese. It's been a growing point in our bond. As I see Owen, waiting for me at the end of the aisle, emotion rears her head, and I feel hope, such hope. In a flash, I see the hardships of my life, all the holes I found myself in, all the mistakes I made, all the pain I wish I could've avoided. Yet, the flash is over quickly and replaced by awe. Somehow God had me all of this time.

He led me to this extraordinary moment. Both Isabella and Owen are my proof that miracles exist and that God can carve a path out of any dead end. I try to smile at Owen, but the tears start flowing instead. This isn't a shock to the system type of love, the kind I kept looking for. This is better. This is enduring. This is the type of love where I don't feel helpless but instead feel strong. This is the kind of love where every day we make the choice to be each other's partner no matter what may come. This is admitting we don't have all the answers, but we want to discover them with each other. This is knowing we are different, unique individuals, but together we are elevated to become more of who we are.

In this moment, I also realize that it isn't this marriage that is my answer to everything; my answer to everything is my journey with God. I always thought I was in charge of my life with a perfect plan, my successes, my failures, ignorant that God even existed. I believed that I was limitless, but when things went wrong, I blamed myself or the cruelty of others. Often, when life would get overwhelming, I would close my eyes and picture that silk butterfly kite, yearning to be set free yet unable. I chose to believe the kite wanted to stay in line with me, soaking up a moment before the day it would escape to new heights. Someday I would escape too. I would stay in that image, quieting my mind until I had the courage to take the next step in my day.

I tried to pinpoint my own yearning for an unrelenting connection to something more, time after time in my life. From my parents to Nanny, to an imaginary grandmother who lived overseas; from Aunt Katie to my boyfriends, to my first husband, to my father's approval and protection; to Joyce's friendship and my bosses and my job—this journey to find that acceptance has been filled with despair, heartbreak, and incredible favor. In each trial, though, I discovered more of myself, more of what I was capable of, and more of what I wasn't capable of *alone*. I look back and see now, not only how high

I've risen but also who is holding the string. My horizon kept expanding until it led me to know this soaring feeling I've been looking for has always been God.

God—this indescribable force beckoning me to let go, to trust, and to simply be loved.

As I reach Owen at the altar, I look straight into his eyes. For a moment, time stops, and all I can see are the fingerprints of God all over him and all over our story. Sunlight pours in through the church windows, dancing upon the pews, and I know this is exactly where I'm meant to be. I sense my own set of wings, placed there by my Creator, and know they've propelled me here into a metamorphosis of purpose, strength, and courage. I'm ready to emerge into whatever is next. I'm not finished yet.

Acknowledgments

This book is my childhood dream coming to fruition. At five years old, I had a burning wish to write stories for a soul yearning to help people even though I hadn't yet experienced much of the journey. I would like to thank my childhood heart for never giving up on that dream.

I owe an enormous amount of gratitude to my honest friend, the passionate co-owner of Acorn publishing, best-selling author and editor, Holly Kammier. Holly consistently believed and encouraged me for over a decade to put my story to paper. She helped me overcome my doubts and devoted endless hours to editing my manuscript, even helping finalize the book title and all other details.

This book would not be possible without my first editor, Jessica Hammett, who had a gift in being able to capture the essence of my voice and manifested raw ideas into beautiful writing that flows throughout this book. This work is a showcase of her talents in composing such coherent sentences and paragraphs; our collaboration was the most pleasurable experience. She is a bright rising star!

Giving myself the permission to pursue this passion and believe in myself was a true breakthrough in the self-love journey, and I owe much of that to the wise counseling of Bill Smith.

This book reflects the entire Acorn Publishing team and their professional dedication to its success. I would like to especially thank the talented Lindsey Carter, who served as the book's final content editor, Leslie Ferguson the book's line editor, as well as the brilliant creative team at Damonza for the design of a remarkable book cover.

This accomplishment is inspired by all my loyal family and friends who have enlightened me during our conversations and supported me along the journey.

Above all else, this is a testimony of God's mercy and love.